TITAN:
The Midnight Hour

By Hugh Beckstead

Illustrations by Megan Furesz

Best wishes

This Book
First Read By

Teanna Parton

Contents

Chapter 1: Michael and Carly

Dusk sweeps over Delta City. Long shadows like steely fingers creep across the vast metropolis. Dark clouds linger and hang low over the horizon with the promise of rain to come. The last rays of sunshine slice through the dark blue grey clouds in shades of orange, purple and red. The vast and lush expanse of Campbell Park begins to empty, like an open invitation along the city's coastline. Only the long shadows of trees play across the open sports fields. Benches and long winding trails looking over the ocean lay vacant.

With the remaining daylight the citizens of Delta City head indoors. The people pass one another without waving or saying hello. Most hardly look up at all. They move about the city oblivious to everyone else around them. Shops and markets across the city abruptly close, pulling down metal shutters and gates. The only activity that freely flowed was the congested arteries of the highways and train lines full of local commuters. It's far safer to seek refuge as the seedy underbelly of the city shows itself to the shadows of the night, and the citizens of Delta City seem to know it.

From the open seas cradling the edge of the city, through the dense green foliage of Campbell Park, across the smooth cold concrete business skyscrapers of downtown, to the high rise condos and trendy shops of midtown, and the massive homes and clean streets of the west end, the entire city seems at the mercy of the dark of night and the fear it brings with it. Yet, in the tougher, duller looking east end, amid its older bungalows and apartments, hope could be found. In what was once a friendly blue collar neighborhood but had since turned into a breeding ground for thugs and criminals, a hero lies in waiting.

On an apartment rooftop in the city's east end Michael Novak sat with his girlfriend Carly Edwards and contemplated what the future might hold for them. They still wore their dress clothes, Michael in his shirt and tie and Carly in her formal dress. They had just graduated from middle school. It is a day they have talked about in great detail for sometime. After the flurry of activity that has surrounded them all day,

Michael wanted nothing more than to be alone with Carly in their own special spot.

For years now they have escaped the outside world by retreating to this rooftop. Carly's parents lived on the top floor and Michael only lived a block away. Here, four stories above the world, on top of Carly's home they have made a sanctuary for themselves and their closest friends. It was also the place where he first told Carly of his love for her this past spring. Carly's best friend Monica Garner, and Michael's two best friends, Perminder Singh and Dave Chang, are the other part of the group that could usually be found there after school and on many weekends. It seemed to Michael that many great memories had been made on the roof.

Like scavengers the group had managed to furnish their sanctuary with an old bus bench that Michael, Dave and Perminder found in an alley. The bench was made acceptable after Carly and Monica got the boys to scrub it clean with a bucket of soapy water. They had also managed to salvage an old plastic patio set complete with three chairs and a table. It had been cracked and patched together with duct tape several times, but Michael insisted it still had lots of mileage left in it. There was also sporting equipment and magazines littered all over the rooftop. It was there that Michael and Carly were able to truly feel at home.

"Can you believe it, Michael? It's finally here . . . graduation!" Carly said, exuding sheer delight. "I mean, I know it's only middle school, but I'm just so glad to be done and moving on to the next phase of our lives. I just can't believe it, high school, finally!" Carly faced Michael with a triumphant look.

Michael gazed at her lovingly as she stood basking in the warmth left from the early summer sun, her dress fanning out around her. Carly was considered truly beautiful by many. She was quite tall for a young woman, but also quite fit making her come across elegant and graceful. With shoulder length auburn hair, high cheekbones, a perfect complexion and big brown eyes, it was hard to disagree.

"I know, but it's funny how some things never change. Just yesterday I caught Dave and Perminder playing on the monkey bars in the park," Michael said, beaming back at her, his usual playful self.

Carly responded with a wry smile. "Stop it. You know what I mean. I'm just so excited!"

"I know it is pretty sweet, isn't it?"

"Wasn't the ceremony beautiful too?" Carly asked, staring at the grey clouds on the horizon seeming not even to hear Michael.

"Yeah, sure," Michael responded, not really knowing what she meant by beautiful. A ceremony like that was not typically what Michael or any of his friends would have called beautiful.

"Did you see poor Julie Becker though? I feel so bad for her. I mean, her brother Brad is still missing and it's been like two weeks," said Carly.

"Hmm, I know. Do you think they'll ever hear from him, you know?" asked Michael, not knowing quite how to word what he meant.

"I don't know. I mean, Brad always thought he was invincible. I think he finally got involved in way more than he could handle. I was talking to Julie before the ceremony and she said that Brad was desperate for some quick money so he could move with his girlfriend when she goes away to college," said Carly.

"I don't know. I just can't see someone like Brad getting involved with any kind of criminal activity," Michael said, as he scratched his head still trying to picture it.

"Yeah well, we are talking about Mr. Midnight here. The rumors and talk about him have been getting worse recently, it seems. I mean, come on, Michael, Brad wouldn't be the first person from our neighborhood to fall into that kind of mess."

"What? Just the other day you were telling me that the possibility of a crime boss like Mr. Midnight, one where no one knows his name and who wears a mask, is impossible. 'Nothing but urban legend,' I think you said. Carly, I do think that you are changing your mind," Michael replied.

"Well, now you're just putting words in my mouth. I don't necessarily mean that he did any work for *the* Mr. Midnight, but I do think he got into some trouble, and I think it may have been more than anybody wants to admit. Let's face it there are some bad elements in this neighborhood these days," she said.

"Yeah, but Brad? I just can't see him being involved in a robbery."

"Unfortunately, money can make people do strange things, things they wouldn't normally do."

"That's like the third person from our neighborhood that we personally know who's been rumored to have gotten tangled up in the Mr. Midnight story," said Michael.

"I know. I just keep thinking about poor Julie and her family."

"Don't worry, I'm sure the police are doing everything they can to find Brad," Michael said, attempting to calm her.

Michael reached out and placed his fingers beneath her chin and gently raised her head. He saw true fear in her eyes. He knew that Julie was a friend of Carly's. He really only knew Brad as a friend of his brother, Vince. Just the day before Michael had overheard Vince and some of his friends talking about how Brad had been bragging that he had landed a great job making big bucks. Michael knew that when people from the neighborhood talked about quick, easy, and most importantly big, money they were usually involved in something shady.

Michael kissed her tenderly. As he took in the moist sweetness of her lips all the troubles of the world seemed to just melt away. He then pulled back, and held her tightly in his arms, trying his best to soothe her.

They gazed into each others eyes, enjoying the moment they had waited the last three years for: graduation into high school. Carly tilted her head to look over the ledge below them, and Michael followed her gaze. Below, three young children were playing a game of tag on the sidewalk and around the cars parked on the side of the street. They seemed to be savoring every last second of the fading sunlight until they were forced to go inside for the night. Already Michael could hear Mrs. McCleary calling out to her daughter Carolyn to come in. For a time they both sat silently watching as the children finished playing. Michael couldn't help but think how not long ago it had been them down there playing. In those days they had not a care in the world, dirty and scabby kneed from a day of nothing but playing around. During those few short years they were not called at the first signs of dusk. The neighborhood was a different place then, a safer place, as was much of the city.

Again Mrs. McCleary's voice cut through the quiet evening, this time slightly more distressed. The calls of the other parents were quick to follow. Eventually the kids all seemed to realize that they had pushed their limits as much as they could, and slowly made their way up the street to each of their homes.

When the children had gone and the street was empty again Michael and Carly both stood on the rooftop and looked out over the neighborhood with the city skyline as their backdrop. He stood directly behind Carly with his arms locked around her. A warm breeze enveloped them, bringing summer smells that filled their senses. The smell of fresh cut grass, burgers on the barbeque waved over them. They watched as the sun slowly faded from view behind the skyscrapers of downtown.

It wasn't always like this for them. For a long time they had a friendship, one that eventually blossomed into love as the two grew older. Michael remembered the first time he laid eyes on her and how his heart had skipped a beat. It still did, whenever he saw her. Michael had been transferred to the same school that Carly attended in the middle of first grade when he and his older brother had come to live with their grandfather. Carly was the first person to welcome him, making him feel right at home. The two were instantly friends. Ever since then they were virtually inseparable. As their friendship grew and matured Michael had always hoped it would blossom into something more.

Michael would often look at her; stealing glances when her back was turned and then blush brightly when she would look up and catch him. He took any excuse to be with her, even over hanging out with Perminder and Dave. For a while he held his feelings in, worried how it could affect their friendship, and terrified of finding out that her feelings were not reciprocated.

By the time they were both starting their final year of middle school their romance had begun to blossom. Michael noticed Carly beginning to return his gestures of affection. She would hold out her hand for him to take on their way home from school. She would give him a long tender hug when he did well on a test she had helped him study for. All of this only helped give Michael the confidence he needed to tell Carly how he truly felt about her. It had taken all the courage he could muster, and she had answered with their first kiss. From then on they were boyfriend and girlfriend. Their friends and family seemed to hardly notice the change. They were the perfect fit, Michael was noble and strong and Carly compassionate and intelligent.

Without Carly's tutoring Michael's grades likely would not have been good enough for his college level high school courses. Carly was always able to keep him focused on his schoolwork and encourage him when he felt like he could not quite grasp an assignment, and push him to reach for that little extra. Of course, without Michael, Carly would have studied so hard she would have had a complete meltdown.

"Well, Did you ever get around to getting your class schedule done for the fall?" Carly asked.

"No, I haven't, but I will, I promise,"

"Michael, you can't keep putting things off until the last minute. You have to start planning for your future now. I had my classes picked two months ago. You know that I plan to…" Michael interrupted before she could finish.

"I know, I know," Michael said. "You've only told me about a million times. I know you've always had a love for science, and of animals. So you're going to focus your studies on science, and just like your dad, do research in veterinary sciences." Carly broke into an embarrassed smile. Michael knew all too well what Carly was trying to get at.

"And don't worry; I know you'll do great. You'll probably end up saving the polar bears or curing cancer in iguanas, something cool. I know it's important, but how am I supposed to know what I want to be doing two months from now let alone four years."

"Just promise me you'll go as soon as possible."

"Don't worry, I will," he replied.

This was a common subject between them; trying to push Michael to set goals in life. He seemed to have no direction at all. He just hadn't found his calling yet. At fifteen, he figured, why worry about it. He envied Carly for finding something she was good at, and so passionate already. Ever since she was little all she talked about was animals and what she planned to do to help them. Carly knew more about animals than anyone, and would always enlighten Michael with some new fact. Thanks to her, Michael knew that Alaskan king crabs have no known enemies, and that sea turtles are immune to jelly fish stings.

For his high school years Michael envisioned some kind of career in football or basketball. He seemed to have an aptitude for all sports. He had won awards in basketball, and had been a letterman on the Eastside Middle school football team.

"It will be hard to get over to the high school though now that I work," Michael stated, boastful and changing the subject coyly.

Two weeks before Michael had gotten a job at the local market, Caruthers Grocery. There was little work available in the neighborhood for someone Michael's age. Mr. Caruthers always hired local kids around fourteen or fifteen to be his stock boy and delivery person. Landing the job had been a real coup for Michael.

"Ooh, look at you mister working man. Your grandpa must be so proud of you."

"I think so. He's talked about that more than me being about to start high school lately. He just keeps saying how proud he knows my parents would be of me."

"Well, good your parents would be proud of you."

Michael's parents had been killed in a car accident when he was five. He remembered very little about them, only vague snapshots which he wasn't even sure were real. He remembered cloudy images of his parents playing with him at a beach, running and playing in the sand and water. There was another of them taking him and his brother Vince to the zoo. He recalled his father holding him high to see the lions. He wasn't sure anymore if the faces he saw in his memory were his own or just from pictures his grandfather had around the house.

His grandfather had told him about traits his parents, Kevin and Kathy, had had. Kevin Novak was a city alderman and prominent figure in the community. Kathy Novak was a teller in the local bank. Both were outspoken advocates for their community. One night after a city fundraiser, their car went over an embankment and crashed into a tree. They were both pronounced dead before they reached the hospital. The only thing Michael could really remember about the events surrounding his parents' deaths was seeing his older brother crying at the funeral. Vince was eight when they died, and remembered much more. Due to their age difference, their parents' deaths seemed to have had a harsher effect on Vince than on young Michael. The boys were then sent to be raised by their grandfather, Dale Novak.

Grandpa Dale was blind. Because of his handicap, he had had to fight for the right to raise his only grandchildren. He was their only living relative. Grandpa Dale lived alone as his beloved wife Emma had passed away some years before. There were many who thought an old blind man was incapable of raising two young boys. Social workers, lawyers, and concerned onlookers couldn't have been more wrong, however. Dale Novak proved many times during their growing up that you didn't need eyes to be able to see everything. He became the cornerstone of the boys' world. He always made sure they were well fed and clothed. He was always in attendance at their school functions or sporting events. To the boys' amazement he always knew when their homework needed to be done and what their grades were. Dale was a gentle, caring, loving man, who always supported and encouraged them in all aspects of their lives. Michael loved his grandfather and always strived to make him proud.

Vince, on the other hand, had been expelled and was always in trouble. Vince had broken their grandfather's heart many times. As they hit their teens the boys began to drift farther and farther apart. Michael no longer felt any sense of closeness to his older brother. In fact for years Michael felt that Vince was jealous of him, and would take any opportunity to tarnish Michael's image.

Carly brushed a stray strand of hair off his forehead with the back of her hand. They locked eyes and she infused him with a warm smile that was quickly returned.

"you know, maybe I will just skip the whole high school thing and go work at the docks." Michael joked, knowing he would get a reaction from Carly.

"Just because he is the only person to just leave this neighborhood after high school and succeed does not mean you should turn out like that. I mean, I just don't trust him. No matter how much you three stooges like him," she said, referring to Michael, Perminder, and Dave.

"Oh come on. Dylan's not a bad guy. He's worked hard, and now the guy is drawing big fat paychecks. Nothing wrong with that," Michael said with admiration.

"Yeah, and with hard honest work I'm sure," Carly added sarcastically with a slight wrinkle of her nose.

"Come on, don't be like that. Dave and Perminder love him."

"Yeah, it's not really hard to impress them," Carly said curtly.

"Well, I think Monica is in love with him too," Michael said, knowing he would get a rise from Carly mentioning her best friend with Dylan Thompson.

"She is not," snapped Carly.

"Yeah, well just watch the next time he comes around, and see how she acts towards him," Michael said smiling.

"Michael, that's gross. Dylan Thompson is too old for Monica. He barely finished high school, and he was always in and out of trouble. He only seems to look back at poor people from the neighborhood long enough to show off his new wealth and success. I wouldn't be surprised if he actually works for Mr. Midnight," Carly said.

"There you go with that whole Mr. Midnight thing again. You know, I'm starting to think you do think he exists," said Michael, unable to stop himself from smiling as Carly became more flustered.

"I never said he didn't exist. I just said it was improbable," Carly replied.

"Sorry, my mistake. But you know that Dylan doesn't work for him. He's an assistant manager at the shipyard."

"Well neither of us has seen him working there. I mean, he works at the docks. That's the least reputable place in the city."

"That doesn't mean that he's working for a known criminal. I think he's a good guy." This was an old argument, and one that he knew he could not win easily with her.

"It doesn't matter. What's important is that we are about to go into high school!" Carly stated.

Michael squeezed his arms even tighter around her. Some final rays of the setting sun pierced through the gathering clouds and blanketed the two of them. They both gazed lovingly into each others' eyes. Suddenly they were disturbed by the sounds of approaching police sirens, screeching tires and gunfire.

Chapter 2: The Museum Heist

Michael and Carly watched intently from the rooftop as the parade of police lights and sirens made its way from the end of the downtown district into their own neighborhood. Leading the way was an old white panel van with its back door open and swinging wildly. The van was weaving through the heavy traffic in what appeared to be an attempt to lose the police. Police cruisers closely tailed the careening van. As Michael watched two helicopters hovering just overhead, all the van's attempts seemed to be in vain. Occasionally a loud pop and crack could be heard coming from the van, and Michael didn't think it was the engine misfiring. Someone in that van was shooting at the police. Every time the gun was fired he could feel Carly cringe. As he rubbed the gooseflesh from her arms he found himself hypnotized by the scene that was about to charge down their own street. Even from three blocks away Michael could see the van's back doors swinging, and with every pop he saw puffs of blue smoke from the open back doors. He could only wonder as to how many people were actually in the van. With a trail of over half a dozen police cars, it felt as though the van were heading right for them.

"Oh, Michael, tell me I'm not seeing this," Carly said, unable to look away.

"Well, you're not going to like what I have to tell you then. Just cover your eyes and I'll let you know when it's over," Michael replied. Carly's hands were covering her mouth.

Michael could see people from the neighborhood looking out from almost every window and doorway trying to see what all the commotion was about. Both he and Carly watched, speechless as the van made its way right toward their front door. It felt surreal, like something from a movie, to Michael as the van swerved into a line of parked cars sending up sparks and bits of debris as it attempted to keep the police at bay.

Finally, he watched the van careen recklessly through the narrow street right below them. He wondered why the police were suddenly staying so far behind the van. Then he heard the loud crack and saw the smoke again, and then he soon understood. He spotted the cracked windshields and the bullet holes in the hoods of the cruisers even from up high on the roof. Still, he thought if the police didn't stop this van soon there was no telling how many innocent people might get hurt.

Michael suddenly thought of the children that had been playing in the street only a few minutes ago. He peered around at the watchful eyes, and saw how they recoiled with fear every time the gun was shot at one of the police cruisers. He watched the Thompsons, an elderly couple who lived across from Carly, retreat from their balcony and watch intently, peeking from their kitchen window. The people in this neighborhood were already afraid of the rising crime rate, but the sound of gunfire while there was still daylight left was still new and frightening to them. It was yet another stark reminder of how far the condition of their neighborhood had gone.

Just as the van came to the end of Carly's block it tried to make a sharp left turn to put some distance between it and the police. Beaten and battered, the van struggled to make the corner. It started to lose control, swerving wildly, sending up plumes of smoke as the tires struggled to grab hold. With tires screeching, the van leaned over on two wheels leaving a trail of debris falling out the back of the open doors. Several black sacks hit the street, exploding into pools of gold and silver. Among the flailing debris a small band of gold and spark of blue could be seen sailing through the air. The van finally crashed over onto its side. It went sliding on its side down the road with a trail of sparks and smoke. The van carried on about thirty feet before colliding into a row of parked cars with a loud and thunderous crash that seemed to shake the very foundations of the buildings in the neighborhood.

"Holy…" Michael could get no other words out. He was speechless. Both of them were now leaning over the building ledge unable to look away.

As the dust settled from the crash, the only sound that could be heard was the police cruisers closing in. Everyone who had been watching seemed to wait breathlessly to see if there would be any movement from any of the vehicles involved. Michael thought that no one would be able to walk away from such a crash. He hoped that no one had been in any of the parked cars when the van hit.

Suddenly a hand emerged from the shattered passenger window of the van. Shaky and unsteady, one of the thieves crawled out and landed on the road with a thud. He had a gash on his forehead, sending thin lines of blood down his face. A black ski mask rested rolled up on the top of his head leaving his face exposed to onlookers. His pants had a tear at the knee and his leg was bloody. The man glanced around quickly at the dozens of faces that were peering at him from all the windows of the neighborhood. He hobbled back toward the van, reaching out to grab at something that sat out of sight. When he looked up and saw the lights and sirens bearing down on him, he abandoned his attempt and fled. As fast as his battered body would carry him, he limped off down an alley and disappeared empty handed. Just then a second hand emerged, and a long narrow face poked out as the police descended on the overturned van.

"Have you ever?" was all he managed. Michael still found himself speechless. When he glanced over at Carly she simply sat unmoving, fixated on the scene.

Michael could not believe what he had just seen. He grabbed Carly by the hand and ran to the rooftop exit. They bounded down the stairs two at a time, leaving Carly struggling to keep up with him.

"Michael, where are we going?" Carly asked.

"We're going down there," Michael replied.

"Michael!" Carly said firmly. She pulled Michael's hand yanking him to a stop right in front her family's apartment, number four fifteen. She seemed startled by his sudden need to run down to the scene. "I think the police will have things under control. We should probably just stay here."

"Yeah, but..." Michael began.

Suddenly the door to Carly's apartment flew open. Her mother, Carol, stood before them wide eyed and panicked. Mrs. Edwards was a short, full-figured woman with wide framed glasses that covered much of her face. She was always dressed stylishly and would never be caught without her makeup and hair done. As she stood in her doorway facing

Michael and Carly she still wore the dress she'd had on during the graduation ceremony.

"Good heavens, there you two are," she said grabbing their wrists and pulling them inside. "I was so worried that you both might have been down there." She turned and pointed towards the window facing the street, not seeming to know how to refer to the scene. "I want you both nowhere near that horrible mess out there."

"We're okay, Mrs. Edwards. We were just gonna go down there and make sure that everyone was alright," Michael said. Carly simply rolled her eyes.

"Oh, no you don't. You two are going nowhere until the police have said its all clear," Mrs. Edwards said, slowly making her way in to the living room. She sat down on the old green sofa and stared at the TV, clutching her hands over her mouth.

Michael and Carly watched intently from the window as more emergency workers and vehicles arrived. Michael saw the frightened look on Carly's face. He wrapped his arm around her, and he felt her flinch as rescue workers dropped some heavy metal equipment that sounded chillingly like the recent gunfire.

"I can't believe something like this could happen right here. I know things are getting bad, but something like this seems crazy," said Carly. Michael pulled her in tighter and kissed the top of her head.

"What happened, Mrs. Edwards? Have they said anything on the TV yet?" Michael asked, turning to Carly's mother.

"Some men robbed the museum. Apparently there was some big fancy diamond on display," said Mrs. Edwards.

"It's called the Faith Diamond, Mom," Carly said, never averting her eyes from the scene.

"Yes, that's the one. Only they took even more than that. They got away with all kinds of things. Well, maybe they didn't exactly get away. They've left a trail of destruction across the whole city, at least that's how they've said it on TV. It sounds like they even shot one of the museum security guards, but I haven't heard his condition yet. They shot at policemen too. Luckily none got hurt. Oh, this is just dreadful," said Mrs. Edwards. She never took her gaze away from the TV.

"Mom, where's Dad?" Carly asked, turning sharply toward her mother.

"He had to go into the lab after your ceremony. He should be home soon. This is the one time I'm glad he's coming home late, let me tell you," said Mrs. Edwards.

"I'm going to call his cell," said Carly, heading to the kitchen phone.

"You should phone your grandfather, Michael. He'll probably be worried sick until he hears from you," said Mrs. Edwards.

"I will, Mrs. Edwards, definitely before we go to the grad party," said Michael, knowing his grandfather would be listening intently to the radio, getting all the details.

"Oh, I don't know if I like the idea of you two going out so late to this party," said Mrs. Edwards.

"You don't have to worry, Mrs. Edwards. It's just at the school, and their bussing us all home after," Michael answered.

"All the same, I just won't rest easy until Carly gets home."

Michael came over and sat on the arm of the couch, and started to watch the news footage of the police chase. The footage showed the van as it wildly flew past commuters on the busy downtown roads. It struck Michael as funny that he had never noticed the big dents in the sides of the van as it came right below them. It seemed, according to the footage, that the van had ploughed through several cars and at least one glass walled bus stop as it frantically tried to evade the police. The cameras had also managed to get a shot of the maniacal gunman who stood at the back of the van as the doors swung about. The gunman clutched the side of the van with one hand, and with the other leveled a massive handgun at the police. Suddenly Carly's building and their street flashed onto the screen. The chase finale began to then show repeatedly on the screen. 'Police chase ends in east side.' The caption read. It felt odd to Michael to see his neighborhood on the TV, especially with such notoriety.

As Michael sat, eyes glued to the TV footage, he pulled out his cell phone and dialed his grandpa. The line rang busy so Michael closed his phone and slid it back into his pocket. He would have to try again later. He was sure that some of his grandfather's friends had phoned to talk about the big story outside and no doubt how such things never seemed to happen back in their day.

"He's just leaving the lab now," Carly said, returning to the living room.

"Oh thank goodness," said Mrs. Edwards, dropping her hands from her face down to her chest.

"Carly, the police have just taped off the area, and people are starting to gather. Can we please go down there now? I'm sure some of our friends will show up," Michael said, practically pleading. He couldn't quite put into words the exact reason he felt the need to head down to the crime scene, but he knew he had to and just hoped Carly would agree.

"Alright fine, but I don't know what your fascination is with getting down there to see something like that," said Carly, her hands firmly planted on her hips.

"You two be careful and don't stray too far," Mrs. Edwards called after them.

The police worked fast cordoning off the area. Paramedics and emergency workers were quick to contain the crash and cope with the injured. As police and paramedics hustled about containing the scene, people from the neighborhood began to gather and watch with curiosity behind streams of yellow police tape. Everyone watched intently as two of the men in the van were carried off on stretchers. Both were loaded into ambulances, but neither received any sympathy from the gathering crowd. The others were still being carefully extracted from the dilapidated van. All the onlookers were talking amongst themselves, sharing what they had each seen, each believing that they had had the best vantage point to see the chase, and the crash that ended it all. The sun, no longer visible, cast a purplish glow over the street.

Most people from the neighborhood had experienced crime, but even a scene like this was new for most neighborhood residents. Fear and morbid curiosity lured people to the edge of the police tape. Many seemed to think that a closer look would help them understand what had just happened. Michael and Carly were now among the crowd on the street, trying to get a closer look. From overhearing the random conversations around them they learned that no bystanders had been hurt in the crash, and by some miracle there had been no one in any of the cars or on the sidewalk as the van crashed.

"Ooh, Carly, over here," said Monica, waving at her. "Carly, oh my gosh, can you believe this?" she screeched from across the crowd. Her dark hair was still up and she still wore her grad dress. She clearly seemed out of place, but it didn't faze her.

Carly made her way to talk with Monica as Michael surveyed the damage. Michael could vaguely overhear the two girls as he stood at the edge of yellow tape. He suddenly felt his foot lightly knock into something small, and heard it skid across the pavement with a metallic sound. He had barely felt it, but still looked down to see what it was.

It really didn't seem like anything extraordinary at first. He had only knocked it lightly and it had slid a foot away. It was a ring, the last light of the setting sun reflected off its golden band. Michael could almost feel some kind of power emanating from it, drawing him closer. Without thinking, he bent down and picked it up. The ring was a gold band with a small blue gem on its face; there were also several hieroglyphs that ran along the band. He was mesmerized, unable to look away from it. Its blue gem seemed alive to him as the centre appeared to swirl and dance. It sparkled like no ring Michael had ever seen before. He started to forget all about what had just happened, or about the people and police all around him. All he was focused on was the ring. He took his eyes off the blue gem only long enough to look at the strange hieroglyphs that ran up both sides of the ring's band. He delicately ran his thumb over the markings. The ring began to tremble slightly in his hand.

"Hey Mike," said Dave from behind him, pulling Michael out of his trance. "Can you believe this?" Dave still had his dark hair immaculately done, and instead of his usual jeans and t-shirt, was dressed in a shirt and tie from graduation.

"I know this is crazy!" said Michael. He glanced down and saw that the ring no longer trembled, and wondered if he had even seen it at all. He found himself completely unable to let go of the ring, so he quickly shoved it into his back pocket, almost forgetting about it the moment he did so. With everyone so distracted, no one seemed to notice.

"I was just on my way to the grad party when I heard the sirens. Next thing I know I've gotta duck into the coffee shop for cover," said Dave, pointing his thumb back over his shoulder at the coffee shop at the end of the block.

"Wow, at least you had somewhere to duck into," said Michael, trying to peer past the crowd to see some of the action.

"Man, Perminder will die when he hears he missed this," Dave said.

Emergency workers were hard at work erasing the scene from the neighborhood. Police and emergency equipment were attempting to pry the getaway van from the row of smashed cars. A flatbed truck waited on the other side of the grisly scene to haul away the dilapidated vehicle. Bits of glass and chunks of plastic and metal littered the ground all around the crash site. Oil and other fluids stained the pavement.

"Hey guys, the police are clearing the area. Let's head back up and watch from the roof," said Carly, appearing from amid the crowd. She was alone now as Monica had left.

"Not me. I'm going to head to the party. I'll see you both there?" said Dave.

"You bet. We'll head there in a while. You know, so we can be fashionably late," said Michael with a wave to his friend. Dave casually walked along the line of police tape, taking his time leaving, trying to see as much as he could before he passed by.

Michael followed Carly back to the rooftop. From there they watched the rest of the spectacle as the police continued investigating the scene. The paramedics had hauled off another man from inside the van. He had looked pretty beat up. The van itself was currently being cleaned out by investigators, who were collecting and bagging everything they pulled from the wreckage. The police had the hardest time getting many of the older people from the neighborhood to clear the scene. The crowd only seemed to grow as Michael and Carly left. The entire neighborhood had heard of the incident, and many apparently wanted to come see for themselves. Michael kept an eye open for his grandpa. It wouldn't be unheard of to see Dale Novak walking that far with his cane leading the way. Blindness had never slowed the old man down. However, Michael's grandpa was nowhere to be seen. Michael reminded himself to phone him soon.

After some time, things finally began to calm down. Night had long since arrived and the steady hum of glowing streetlights were the only noise now heard from the roof. Carly moved over to a couple of patio chairs in the middle of the rooftop and Michael came to join her. The chairs creaked, and Carly feared they would break as they sat down. Michael hardly seemed to notice and simply plopped down, resting his feet on the inflated pool edge. Last summer Dave and Perminder had brought a kiddie pool up to sit in. It lasted all of a week. Then the water started to turn green and Carly had to drain it herself. No one seemed to notice.

"Can you believe that?" Carly asked, motioning to the street below.

"Yeah I know. Who would have thought we would ever see anything like that? Makes you wonder what's going to happen next," said Michael.

Michael made a disgruntled face and began to shift irritably before shoving his hand into his back pocket. Before Carly could ask what was wrong Michael reached into his pocket and pulled out the ring.

"What is that?" Carly asked, peering curiously at the ring.

"Found it down there," Michael said motioning to the street below.

"Where down there?" asked Carly.

"Down by the police tape when I was watching everything."

"What? Michael did you take something from the crime scene?"

"No, it wasn't like that; it was outside the yellow tape. Honest," Michael said.

"Why would you do such a thing? Do you have any idea how much trouble you could get into if you get caught?"

"No, no it wasn't like that. It was..." he began defending himself, when suddenly something strange happened. The ring began to glow a bright brilliant blue and tremble about in his palm.

"Oh my goodness. Michael what's happening?" Carly asked, her mood suddenly turning to shock at the sight of the glowing ring.

"I have no idea," Michael said surprisingly calm. "It feels so strange."

Michael Novak, you have been chosen, said a voice that seemed to come from out of nowhere. The voice had a resonating deep baritone ring to it. It was simultaneously ominous and soothing.

"What the...Did you hear that?" Michael asked still grasping the glowing ring.

"Hear what? What's going on?" Carly asked, her voice full of fear.

"Are you telling me you didn't hear that voice?" Michael asked.

"All I've heard is your voice," Carly answered.

"No, it's not mine. It's someone else's. I don't even know where it came from."

Michael you have been chosen, the voice repeated.

"There it is again," Michael said, suddenly leaping to his feet, and looking around for the source of the voice.

"Michael put that thing down please. We'll take it back down to the police," Carly pleaded, panic creeping into her voice.

"I don't think I can," Michael replied.

"Of course you can. Just…" Carly started.

The glowing began to intensify. It started to buzz loudly in his palm. Michael looked at the ring, his eyes going as big as saucers. The blue glow seemed to spread. Soon his whole body seemed covered by it. Michael clenched his teeth and his mouth drew back, as though he expected some jolt of pain. Still, he never let it fall from his hand.

"Michael, I'm going to go get some help. Just hang on," Carly said, her voice faltering. She stumbled slightly as she ran towards the door.

"Wait. Don't just leave me," Michael begged.

"I'm scared. I'm just going down to get my dad or somebody," said Carly, still making her way to the door. Her hands fumbled blindly behind her, grasping for the door knob.

"Carly, I'm starting to feel something weird," said Michael. He held out the ring as though to protect himself from it, yet he never released it from his grasp.

"Michael, please, just hold on…" Carly began.

Suddenly, without warning, Michael was struck by a big flash of blue lightning.

Chapter 3: The One Chosen

Michael felt the heat and force of the blast envelope him, but he was perfectly fine. His only thoughts were that Carly had been hurt. As the smoke from the blast began to dissipate, Michael saw that the force of the lightning blast had sent Carly sprawling to the hard surface of the roof. She was face down and slightly winded, gasping for air. He could see a thin blanket of smoke float by her. He watched intently, too frightened to move as she propped herself onto her elbows. The heat of the blast still hung in the air.

"Carly!" Michael yelled out in fear.

Finally breaking the spell that seemed to have been locking his legs in place, Michael ran to her side. As he reached out to touch her, he saw that his arms no longer resembled his arms at all. He was now wearing something over his hands and forearms that he had never seen before. He stumbled backwards from the shock, his eyes scanning his arms, trying to comprehend.

"Oh my God, Carly! I think something weird's going on here," Michael said in a wavering voice.

"Michael…." Carly began. As her words trailed off Michael dropped his arms to look at her. He was relieved to see that she looked uninjured, but her wide eyed look of fear and confusion did not make him feel any better.

"Michael!" Carly squealed again. "Is that really you under there?"

Standing where Michael had been a moment before was a man looking only vaguely familiar. He wore a yellow bandana on his head that came down over the top of his face right to the tip of his nose, the ends of which flowed out the back in two long flowing strands. He had a tight yellow sleeveless shirt that had small fanned-out blue shield guards at the top of the shoulders. Emblazoned on the chest was a big letter T, its stem ending in a jagged lightning bolt shape. His pants were blue and had a yellow belt which also had ends that came out in two very long strands that seemed to sway and billow in the wind. He wore yellow boots that had two horizontal blue stripes that ran around the back of his calves. As well as blue arm guards that ended in a pair of fingerless gloves, the ring shone brightly from his right middle finger. Sheathed on his back he had a large staff that had a blue jewel embedded in the end. Smoke still danced and swirled around him in long thin tendrils.

"Michael...is that...you? Please tell me that's you," Carly asked again. Her hands had begun to shake slightly; her bangs were now glued to her head with sweat.

"Yeah, it's me. At least I think it still is," he said, as he examined himself. He strained his neck trying to get a good look at himself all over.

"Michael, what happened? Are you hurt?" Carly asked.

"No, I feel...fine. A little weird but actually really good," Michael replied, shocked.

Michael had no idea what was going on. There hadn't even been any thunder around or any other lightning. It seemed to come out of nowhere and strike him, like it was aiming just for him. He could now feel a surge of power flow into his veins.

"I actually thought you were the one who got hurt there. Are you okay?" Michael asked.

"Jury's still out on that one. I mean physically, yes, but mentally..." Carly responded.

"Maybe this is all a dream and I'm actually really hurt and on my way to the hospital."

"If this is a dream then I'm having it too."

Michael Novak you are the one chosen to be the next Titan.

The same voice came again and now Michael was determined to find its source.

"Did you hear it that time?" he asked Carly. She only looked at him with wide, questioning eyes, shaking her head.

"Who are you? What's going on here?" Michael said, looking up and seemingly asking no one in particular.

"Michael, I'm scared. What's going on? Who are you talking to?" Carly asked timidly.

Michael could not remember a time in his life when Carly had ever been genuinely frightened. The fact that she was now did nothing to calm Michael's nerves.

"I don't know. Why can't you hear it? There's this voice that keeps telling me..." Michael began.

There is little time, and there is much that you need to be taught.

"There it is again! Are you telling me you can't hear that?" he asked Carly. She shook her head again. She remained motionless, barely able to speak.

You must leave here and come with me, alone. Your training must begin. You must be taught the way of the Titan.

"What? Just go, like that? I don't even know who you are," Michael said, looking up into the evening sky. "Where exactly are we going, and for what?"

"Go? Where do you want to go?" Carly asked.

"I don't want to go anywhere. It's this voice," Michael said, not knowing what else to call it. "He wants me to go. I have no idea what's going on here."

"That makes two of us," Carly said, completely exasperated.

All will be explained to you. Now come, we are wasting precious time.

"Why should I go anywhere you ask me to?" Michael asked.

"No Michael, you can't go anywhere. I mean, look at you," Carly said. "I really don't think you are in a state to be going anywhere."

You have just been transformed into Titan. The ring has sought you out above all others. You have been chosen among many to hold the power of Titan. You now have many special powers, and they need to be explained and shown to you, so you may understand how to use them. Now we must go somewhere private so I may teach you.

"I don't know why I should go anywhere with you. None of this is making any sense," said Michael.

Look about you. Look at the transformation you have already undergone. Do you not wish to know how this can be? If you wish to know the answer to your questions you must trust in me.

There was a long pause as Michael continued to look himself over in wonder. Carly also could not stop staring at him, but it was with a lot less wonder and a lot more confusion. Finally Michael answered.

"Alright," Michael agreed. "We better not go far, or for very long." Michael was willing to follow the voice on instinct. He needed to know more. All he really knew was that something major was now happening to him, and he had to get to the bottom of it.

"Alright!" Carly said loudly. "What do you mean alright?"

Michael tried to take a step closer to comfort her, but she drew back.

"It's going to be okay," he told her. "I'm gonna go and find out just what's going on here." He paused, looking her over, not quite knowing what else he could say to put her at ease. He could only imagine how he would feel if he saw Carly go through what he just had.

"You have to trust me. I really have a strong feeling here. I have to do this. I mean, look at me, don't you want to get some answers to all this?" he asked her, gesturing at his new appearance. "I'll be back before you know it. Please don't say anything to anyone about this while I'm gone. I don't need to freak out anyone else," he pleaded.

She gave him an angry look. She seemed offended that he would even have to ask her to keep things quiet. Of course, Michael thought, who would believe any of this?

"Okay," she said in a voice that told Michael she was still very unsure. "But I'm going to wait right here on the roof for you to get back."

"Okay," he said in his most reassuring tone. He had no idea how long he would be, but he knew there would be little point in arguing.

Then he turned and faced the edge of the building, looking out over downtown. "So," he said to the voice. "Where exactly do you want me to go, and just how do you want me to get there dressed like this?"

Do you see that building due north, the tallest one?

"Yes."

You're going to jump to it.

"WHAT?" Michael said, suddenly wondering if Carly's bad feelings were on target. "Are you crazy? That's the Empress Building. It's the tallest building in the whole city." He was trying to keep his voice down so Carly couldn't hear. "Do you have any idea how tall that thing is, and how far away? Just how do you expect me to do that?"

Leave that part to me. You just leap for that building. Don't worry, you are perfectly safe. I will help you this time. I will give you a little push.

"This time? You know, I'm starting to have second thoughts about this already," said Michael.

Your first test is to trust me.

"Trust you? I can't even see you,"

You must not be afraid. In time, when you are transformed as Titan, you will learn how to do this all by yourself with the greatest of ease. Now jump for that building!

"You mean you want me to get dressed like this again?" said Michael, this time with no response from the voice.

Michael couldn't believe what he was hearing. Then he looked himself over, and figured that enough unbelievable things had happened tonight, so why not believe he could leap across the city. If he could survive being struck by lightning and transformed into this, then why not jump across the city to its tallest building.

"I can't believe I'm about to do this," Michael whispered as he looked at the Empress Building.

Michael turned back and moved to the middle of the roof. He took several big breaths, then started to run to the edge of the roof. Carly couldn't help letting out a high pitched scream, as she saw Michael run for the ledge. Michael eyed the ledge carefully then hit it with his right foot and with all his might he shot himself off the roof and into the air towards the Empress Building.

When Michael shot off the ledge Carly gasped and ran toward him. As she ran, her jaw dropped. She watched Michael launch into the air toward downtown. He flew so high that he faded from view in a streak of blue and yellow.

As Michael took his initial leap off the buildings edge he thought at first that he had made a terrible mistake and that he was going to fall to the ground. Yet as soon as his feet left the ledge, he found himself soaring through the air. He could suddenly feel a giant push from behind that propelled him upwards. It felt as though he had been plucked from the air by an invisible giant and was being whisked across the city. His heart raced as the city flew past him in a streaking blur of halogen lights. He squinted his eyes against the rushing wind. The low buildings of the east end quickly led to the midtown high-rises and beyond. The wind blew the ends of his bandana and belt back at ninety degree angles. Michael felt as if the breath was being sucked from his body. An intense sense of fear and excitement sent shockwaves through him. He was soaring across the city at an incredible speed, yet time itself seemed to be slowing down.

As the Empress' rooftop began to rise towards him, Michael suddenly had visions of being splattered all over downtown Delta City. He quickly prepared to land. He stuck out his legs and prepared for impact. He began kicking in a running motion as the rooftop came into view. As he landed he lost his balance and fell after only a few steps, and ended in a full somersault. He scrambled to his feet, and stood atop the downtown skyscraper. He dusted himself off as he looked out over the city in complete shock.

"Oh man! Oh my God that was incredible!" Michael shouted in absolute awe, as he looked back, trying to spot Carly's apartment from the Empress. "Carly and the guys are never going to believe this."

Michael's nerves felt on edge. He had never even been on a plane in his whole life. Yet he had just flown across the city, only to find himself on the roof of the city's tallest building. The downtown spread out before him in a jungle of illuminated concrete mountains, the East end fading off into the distance. East end living is generally not one of luxury. Michael rarely found occasion to stray more than several blocks out of his neighborhood. He had only ever seen The Empress from a distance. His school had gone there on a field trip once but Michael was forced to miss it after catching a severe cold. Now Michael Novak was sitting atop the city's biggest landmark. This was shaping up to be the most amazing night of his life.

"Whoa!" exclaimed Michael again, this time to the voice. "How did you do that?"

That I will show to you later in your training.

"What's all this training about? Okay, if I can be perfectly honest, this is all starting to freak me out just a little," Michael said. "I hope you're ready to tell me a few things now. Because I really want...no, I need to know just what's going on, and what on earth I've gotten myself into."

Where would you like me to start?

"Well, I want to know everything. What's happening? Who and where are you?" asked Michael, sounding a little agitated. "And please don't tell me that we have to fly off someplace else first, because I like it right here with something solid under my feet."

Very well, I am Azure. I come as an envoy from the gods with these powers, to act as the chosen human's guide. I am here to aid and assist the chosen human in understanding and using his newfound powers. I can never help. Even if I were to want to, I cannot. I am here only to teach and offer advice, and to guide the chosen Titan's decisions. As well to make sure you fully grasp the vast powers you will be granted. You will only ever hear my voice. My body is elsewhere.

"Okay, so that big mystery is solved, I guess," Michael said with sarcasm. "So maybe now you wanna tell me just what's going on here. What is all this about?"

I shall start from the beginning.

"Yes please."

Michael walked over and sat on a heating duct with an amazing view of the city. He wanted to be perfectly comfortable while he listened.

Many centuries ago, the gods of old decided that the world needed a hero to come and protect the people from the evils that they faced. The old gods thought the best one to take on this responsibility would be a human. As a human would be able to best relate to and understand the troubles of this world, this was far better than sending one of their own. They could choose no ordinary human to challenge the evil forces that threatened the world at those times. So they forged a ring, the ring that found you earlier tonight, and put within it many powers of their own to aid the chosen human. The ring was charged to go and search out the most appropriate human host. The ring would then grant these powers to the chosen one. When controlling these powers that human would become the most powerful person in the world. They would become Titan. As Titan, each chosen one must act as protector and guardian of the regular law abiding citizens around them. There have been sixteen Titans chosen throughout history. As each Titan's time would come to pass, a new Titan would be chosen to be a champion for its people. You are the seventeenth.

Azure paused as all this information was being processed by Michael. Finally Michael asked, "So why me? Why now? Where has this Titan been all this time? How come I've never heard of any Titan before?"

About a million other questions were swirling around in Michael's head, but he thought that these ones were the most important for the time being. Finally Azure began to speak again.

As the gods of old began to be forgotten in the new world, their old ways died with them. Their world has now passed on to other realms. Yet the powers that had been granted to the power ring remain. They have been held in limbo for many centuries. There has not been a chosen Titan for close to fifteen hundred years. The gods however did not entirely disappear, but rather took a backseat to the goings on of a world that had long forgotten them. Now however, new evils set about plaguing this world and a hero is needed. But only the bravest, noblest and truest of heart is capable or worthy of controlling the responsibility and the powers of Titan. The ring was to search out the most worthy person to carry this responsibility. That person, Michael Novak, is you.

As Azure spoke this last sentence it hit Michael. Chosen, he thought, for something like this. He could barely believe that this was all true. For the first time Michael felt truly special and important. Michael had never been chosen for anything in his life.

"What is with this costume anyway? Isn't it a little much?" he asked.

Your uniform shall be a beacon, a symbol of hope to all around you. No Titan has ever worn the exact same uniform. There have always been similarities however, such as the Titan symbol on your chest. This uniform is very important to who you shall become and what you will represent.

"I just thought maybe we could talk about it a little before we finalized it. You know maybe make sure it was fashionable in today's world."

The uniform has been chosen. It shall be yours.

Michael could tell that there would be no more point in trying to convince Azure that something a little more modern and up to date could be chosen.

"So, okay then, you're telling me that I've been chosen to be a hero, to be this Titan? Are you sure no one else has turned the job down? I mean, it's just me, me and no one else? How could it have chosen me for something so big? I'm only fourteen. I'm honored, but aren't I a little young?" Michael asked.

You are of average age of the Titans I have trained. The youngest was twelve. No, your age is irrelevant in regard to the power you will have. As I have said the ring chose you for good reason. The ring sought you out and you alone. It was no coincidence that you came to be in possession of the power ring tonight. The ring was searching for you. Of everyone, you most represent what the ring stands for. You may decline the responsibility if you wish. If you accept, it will take very hard work and dedication.

Azure said this in a milder tone of warning that almost made him sound human to Michael for the first time.

Your duty as Titan to protect the world from evil, must come above all else. By no means will these powers make your own life easier. At many times your life will very likely be in great danger. Others could also find themselves in danger simply by association. It is a very big decision. Unfortunately there is no time to waste. You must tell me now, do you accept?

"That's it?" exclaimed Michael. "You want me to give you an answer just like that?"

I am afraid so.

"Don't I at least get a minute to think it over?" asked Michael.

All right I will give you one minute.

"Wow, that's so thoughtful and considerate of you. This is the biggest decision of my life, and you want me to make it in just one minute?" Michael paused and Azure did not respond. "Okay hold on one minute," said Michael.

Michael stood in silence, thinking. He wished that he could see Azure. He had never known it could be so difficult to talk to someone that you couldn't see. He thought about what Azure had told him. About the powers, his responsibilities, and even the risk involved. Finally Michael came to a decision.

"Okay, I'll do it," Michael said triumphantly.

Very well, from now on as long as you are in this form you shall be known to the world as **Titan**.

Chapter 4: Mr. Midnight

Ned Baker was currently discovering what it was to be completely and utterly lost and alone while being trapped in a city of millions. All Ned needed was to find somewhere secluded so he could think things through. Yet in a city so vast, he seemed unable to find one isolated corner. He was deathly afraid that everyone he saw was watching him suspiciously, some even recognizing him. Trying to avoid eye contact, he hunched way over, as though he were walking into a heavy wind. Paranoid, he convinced himself that everyone knew him, and that he would be found and caught any minute. Such is the life, he thought, of someone wanted by the police.

Of course Ned wished he wasn't the only member of his crew to escape from the botched museum heist. The cops had swarmed the upturned getaway van so fast that no one else was able to get out. While the van was flipping over and over, Ned had been tossed around, and had smashed his knee on the metal roof. It was gashed open and aching. It left him limping severely, making any quick escape impossible.

When his knee hit he lost his grip on the bag of goods he had been carrying. He had been dazed as the van came to a stop and he started to crawl out, never once attempting to grab any of the loot. As he escaped the van, the spectators watched him closely, causing him to pause momentarily before fleeing.

With so many valuable goods, and his partners, still sitting in the van Ned had a choice to return to the van or escape. He chose the latter. Looking back, he should have at least grabbed something, anything, on his way out. Not once did he consider any of his partners in the wreckage. He just needed something to bring to his boss, Mr. Midnight.

As he was trying to limp away, he had heard a low whimpering coming from inside the van. His partners were begging Ned to help them out of the wreckage. Ned had suddenly froze, wondering what to do. He felt the urge to reach into the van, past his partners, and at least grab a sack. The police cruisers speeding up to the scene made the final decision for him, and he turned away empty handed. As he made his first step he put all of his weight down on his injured leg and it sent him sprawling to the ground. Ned quickly got back up, ignoring the throbbing pain in his knee. He limped as fast as he could up the street and down the first alley that he came to, vanishing into the darkness.

After escaping he spent the rest of the day trying to lay low. It was difficult as his face and name were on every radio and TV in the city. He had decided that it would be best to wait until dark before making his move to some place safe. With great trepidation he would begin to make his way from the east end of the city down to the docks, the shadow of downtown. Until then he would use the time to rest his wounded knee, which still trickled blood down his shin.

Ned pulled his cell phone from his pants pocket and was relieved to find that although cracked in two places from the crash it still picked up a signal. He tried phoning several of his friends, but none answered. By now many of the people he knew would have heard about the botched heist. No one who knew of Ned's situation would even consider getting in touch with him. He realized he was now truly alone. Ned couldn't blame them really. He would have done the same if any of them had been in his position.

He finally hid in an alley about twenty blocks from the scene of the accident, in an isolated little spot behind an office building where someone had thrown away some chairs. The chairs had torn fabric seats and rusted metal legs, but they still sat just fine and sure beat sitting on the ground. Sitting in a dirty alley waiting for the cover of night, Ned tried to formulate a plan.

Soon Ned would head to the base of Mr. Midnight. By now his boss would have heard the full story of what went down. Ned wished that there was someone else with him to help shoulder some of the blame for what had happened. His boss was not famous for being very forgiving. As the moon drew higher and higher into the sky, Ned began to make his way slowly towards Mr. Midnight.

Ned wove his way through the back alleys and deserted streets of downtown. He stuck to the shadows, doing his best to avoid all contact with people. This became much easier as the tall buildings and bustling streets gave way to the grittier quieter area of the docks. At night the docks were mostly vacant. The only activity you were bound to see was surely illegal. Ned approached the downtown harbor that served as Mr. Midnight's headquarters. He had come across only two police cruisers on his journey, and saw them far enough in advance to duck out of the way. The few times that he had seen other people on the street they had noticed him limping, but none seemed to recognize him from the TV news bulletins. Paranoia set in as Ned crossed fewer and fewer people along his journey. He was starting to believe going to see his boss might be a bad idea. Yet when he tried to think of another plan he came up empty.

He had rehearsed on his long walk back what he would say in his own defense. All the others had been caught. Ned planned to use that to deflect the blame onto them. After all, he hadn't been the one driving, or shooting at the police. That's it, he thought, Sam was surely to blame since he was the one who went nuts and started shooting. Although, he thought, it had been him who had been distracted by that strange ring in the display case.

He wished that he could just block out the lasting image of the ring from his mind. The ring had been the cause of all his grief. The heist had gone like clockwork, just like they had rehearsed, until he had spotted the ring amid the museum's displays. It had not even been on his list of items to steal, yet he had been so mesmerized by it he simply was unable to leave without it. It had been the thought of the ring that had made him stop as he exited the van. He had wanted to go back and retrieve it, but the police had made that impossible. Of course being distracted would be information that Ned would not bother to tell Mr. Midnight. He was more scared of facing that man and having to tell him firsthand that his crew had failed than he had been of anything in his life. Ned had actually never had a face to face meeting with Mr. Midnight, and had been hoping to never have one.

As he approached the front of the building, it stood like a concrete and glass monolith. It was a vast block of concrete with small panels of windows slapped on the outside. It gave the visual of soullessness, and a cold hard sense of power. Just the sight of it sent shivers of dread through Ned's body.

As usual there was one guard on duty out front. A giant gorilla of a man in dark glasses towered over the entrance. As soon as he spotted Ned coming the guard shot one mammoth arm out and pulled the front door open for him to pass through. Ned slowed to a point where he hardly seemed to be moving. His mind quickly flashed to the foreboding image of his boss, whose appearance Ned had heard about plenty of times. He wondered if he shouldn't just turn around now and make a run for it. Maybe he could just lay low for a while. Then, feeling the eyes of the guard bear down on him, he headed into the building.

The entrance of the building was set up much like the main floor of a grand hotel. There were lounges and a bar, and even music playing softly. Not wanting to be noticed, Ned dropped his head down and quickly tried to make his way down the long hallway to the bank of elevators at the far end. He wanted desperately to avoid the looks of disapproval or sympathy of the few people hanging around. As he shuffled his way through the lobby, he couldn't help but hear the low whispers that followed him. Waiting for the elevator was the longest twenty seconds of Ned's life.

He wanted more than anything to turn and run out of the building. More than once he had seen failed employees making the doomed journey to Mr. Midnight's office. Ned had always wondered what he would do if he were ever in that position. Ned had often wondered about the things he would say and how he would act in front of Mr. Midnight. Now, his mind was at a total loss. He knew he would be lucky if he was able to speak at all.

Before the elevator door could even fully open Ned rushed in, pushed the button for the top floor, and faced the back until the doors had closed. As the elevator came to life and began its climb Ned's stomach began to do somersaults. The elevator seemed to crawl. The melodious dinging chime of the floors ticking by felt like torture.

Finally the doors opened at the seventh floor and Ned started down the narrow hallway that led to Mr. Midnight's office. Ned always assumed the rumors of this floor were largely embellished, but judging by the cold, sterile look of the passageway to the office door, he started to think that all the rumors were true. The hallway was the exact opposite of the lobby. The hall was narrow, brightly lit, and painted stark white with no pictures, clocks or anything on the walls.

At the end of the hall was a large set of black double doors. Ned tried to gather all of his courage. On the other side of the door was the sum of all his fears. Just as he was raising his hand to knock on the door he saw a small camera staring at him from the top left corner above the doors. He immediately froze. He knocked firmly and after a moment the large doors swung open. Ned swallowed hard, wiped his sweaty hands on his pants and walked in.

At first Ned thought that the room was completely black, but as his eyes adjusted he saw that the room was large and lit with only the glow of the streetlights and the moon filtering in. The moonlight cast an eerie glow, making it hard to see the darkly dressed figures in the room. There were two large guards standing on either side of the door, both even bigger than the one at the entrance. Ned walked between them and up to the large desk that sat at the other side of the room against a large bank of windows. Mr. Midnight loomed larger than life behind the desk. He wore an all black suit with a red tie and a black fedora, just as Ned had heard. Concealing his face was a solid gold mask. Ned started to bite his bottom lip. Mr. Midnight sat upright with his elbows resting on the desk and his gloved hands folded in front of his face. He was silent for several moments, as though quietly passing judgment over Ned. While he sat, the guards remained silent. The only sound in the room was the thundering beat of Ned's heart.

To Mr. Midnight's right stood his loyal and deadly female bodyguard Kaizen. She was the only one in the room whom Ned had ever seen. She was cold, emotionless and intimidating. Her face was simultaneously beautiful and hideous. Almost as much rumor and mystery surrounded her as it did Mr. Midnight himself. She had been scarred long ago and had a silver plate covering the top right part of her face. She had also lost her eye in the same injury, a glowing red mechanical eye shone where her own once was. Her real eye was now glaring at Ned. Her body was feminine but very athletic and muscular. Ned had once seen her fight off five full grown men.

Standing alone in the middle of this scene, Ned felt like a little minnow that had been dropped into a shark tank.

"Mr. Midnight, sir," Ned began in a weak and shaky voice. "I just want to s..."

Mr. Midnight gently raised one gloved hand, silencing Ned.

"I give you a simple job," Mr. Midnight interrupted, his voice sounding smooth and venomous. "And not only do you and your team not complete it, but you show up here at my doorstep with every policeman in the city knowing who you are and hunting you down. The rest of your team is in jail, and telling lord knows what to any policeman or lawyer that will listen." Mr. Midnight paused looking him over while Ned stood there frozen, his eyes wide with fear. "On top of it all, you stand here before me empty handed."

"I...I'm s-sorry, sir...b-but..." Ned tried to say, but the harder he tried the more he seemed to stammer. He couldn't remember his hands having ever felt so hot and sweaty before. Giant beads of sweat rolled down his forehead and back. He could remember his rehearsed speech no more than the answer to two plus two.

"SORRY?" Mr. Midnight suddenly roared, this time slamming his hand down on the desk, looking as though he was about to get up and pummel him. Ned cringed.

"I cannot stand for sorry I'm afraid," Mr. Midnight seethed.

"Sir I can explain. I mean, it was our driver you see. He had us tailed by the cops as soon as we left. And one of the other guys, Sam, he kinda' lost it. He just started shooting at the cops," Ned said, trying to explain. He could see however that none of it was working. All of his rehearsed speech would be useless here. Then Mr. Midnight once again raised his hand to silence Ned.

"I am not interested in your pathetic excuses," Mr. Midnight said flatly.

"B-but, sir, please, can you give me a chance to explain?" pleaded Ned.

"Alright," said Mr. Midnight. "Can you explain to me how you alone managed to escape, and without any of my cargo?"

Ned's jaw simply hung open. He was speechless with fear.

Mr. Midnight relaxed into his chair and then made a slight hand gesture to Kaizen, who quickly jumped to life at his side. She stepped forward and snapped her fingers at the two guards by the doors. Before

Ned could register what was going on, the two guards had stepped forward and grabbed him by either arm. Both towered over Ned, their grip on his arms like vices practically lifting him clear off his feet.

"Please see to it gentlemen that our friend Ned here," Mr. Midnight said to the men, "understands that ineptitude of this kind simply cannot be tolerated in my organization."

Ned felt his insides almost hit the floor as he was suddenly being dragged out the door towards the elevators. He thought of trying to scream or struggle, but knew it would be useless. He wasn't even sure he could will his arms or legs to move. Maybe he would have been better off if he had just let the police capture him after all.

Ned knew he was about to find out just what had happened to all those other sorry souls who had made the same trek up to the seventh floor. He started to wonder what sort of rumors would start to circulate about him. He supposed he would never know. Ned had not cried since he was in the third grade when his dog had died, but now tears began to trickle down his face. Before they had even reached the elevators he was sobbing.

As Kaizen went to close the doors behind them, Mr. Midnight stood and paced in front of the windows that looked out over the city, his city.

"So many plans for so long, and now so close to seeing them come to fruition I feel surrounded by people I cannot trust to do a simple errand." He paused, looking over at Kaizen who was once again at his side. "The only one I can ever really trust besides myself is you Kaizen," Mr. Midnight said, agitated.

"For a long time Delta City has been at the mercy of Mr. Midnight and now so close to bringing the city to its knees and having it completely in my grasp, fools such as this could threaten it all," Mr. Midnight said. "I am not about to let it slip through my fingers. See to it that Ned is made an example of. Now after years of planning and hard work I have the ultimate plan, and I will not allow anyone's stupidity or mistakes to ruin it."

Kaizen stood solidly and said nothing in reply. She simply gave a firm nod of understanding.

"Much is happening, Kaizen," Mr. Midnight said without looking her way. "My syndicate is at its zenith as we speak. Our competition and enemies are vanquished; the police are helpless to stop us. The coming weeks will see that things stay in our favor for some time to come. We must be on our guard. I will not lose this city to anyone."

Mr. Midnight walked down the length of the room to a large cabinet mounted on the wall and opened it. Inside was a shiny silver instrument roughly the same size and shape as a handgun. This was unlike any other gun, however, and Delta City was about to find out just how much so. Despite all the problems he had encountered, it would take a miracle for someone to stop what he was about to unleash upon the city in the coming days. The full details of his plan were nearly complete and it would give him absolute control. As of now the residents of Delta City said his name with awe and fear. Soon they would be afraid to say his name at all.

Chapter 5: Titan Training

With Azure's decree still ringing in his ears, Michael looked down at himself finally taking in the transformation that he had undergone. He no longer looked like plain old Michael Novak. He felt the surge of power coursing through his veins. He was so full of energy that he thought he might burst. So much had happened in such a short time. Michael wasn't even sure how he would convince himself of it, let alone anyone else. It all felt so dream like. It also felt weird every time Azure called him Titan out loud, but Michael was sure that in time he would adjust to the name change.

"So, what exactly are all these powers that I have?" asked Michael, brimming with excitement at the possibilities that lay ahead.

As Titan, you will possess great power. You will have heightened strength that will make you the strongest living human on this planet. Take care however as your strength will be far from limitless. As well, you have accelerated speed and agility. You will also have the ability to jump large distances with the greatest of ease, as we did earlier.

Michael smiled as he recalled the rush he felt from soaring through the air across the city. If his other powers were anywhere near as cool as that, he couldn't wait to try them out.

Also you will find that you will be nearly invulnerable, and cannot sustain injury easily. Should you, your wounds will heal faster than the normal rate of other humans.

Lastly, your staff is also one of your greatest weapons. You shall find it most useful when defending yourself, and in attacking your enemies. It is indestructible, so you need not worry about its safety. The jewel at its end has the ability to harness and shoot lightning at any object or enemy. This however is not a power that you should rely on, as you will only be able to use it a small amount before it's energy is depleted, and needs to recharge itself.

"Alright then. Is there anything else I need to know, or am I ready to just jump into this and start busting up bad guys and saving the day?"

Michael was busy flexing his newly heightened muscles and taking swings at the air with his staff as he spoke.

He felt energized and empowered with his new abilities. Some deep part of him knew from the moment he had laid eyes on the ring in the gutter that it was something important. As soon as his eyes had locked on it, it had drawn him in. Of course he never, in his wildest dreams, thought that this in any way would be a part of his future. Now that it was, he wanted nothing more than to fulfill his new obligations, and put his new powers to use.

You are almost too eager, Titan. It may get you into trouble. You must learn patience if you are to be effective in your role. Before you start your duty as Titan you must first know how to use all your new powers comfortably and safely. Your own safety and that of others is paramount. Now let us begin.

Over the next several hours Titan, staff sheathed to his back, ran through what he thought of as the standard obstacle course for new superheroes. He wasn't sure if it would really help once he found himself in real battle, but of course it couldn't hurt, he figured. Azure seemed to want to have Titan ready to be able to, as close as possible, fulfill his new duties by sunrise.

Much to his dismay, Titan was first made to practice his jumping abilities. Michael Novak had never done particularly well with heights. Being Titan did nothing to squash his fear. The first great leap he had made was actually done by Azure. Somehow it had all seemed so much less frightening when he knew that Azure was doing the real work and he had just been along for the ride. So he was in for quite a shock when it was his turn for his first solo jump.

Now that you have gained trust in me, your next test is to jump to that large building directly east of us.

"You mean that huge one with the big antenna on top?" Titan said. He couldn't help thinking at the same time how he would not have chosen to jump right to the next tallest building in the city for his very first attempt.

Yes, that is the one

"Are you kidding me? Don't you think I should try something a little easier for now, and then work my way up to the mammoth skyscrapers?" he said, unable to believe what he had heard.

You need not worry. I am your guide. I am here to watch out for you. I would not ask it of you if I did not believe you were capable of doing this. If you are focused you will find your mind and body able to adjust naturally to t he challenge. It will not be as hard as you think.

It was going to be much harder than he had originally thought, Titan was sure of it. There was no way Azure could be right about that, he thought. It seemed far to Titan's eyes. It was hard not to wonder if maybe Azure was a little out of touch with the whole guide business after such a lengthy lay off. He knew, however, there was no sense delaying the inevitable. He started to walk over to the far edge of the building so he could get himself a good running start.

"Okay on three then," Titan said. In a sprinter's stance, he prepared himself, rubbing his hands together vigorously.

Titan, you greatly underestimate your strength. You will not need that much of a run to make it with your powers.

"Alright, but I don't see how I'm gonna know how much energy to put into it," Titan said, walking back over the roof closing the gap to the edge.

Focus on your goal. See where you want to go clearly in your mind and you will do fine.

Titan stood still, focusing on his target several blocks away. He began taking deep breaths, and concentrated as hard as he could. Finally when he thought he could prepare no more, he took three big steps towards his target and launched himself into the air.

"Wahoo!" Titan yelled, with excitement and all the remaining air in his lungs.

The same sensations began to sweep through his body as on his first jump from Carly's rooftop. The air rushed past him in a deafening roar, with the wind causing him to squint slightly against its force. The building he was jumping towards started to come much faster than the last one. Suddenly he realized that Azure was right. He had underestimated his own newfound strength, and was about to completely overshoot the rooftop.

"Oh no, pull up. Gotta pull up!" Titan yelped.

Titan quickly threw all his weight down towards the rooftop as hard as he could. He found himself suddenly in a steep decline. He hit the rooftop hard with a thud and bounced into the air, and then rolled to a stop only a foot from the building's edge. Titan yelped as he leaped to his feet, rubbing his right forearm furiously as he had smacked it on the hard surface of the rooftop. At first the pain was intense and he truly feared a broken bone. Lightning bolts of pain shot up his whole arm. As he inspected his forearm he could already see a deep purple bruise forming where it had hit. Then to his surprise, as quick as the bruise surfaced it disappeared. The sharp pains faded as well.

"Uh...whoa! Okay, I think that went well," Titan exclaimed. He couldn't stop looking at his once injured arm. He expected the bruise and pain to suddenly reappear. He looked around at the city below him with a broad smile. "I mean no broken bones, no loss of life. We're doing well here, don't you think?"

Yes, very fine indeed. Okay, now again. This time, you pick where you jump.

"I was kind of thinking about having a little break. You know, enjoy not putting my life on the line for a minute," Titan said.

There is no time for breaks tonight. You still have much to learn before daybreak. This city desperately needs a hero, and I plan to have you ready to fill that role by morning. Now, jump again.

"Okay, okay," Titan said getting back to his feet. Under his breath he said, "Man, what did I get myself into here? Sheesh."

Titan looked out over the city. He was surrounded by tall buildings. He chose one that was much closer this time. His target seemed much more attainable. He jumped to the building across the street. It was over twenty stories tall, but half the distance and presumably safer. He still managed to land on his face, but jumped up and dusted himself off quickly.

"Hey, I think I'm getting the hang of this," Titan said, wiping dirt from his face. "My landings are still a little touchy though."

Very good, now again.

"Um, how many jumps do you want me to do tonight?" Titan asked.

As many as it takes for you to feel completely comfortable.

"Okay then," Titan said, letting out a big sigh. "Next jump comin' up."

As he lined up for his next jump, he couldn't help but think again that this superhero stuff was way harder than he would have thought. However, as soon as he thought of himself in that light, superhero, he felt a strange excitement creep through his body again. It was these thoughts that kept him going as he acquainted himself with his new jumping ability.

Soon Titan felt like an old pro, even though it had only been just over an hour. He felt like he had literally jumped around the entire city from rooftop to rooftop. He had even jumped from the roof to the ground and back again. Luckily his landings were also getting better, so he never needed to test the boundaries of his durability. As he continued he had begun to fell much more comfortable with the heights as well.

Now, Titan, we will test the limits of your newly increased strength.

"Yeah, now we're talking. What do you want me to do first?" Titan asked with great enthusiasm.

First, you must learn the full measure of your strength.

"Okay, how do I do that?" Titan asked.

I think we will need a safer, more discreet place to do this.

"How bout that construction yard three blocks over?" Titan said, pointing due east to the construction site of another downtown skyscraper. The total size of it was an entire city block.

That should do just fine. You must go there at once and we shall begin.

Without hesitation this time, Titan leaped from the window ledge he had been perched upon and dove straight at the centre of the construction site. He landed on his feet, kicking up a cloud of dust as he did. Titan had heard from his grandfather and Carly's parents about the building that was being erected here. It was to be a giant, state of the art facility. Currently it was nothing more than a metal frame that looked to Titan like a giant robotic finger trying to touch the moon. Mounds of dirt, concrete, and steel beams lay all around it. The streetlights illuminated the area, giving it an eerie glow. Several bulldozers and backhoes and other pieces of heavy machinery were scattered all over the site, like silent sentries waiting to spring into action. With a seven foot fence circling the perimeter, no one could see Titan from the street. Since the site was also in the middle of a business district, all the windows from surrounding buildings were currently dark and vacant. There was not a single person anywhere, making it a perfect training ground.

"So what do you want me to try breaking first?" Titan asked, interlacing his fingers and stretching his arms out.

You are to break nothing here. You will simply attempt to lift different objects so you will have a sense of your limits.

"Right, yeah of course. That's what I meant," Titan said, clearly sounding a little disappointed.

You will go and attempt to lift and move as many of the objects here as you can. This is not a test where I will watch over you. I can provide no assistance. Here you will go on your own, and gain an understanding of the strength you now possess.

"Okay, I think I get it. I'm ready. When do I start?" Titan asked.

Whenever you wish.

He was hoping that Azure would just continue to tell him what he needed to do. He had already been through so much tonight that thinking on his own seemed just a little out of reach.

Not knowing where to start, Titan walked over to a group of big concrete cylinders that seemed to stand about twice as tall as him. He had no idea how much they weighed. Titan squatted down in front of one, clenched its base in his hands as hard as he could, and heaved upward with all his might. With his powers, the cylinder was nowhere near as heavy as he had thought. At first, as it began to rise off the ground, a wide grin broke out over his face. That quickly faded however when Titan realized that he had again underestimated his new powers, and had lifted too hard.

The cylinder had come up in the air, until it hung over Titan's head. It teetered above him until it was almost out of his grip altogether. He had almost gone from lifting the cylinder to throwing it. As he tried to keep his grip on it, he began to lose some of his focus. He flinched and closed his eyes, and tilted his head down and away. Suddenly, the cylinder came crashing down to earth, burying Titan beneath it.

As the dust settled around the cylinder, everything was silent. Then the cylinder began to rock back and forth until finally it rolled over completely. Coughing and a little shaken, Titan got to all fours, spitting out chunks of dirt. His arms, chin, and neck were covered in cuts and scrapes. Again he marveled as they all vanished before his eyes in seconds.

"That is just never going to get old," Titan exclaimed.

Titan, are you alright?

"Yeah, just peachy," Titan said, regaining his breath and getting back to his feet.

Very well then, continue.

"Wow, thanks so much for all your sympathy," said Titan.

This time, Titan was not going to be defeated. He walked right over to the cylinder, assessed it, and then picked it up. He was shocked to discover that it felt no heavier to him than a big sack of potatoes. With it high over his head, he held it with one arm, pressing it up and down like a weightlifter.

"Yeah baby!" Titan yelled victorious.

Very good. Not only are you mastering your strength, but you are learning from your mistakes. Now continue with something new.

"This is incredible. It feels pretty light, and this thing weighs like ten times more than I do," Titan boasted.

You will find many incredible things as you discover the true potential of your powers.

While still holding the first cement cylinder, Titan bent down and scooped his hand under another. Suddenly he had two of them up over his head, one in each hand. Pressing them over his head, he wished Carly could have been there to see him.

After setting down the two cylinders without further incident, Titan went about the yard continuing to test his strength. With the greatest of ease, he bent one inch steel rebar into a circle. He was able to crush discarded concrete blocks like they were made of papier-mâché. Absolutely everything he touched seemed weightless to him. It seemed almost impossible to really gauge the true limit of his new strength.

After spending his whole life as regular old Michael Novak, suddenly he was anything but regular. His new powers were truly unbelievable. He still couldn't believe he had been chosen. He was almost waiting for Azure to tell him that there had been a mistake, and that he now had to give all these powers to someone else. For now they were his, and he couldn't wait to use his next power.

In time you will gain even more knowledge of your new strength. For now, however, we will move to working with your staff.

Without being told, Titan pulled the staff from the sheath on his back. He had almost forgotten it was there. Holding it now, he waited for instruction from Azure.

Your staff is the only weapon you will have as Titan to combat evil. Be careful, it is far more than just a blunt instrument. So, now we shall practice firing with your staff.

"Now we're talking," said Titan. "What should I shoot at first?"

It is not always what you should fire at that should concern you, but when. The lightning blasts are powerful and can be dangerous to yourself and to others if you are not careful.

"Okay, I get it. Be careful, and conserve energy. Will do. So, should I go somewhere to practice or what?" Titan said.

You may find a fixed object for target practice in this yard.

"Oh, you mean for once you don't want me to leap all over the city to do something?" said Titan. Azure did not reply. "I'm just kidding, Azure. Don't tell me your sense of humor dried up during all those years of forced retirement. Okay, let's start."

Titan looked around the yard, and was able to find a thick steel beam that was sticking six feet out of the ground. It was perfect for target practice. Titan grabbed a concrete block and placed it on top. He took several paces back until he was a good ten meters from the beam and prepared to fire. Titan, very carefully, aimed the jeweled end of his staff at the block. Nothing happened.

Titan could not figure out how to make the staff fire at all. He tried pointing, he tried to yell 'fire!', and he shook the staff and did all but throw the thing at his target. It simply would not work. Titan assumed that there was another piece to the puzzle he just wasn't getting. This was another puzzle that Azure wanted him to solve.

"Okay, I give up. Just what am I supposed to do to make this thing work?" asked Titan.

The staff is working through you, Titan. All you need do is focus on your goal to achieve it.

"Once again you've explained it all so clearly," Titan said with mounting frustration. "So then all I have to do is point this thing and think..." BOOM!

Before Titan could even finish, a flash of blue lightning shot from the end of his staff. It struck a giant pile of dirt at the other end of the yard, sending up a massive cloud of dust into the air. The concrete block sat fully intact. The blast caught Titan off guard, and he was blown over.

"Whoa! Now, that was cool!" Titan said, getting back to his feet. "I gotta try that again."

Titan's next shot missed once more, this time by about five yards. However he did manage to remain on his feet. He was getting used to making the staff fire. He prepared himself for the way it seemed to heat up and rattle just before it shot, and with the recoil once the shot went off. After only a few seconds of missing his second shot, he fired another. This blast managed to blow off the top corner of the block, sending small bits of concrete flying all over, and knocking the block right off its pedestal.

"Oh man. I hit it. I actually hit it," said Titan staring unbelievingly at the staff in his hands. "Okay, this is now officially the coolest thing that has ever happened to anyone."

In short order, Titan sent a series of similar shots in the yard, six in total. The shots ranged from pieces of scrap metal to chunks of stone or concrete. They were aligned in a giant crooked circle with himself in the middle. He counted to five and then pulled out his staff and fired at every target. He only missed one, and just barely. Feeling a bit like a cowboy in a western, he re-sheathed his staff triumphantly.

"Okay, I think I have the hang of this now. What else do you want to see me shoot at?" asked Titan.

I think that is enough for this evening.

"Are you sure, Azure? 'Cause I'm just starting to warm up with this thing," he said.

You have done well. You have shown great improvement over a very short time. You should be quite pleased with yourself.

"Thanks," said Titan, glad for the acknowledgment. It felt good to know that he wasn't the only one thinking it.

Titan had lost all sense of time while testing the limits and capabilities of his new powers. To him it felt like only a couple of hours. Yet he could already see the first signs of sunlight creeping over the downtown skyscrapers. He was starting to feel at home in his new costume, and with his powers. It had been the most amazing night of his life. It had felt so unreal to him being in control of such powers. Azure had certainly shown no signs of having been out of work for nearly two millennia. Through it all, he was there in the young Titan's ear talking him through everything. As one chapter of Michael's life was ending with his graduation, another chapter was opening with Titan. He simply didn't want this night to end. He felt invigorated.

Suddenly he thought of Carly, sitting up on the rooftop worrying, waiting for him. For all the hours that had gone by, he hoped that she had managed to stay calm. Of course, how could he blame her if she didn't? He had been so caught up in learning to be Titan that he had forgotten all about everything. He started to wonder how he would even begin to tell Perminder and Dave why they didn't meet for the grad party. He hoped that Carly hadn't told her parents or his grandpa. Thinking of his grandpa didn't make him feel good either. He had last seen him at the graduation ceremony. He was supposed to have called, but considering the series of events there really wasn't an opportunity. He didn't know how he could explain it, but just hoped they would all understand. Suddenly, he was no longer feeling so super.

For your last test of the night I want you to take us back to where we started in one single jump.

Titan could not believe what he was hearing. Azure had pulled Titan from his reverie. He had done well learning his jumps and the rest of his new powers, but suddenly this seemed so daunting. Leaping back across the city to a rooftop far from where they were, Titan felt fear build in the depths of his stomach.

"You want me to take us back?" Titan asked in a low voice, "But that's way farther than I've jumped so far. I haven't even nailed those landings yet."

It is far. It is also something that you must be able to do on your own.

"I don't know. I mean, I'm not sure I'm ready. What if I don't make the roof? I'm not even sure all these powers will be able to save me from a fall like that." Titan felt his voice go a little higher and shaky.

You must not show fear. I have watched as you have progressed so much in just one night. Do you really think that I would ask you to do this if I really felt that you were not ready? You must trust your powers. You won't be hurt. It would take far more to accomplish that as long as you are in Titan form. You need to have faith in your ability.

"Okay, I'll do it," said Titan hesitantly. "Should I go to higher ground first?"

Yes, take us higher. Then you will be able to gain bearing and judge your distance.

Titan said nothing in return. He simply leapt to the top of the nearest building. He walked over to the edge of the rooftop, looking towards Carly's. His first jump had almost been a disaster, but he had then started to get the hang of it. Azure's earlier words were ringing in his ears. He had felt the surge of power flow through him all night. It was the same power that had taken him this far. He knew he just needed to believe, and that he could do it. He would be fine.

"Okay, I'm ready. Any parting advice before I try and cheat death here?" Titan said, attempting a joke.

You have nothing to fear. In time, this will be second nature to you. Just remember that height can be your ally as well as your enemy.

He was hoping for a little more straightforward advice, but as always seemed to be the case with Azure, his advice sounded more like a fortune cookie than actual instruction. But he thought he understood, at least he hoped.

"Okay, here goes nothing," said Titan.

For a split second, as he gazed out at Carly's, he started to wonder if he would lose his nerve. Then he carefully attempted to gauge the distance, and strength of jump he would need. He took several steps back, and then leapt into the air with all his might. He felt the cool night air chill his sweaty skin as he sped up and over the city. His heart pounded, and his breath came sharp and fast. The city passed beneath him in a blur as streaks of orange and white halogen flew past. He covered miles in mere seconds, feeling weightless. The fears he had had only moments ago melted away.

Then he spotted his target below him, and hurled all his weight to the roof below. The ground started coming up almost too fast. His brief elbow injury from earlier flashed before his eyes. As he came to impact, he tucked his body in and barrel-rolled to a stop. At first he laid perfectly still, afraid to move, or open his eyes. Slowly he found himself back where this whole crazy night had started. He stood trembling slightly, and looked back in amazement. It had happened in the blink of an eye, and yet in that time he had flown, on his own, across the city from one rooftop to another. Titan then realized that his trembling was not from fear but excitement. The surge of power he felt coursing through his veins was exhilaration at being alive. He glanced over and saw Carly curled up fast asleep on the old bus bench, awaiting his return.

You have done well tonight, Titan. Our work, however, is only just beginning. Tomorrow as the sun sets you must return to this very spot. Then you will go out into the city and we will take your training to another level.

"So, I'm ready to go out and fight crime, just like that?" Titan asked.

Yes and no. You have learned much, but you still have much more to learn. You will learn no more simply by us leaping pointlessly about. You need opponents to face. You also still need much guidance before you are fully ready.

"All right then. Tomorrow night. I'll be here and ready," Titan said, unable to even imagine what that could bring.

Until then you will carry on your daily life and you must say nothing to anyone about your identity as Titan, including the girl. I will erase these events from her memory.

This thought had never occurred to him until this moment. He simply couldn't imagine something so incredible, and not being able to tell anyone. As far as his grandpa was concerned, he was already sure of how proud he would be. Plus, Perminder and Dave, he knew how cool they would find it, and how jealous they would be. Above all he needed to tell Carly, he shared everything with her.

"What? You can't do that to Carly," he said pointing over to where she lay sleeping. "Look, if I'm going to do this then I will need her there to talk to. I have to at least be able to tell her. You don't have to worry, she can be trusted."

Very well, but you must make sure that she tells no one.

"Don't worry," Titan said. "Carly would never tell a soul." He was so relieved to be able to tell Carly. He was not sure he could go through with all this if he couldn't tell her.

It will be far better for the both of you if this remains secret. Simply knowing your identity could put her at great risk from your enemies.

"My enemies?" Titan asked. "I don't have any enemies."

Not yet. They will come. They always do. It is an inevitable part of your new position.

"Why wouldn't you have mentioned that a little earlier, or was that part of the fine print?" said Titan, and answering himself before giving Azure a chance. "Not that it will matter much. With powers like this, no one can stand in my way."

There is one last important bit of information you must know, perhaps the most important.

"What is it?"

Tomorrow you will activate your powers for the first time on you own. These are the words you must know to activate and deactivate your powers.

"Cool, let's have 'em."

To activate your powers you must use the phrase 'Exaudio Fortis'.

"Got it."

Then saying 'Extermino Fortis' will take your powers away, and you will return to your previous form.

"Okay, I think I can remember that," said Titan.

I am glad to see your optimism. Now, tomorrow at sunset, on this very rooftop, we shall continue. You may now practice the deactivation of your powers.

"Okay."

Titan held his hand high above his head remembering what had happened when the lightning had first transformed him.

"Extermino Fortis," said Titan, and as he said it a yellow mist began to surround him. As it vanished he was back to wearing his own clothes, with the ring on the middle finger of his left hand. His whole body seemed to tingle with the last vestiges of the powers flowing through his body.

"Azure?" Michael said, not sure if he would continue to hear Azure's voice or not. "Azure, are you there?" He looked down at the blue jewel in the ring. It once again danced and swirled. Azure did not respond.

He made his way over to Carly. He sat at the edge of the bench and gently stroked her back. She stirred slightly. As though startled, she rolled over so fast she nearly flipped the bench right over with both of them on it.

"Michael, you're back," she said wide eyed, trying to shake off the last remnants of sleep.

"You have no idea how good it is to hear you say my name again," Michael said, as he gently stroked hair away from her face.

"What happened? Are you all right? I was so worried." He could tell by her voice that she truly was scared.

Michael tried to explain all that he could to her about his night as Titan. As the new day's sun began to rise, Carly sat back in amazement as he told her about his powers, about Azure, and all that he had done throughout the night.

"Now you have to promise me, Carly, that you won't tell anyone, not even your parents or Monica or anyone about what happened up here tonight," Michael pleaded.

"Michael please, do you really think I would ever tell anyone?" she replied.

"I know you wouldn't if I asked you. It's just that Azure told me specifically that we can't tell a soul. I wasn't even sure he was going to let me tell you," he said.

"Well, I pretty much already knew."

"I know. I thought it best not to ask how he planned to deal with that fact," Michael said.

"What was I going to tell anyone anyway?" she asked. "That you were transformed by lightning into this masked avenger, and flew off into the night. I spent the whole time worried sick here waiting for you to come back."

"I'm so sorry that you had to wait. I'm even sorrier that we missed the grad party."

"It's okay. I mean, this is incredible. Michael, you just turned into a superhero," Carly said. "Monica did call my cell like ten times. I don't know how I'll explain all this to her."

"Carly, I'm so sorry. At least we didn't miss the ceremony, and it was beautiful, right?" Michael tried to reason.

"People won't know the situation. How will I explain this to Monica, and all of our friends?" Carly asked. "We'll just say something about the police chase, and how it freaked my mom out. Of course, we'll skip the part of our night that involves magic lightning and mystical power rings. I'm sure it was so busy at the party that no one noticed that we weren't there anyway."

"Well, I just feel so bad we missed the whole thing. I know how much you had been looking forward to it," said Michael sympathetically.

"Okay, that's really not helping me get over it right now," said Carly.

"Let's just go in and talk about it," said Michael.

They started to make their way back to the exit, when Carly asked, "Michael it's nearly six and you haven't slept a wink. You should run home and get some rest at least."

"Actually," said Michael. "I feel great, like I just slept for ten solid hours."

"Oh sure," Carly said, with mock sarcasm. "I'm exhausted, sitting here worrying all night while you come back wide awake."

"You know, Carly, I am so glad that you were here to witness all this. Because if you weren't, I would think I had gone completely crazy," Michael stated.

"Everything's going to be different now isn't it?" asked Carly, looking up wide eyed at Michael.

"Yes, I suppose it is," Michael replied with a light laugh. He then took Carly's hand and they headed inside.

Chapter 6: The Gang's All Here

Michael followed Carly to the door to the Edward's apartment still feeling light, airy, and full of wonder from the events of the night before. Carly gingerly turned the doorknob to the apartment and the two of them slipped inside not wanting to wake her parents. They needn't have worried however as her parents sat at the dining room table looking worried and as though they had been up all night.

"Oh thank goodness," Mrs. Edwards declared. She rushed over and grasped hold of Carly. She wore a robe done up tightly, yet her hair was puffed up and her makeup already on as if she had been up all night looking this way.

Michael and Carly looked at each other bewildered and not knowing what to say.

"Just where have you two been?" asked Mr. Edwards. Mr. Edwards looked far less formal than his wife, with pajamas, an open robe and a creased face that had clearly just gotten out of bed. He was a tall, husky man with peppered grey hair and a bushy goatee.

"Daddy, we were just..." Carly began.

"I was talking to Michael," Mr. Edwards said, glowering Michael's way.

"We were just...uh...just at the grad party, and didn't see how late...er...early it had become," Michael answered.

"Son, Carly has a curfew for a reason. This neighborhood is just no longer safe to be running around in after dark. You were told to have her back here thirty minutes after the party ended."

"Dad, I'm perfectly capable of being responsible for myself." Carly added, jumping in to Michael's defense.

"Come on, son, I think it's best you get on home right. I'm sure your grandfather is worried sick about you as well." Mr. Edwards said leading Michael back out the front door and ignoring Carly's comments.

"Now, Les just calm down," said Mrs. Edwards.

Mr. Edwards ignored this as he and Michael stepped into the hall shutting the door behind them.

"Mr. Edwards, I'm really sorry we're so late and that you both were up worrying about us. That was never our intention, and I'm truly sorry," Michael stated, barely able to look Mr. Edwards in the eye.

"Son, we've always liked you and thought you were a good kid, and were fine with you and Carly dating so young. However, if you start to act more like Vincent Novak than the Michael we have come to know then I may not be able to let you continue to date my daughter."

Michael stood there, stunned. He had had to face many comparisons to his brother and his less than stellar reputation over the years, but never from the Edwards' before.

"I'm nothing like my brother, sir, I promise you." Michael tried hard not to show just how deep those words had cut.

"I truly hope you are able to prove me wrong, son, I truly do."

Mr. Edwards turned swiftly and went back into the apartment closing the door leaving Michael alone in the hall. He stood staring at the door for over a minute. Then he turned and shuffled his way to the end of the hall and down the stairs and began his trek home.

As Michael stood at the top of the front steps he saw his friend, Perminder Singh, walking down the sidewalk dribbling a basketball. Perminder was tall and skinny with black hair and dark brown skin. Michael had been friends with him since Michael had moved to the neighborhood. Perminder was the first person his own age he had met after moving. Perminder came from a big family with two brothers and two sisters, and Michael had always marveled at how close Perminder was to his other siblings, even as the baby in the family.

"What are you doing up so early on a Saturday, it's only quarter to eight?" Michael asked as Perminder approached.

"What do you mean? I always get up early Saturday to shoot hoops at the school," Perminder replied, leaning his tall skinny body against the railing. His buzzed hair and round face always made him look several years younger than he actually was. Perminder was always teased about his skinny stature by Michael and Dave. The two of them were both broad shouldered and rather muscular for their age.

"Yeah, I would have thought with all that practice that you'd be better then," Michael joked.

"Whatever. It was super hard to get up this morning though. You know after that wild grad party. By the way, real nice of you guys to avoid me there last night," Perminder said.

"Oh yeah, the grad party. I'm real sorry, man. We tried to find you, but we just couldn't. There were just so many people," Michael said, full of fake apology, hoping that Perminder would buy it. He and Carly hadn't had any time to go over what they would say to their friends. Michael was just making it all up as he went along. He knew no story they could tell their friends would properly explain their absence. Perhaps, Michael thought, they just might believe that we were there anyway. Michael thought it funny how he had to be a liar in order to protect his secret of Titan.

"Anyway, at least I had Dave with me," Perminder said.

"What happened to that girl you took, Stacey?" Michael asked.

"Well, she ended up ditching me for her old boyfriend as soon as we got to the party."

"I'm real sorry, man. Let him deal with her. You could do better than her anyway," Michael said, placing a sympathetic hand on his shoulder.

"So, what are you guys doing up so early anyway?" Perminder asked, changing the subject.

"Ah…well, basically, we just got back now and, well, I kinda got in big trouble from Carly's dad for bringing her back home so late."

Perminder just stared down at the ground and shook his head. Perminder had always been a good listener if Michael needed one and Carly wasn't around, but he was always a little short on advice.

"So, can you believe the action that went down here last night? I can't believe I missed it," Perminder said, completely changing topics.

Michael's first instinct was to tell Perminder about what happened to him last night and how he turned into Titan. He just knew that Perminder would love it, and it killed him not to be able to tell his friend.

"Who would've thought something like that could happen right here in our own neighborhood? I know it's scary, but it's also kinda cool. I mean the police still have that corner taped off," Perminder said, pointing toward the crime scene. "This is the kind of stuff you only see in the movies."

"Yeah, I know what you mean," Michael said. "We were up on the roof when it happened. We had a bird's eye view of the whole thing."

"Wow that must have been great! I was at home and heard the crash. I never came down though. I knew all the good stuff would have been over by then. Figured it would be just as good watching it all on TV. You know, and then I get the commentary and everything. Plus they kept replaying the whole thing for like an hour," Perminder said, while doing a crossover dribble. "Can you believe they still haven't caught that one guy from the van?"

"Yeah, that's crazy," Michael said, suddenly full of guilt. It instantly hit him that if Azure hadn't been so worried about training maybe Titan could have caught this lone fugitive.

"And you know what else? My mom said she saw these weird flashing blue lights later on coming from this direction. Did you guys see anything like that?"

Michael shook his head. Perminder lived on the street behind Carly in an apartment that faced her. So, he no doubt would have been able to see the lightning from the ring. Michael had no idea what to say. He simply shook his head, dumbfounded. Michael knew that Perminder's mom must have been talking about the lightning that transformed him. If she saw then who else could have seen?

Michael spotted Carly's best friend Monica coming down the street, no doubt coming for some post grad gossiping. He decided he'd better get going to work. He thought again how he needed to go home and see his grandpa, but knew it would have to wait. If he was late, even after grad, Mr. Caruthers would be furious.

"Hey, Mike, don't forget we got the three on three tournament coming up. You could do with a little practice yourself," Perminder called to him, holding up his basketball.

"Don't worry, I'll be there and ready to out play you," Michael called back as he continued down the street.

As Michael walked the two blocks to the store, he felt like he was walking on air. He still couldn't shake the feelings he had, as the power of Titan coursed through his body. He could clearly see and feel all the incredible things that he was able to do. At least he could think about it all alone at work. For the first time since his very first shift at the store he found himself looking forward to going to work.

While walking he pulled out his cell phone, and decided to try calling his grandpa before he got to work. It wasn't very often that Michael would go this long without checking in. He cursed as he flipped the phone open and saw nothing but a blank screen. Go figure, he thought, dead battery.

Without warning, he was shoved, and it sent him back a step.

"Hey, loser," his older brother Vince said, glaring down at Michael. "I don't care if you think you're some hot shot now that you're going into high school. You still cost me a lotta grief by not even phonin' Grandpa last night."

Michael knew that Vince was likely lying. He always seemed to be able to hit just the right buttons with Michael. If Vince had any chance at taking some of the joy out of day, even by making him think he had upset their grandpa, then he would do it. Grandpa Dale had always trusted Michael and never shown outwardly how worried he may have been for him at any time. Still, the guilt hit hard. Michael tried not to let Vince's comments get to him. He knew Vince would be taking his anger out on him no matter what. Yet, today of all days, Michael felt empowered to at last stand up to Vince's bullying.

"Shut up, Vince, and get outta my way. I'm late for work," Michael said, realizing after saying it how bad it could be for him.

"What did you just say to me?" Vince said, clearly angry at Michael for being so defiant. Vince straightened his back and puffed out his chest and crossed his large arms. Vince was several inches taller than Michael, and much more muscular. Michael's hair was typically tussled and messy where as Vince's was always slicked back and neat. Other than that, the similarity in the two brother's appearance was outstanding.

"Vince, I'm sorry, but I'm gonna be late for work. Please," Michael begged, his tone suddenly changing drastically.

"Well, you're lucky I'm in a hurry too. I got things to do, but don't worry we'll settle this later," Vince said, shoving Michael aside and carrying on down the street.

All it took was one encounter with Vince to suddenly make Michael feel as far from a hero as possible. Michael thought that having the power and ability of Titan would make him more confident in dealing with everything, especially his bullying older brother. Yet, as soon as Michael ran into him, all of his newfound confidence seemed to drain away. It was definitely something he knew he would have to work on.

At last, a little deflated, he arrived at the little corner grocery, only to find Mr. Caruthers grumpy as usual. As Michael looked up at the clock over Mr. Caruthers head, he saw that he was five minutes late.

"Finally made it eh? I think I've covered with you how I feel about tardiness," Mr. Caruthers said.

"I'm sorry, Mr. Caruthers. It's just with grad and everything, and then I ran into my brother on the way here. It won't happen again I promise."

"You know I gave you this job because I respect your grandfather, and your dad was a good man too. Now don't go making me regret my decision or disappointing either of them. Many other kids wanted this job you know," Mr. Caruthers warned, barely peeking over his bifocals the whole time. The dire warning was nothing new to him. It was the same speech Mr. Caruthers gave any time Michael screwed up in the slightest.

Mr. Caruthers was in his sixties, and had run the little store as long as Michael could remember. He was short with wispy white hair. His body was slender, except his stomach which stuck out. He always looked as though he had a basketball shoved under his shirt.

"Here, I need you to do the stocking and pricing, then run these items over to Mrs. Bennett's place. Just to show you that I'm a softy sometimes, after you're done you can then take the rest of the day off. You know, as a graduation gift from me. I already filled the order for your grandfather. It's ready in the back when you go," he said handing him the list.

"Thanks, Mr. Caruthers, that'll be great," Michael said, trying his best to sound grateful.

Michael practically ran through the store doing all his usual chores. Then, he was off getting everything for the Bennett order. As he worked, he was completely distracted by the previous night's events. He wondered what he could be in for tonight, and what new things he'd learn. He had put the ring back in his jeans pocket, and he was frequently tempted to pull it out and examine its strange marking and mesmerizing stone. After making it to the Bennett house and back in record time, he was finally ready to go. He grabbed the bag for his Grandpa and ran for the door.

"Take it easy there, before you break everything in the place. Then you'll be lucky if you see me give you another day off," Mr. Caruthers hollered, as he scurried out the door.

"See ya, Mr. Caruthers," Michael said, ignoring the old man's grumbling.

He had grown used to Mr. Caruthers' grumpy demeanor. Despite what he might say, Mr. Caruthers had never hesitated to let him go if his grandpa was sick or he had exams to study for. Michael knew that deep down the old shopkeeper had his best interests at heart.

After what seemed like an eternity, Michael went home. Home was a small three bedroom bungalow, only a few blocks away from Carly. The little house looked like many of the other houses on the street. They were small square homes on little postage stamp yards. Most of the houses were white with only the color of the window shutters and fences as distinguishing features. The Novaks had an old faded white wooden fence that went around their yard, and blue shutters with peeling paint. Michael opened the rickety old gate and went around the yard to the back door. He couldn't remember the last time anyone had entered the house through the front door. When he entered the little one level house he knew he would find Grandpa Dale in his big old armchair in the living room, intently listening to the news on the radio.

The old armchair faced towards the kitchen. There was a small, two-tiered end table beside it. The top of the little table held Grandpa Dale's radio, which must have dated back a good twenty-five years. The second tier held a variety of snacks, such as hard candy, chocolates and peanuts. He wore his usual gray slacks and powder blue collared shirt. Michael had long thought that he had a whole wardrobe of nothing but this same outfit. His gray, widow's peaked hair was immaculately combed back, with his trusty black comb in his front shirt pocket. Most of his face hid behind his big dark glasses. His long metal cane with a black plastic handle leaned up against the arm of the chair. Grandpa Dale was sitting forward with his head hung down as he listened intently to the radio. Michael tossed off his shoes and headed to the kitchen table with the shopping bags.

"Michael, how was the celebrating?"Asked Grandpa Dale, a wide smile suddenly breaking across his face, as Michael set the bag of groceries on the kitchen table. Michael could never get away with sneaking in. His grandfather had ears like radar, easily compensating for his lack of sight. He also seemed to be able to always distinguish between the two boys by the sounds they made. "It must have gone well, since you're just getting home." A wide smile spread across the old man's face as he raised his head. "Although, a phone call to allay an old man's weary mind would have been nice."

"Oh yeah, it went great, Grandpa," Michael said, relieved to at last see that he wasn't going completely mad with worry. "I'm sorry I didn't phone you. I meant to. I tried a couple times and got a busy signal. Then my cell died and I just couldn't."

"Well, just try and remember it for the next time you're going to be out all night long. Though I suppose times like this in a young man's life the last thing you want to do is have to worry about calling an old man like me." What would have sounded like a guilt trip from anyone else was said with a smile by Grandpa Dale.

Michael valued that Grandpa Dale would trust him enough to know right from wrong, and avoid getting into trouble, even if his older brother couldn't. However, Michael saw relief in his old face at knowing Michael was okay.

"I did quite enjoy the ceremony, and I'm sorry your brother couldn't make it," Grandpa Dale said.

"I'm glad you liked it. But don't worry about Vince. I don't think it was his thing," Michael responded. As angry as he could get with Vince, he always felt the need to make him look a little better to his grandpa. He hated the idea of him being disappointed, even of Vince.

Michael made his way into the living room, leaving the groceries and wanting to spend some time with his grandpa. He plunked down on the couch that sat under the front window. The two of them had had many conversations here. So many of Michael's most cherished childhood memories with his grandfather came from this very room.

"I'm very proud of you, son, for finishing middle school, and with such good marks too. And I know your parents would be proud as well," Grandpa Dale said, his voice suddenly weakening with emotion. He sat back into his chair and lifted his head up toward the ceiling. Michael was sure that if he hadn't been wearing those big dark glasses he would see tears in his grandfather's eyes. If he saw that, he would be likely to start crying himself.

"Thanks, Grandpa," Michael said bashfully. Michael slowly reached out and patted the back of the old man's hand before resting it on top of his. His grandpa turned and faced Michael again with a warm smile.

"I do still remember my own middle school graduation. Thought I was pretty hot stuff, I did. Thought I was ready to take on the world," Grandpa Dale said. "Then there was your father. He spent about as much time getting ready as your mother did I think. You don't even want to know how long it took him to get ready for his high school senior prom."

"Really," Michael said with a humoring chuckle, as he prepared for the familiar and comforting story.

"Of course, they had just met and started dating around that time, oh not six weeks before. What am I doing? I'm sure I've told you all this many times before. I don't mean to bore you."

"Its okay, Grandpa, I like the story." said Michael truthfully. Grandpa Dale was full of great old stories, and this was just one of many he had about Michael's parents. It seemed to Michael as though his entire relationship with his parents revolved around Grandpa Dale's stories.

Grandpa Dale paused as though in deep reflection before speaking again.

"I trust you were no where near that accident last night. From what I heard, it sounded like it was right by Carly's."

"Yeah, we were fine. Luckily no one there got hurt."

"Well I just hope it didn't dampen the celebration."

"No, not at all. I brought the groceries we needed," Michael said changing the subject before he would have to lie about Titan.

"That's wonderful, son, thank you." Suddenly a look of alarm crossed his face. "Michael, is there something else on your mind you need to share?" Grandpa Dale always seemed to know, no matter how hard Michael tried to hide something.

It would be his first instinct to share with his grandfather the news of Titan, but he suddenly found himself unable to speak. Azure's words rang in his head once again. He wasn't even sure he could possibly put everything into words. What if his he disagreed with it all? What if it simply filled him with worry? Michael just couldn't bear it. What if Azure was right and he ended up somehow putting his grandpa in jeopardy by knowing?

Instead, he found himself saying, "No nothing else new."

"Well okay then. I thought I just picked up something in your voice there," Grandpa Dale said. He might be blind, but Michael could tell that he sensed some things very well. Another awkward pause filled the room.

Well, I am going in this week to get my class schedule for fall" said Michael. He wanted to give him something and didn't what else he could say.

"I am glad that you decided to not let that brain sit and rust for too long..." He casually flicked out the little black comb from his shirt pocket and ran it twice through his thinning hair. His hair looked no different as he put the comb back in his shirt pocket.

Michael spent a good deal of the afternoon with his grandfather, trying to make up for the night before. For the first time since finding the ring, Michael felt like his old self again. Michael talked about his future and he listened to Grandpa Dale talk about the past. Before long, Michael saw that the sun was setting. As much as he hated leaving his grandpa, he knew that he had to get back to Carly's to prepare for his night as Titan.

"Grandpa, I'm sorry but I gotta get going. I promised Carly that I would meet her," Michael said, getting up to leave.

"That's fine, son. You both have fun now. Just be sure to call me if you're going to be late."

"Okay, Grandpa, I will."

Michael headed back through the neighborhood towards Carly's. As he made his way back, a sense of nervousness and excitement began to creep over him. He was so caught up in his thoughts of Titan that he didn't even get slowed down by any of the usual spots of the neighborhood, like the Burger Pit or the newsstand. He passed a whole fresh batch of comics at the newsstand without as much as a second glance. He didn't even slow down when he passed by Jimmy Nelson and Laurie Kane, a couple he and Carly had double dated with at the movies two months ago. They did a double take, but seemed to realize that Michael was completely lost in a dream world. Thinking of his conversation with Carly's dad from the morning only made him more nervous. He no longer knew how he would have to act around her parents. He could only hope that her dad would not be around tonight. As the building came into sight, he saw that not only Carly sat waiting at the front steps but also Dave, Perminder, and Monica. The buildings front steps was another common and familiar meeting place for the group

"Well look, if it isn't big, dumb and ugly," Dave said with a broad smile as he saw Michael coming.

"Well if anyone knows dumb and ugly, I guess it would be you," Michael joked back.

"How was work?" Carly asked.

"Good, Mr. Caruthers gave me the afternoon off. So I went to see my grandpa."

"Yeah, did you tell him how you stood up all your friends at the grad party?" asked Dave. His eyes were drawn in a grimace. Yet, with the tone he used Michael couldn't tell if he was kidding or serious.

"These guys haven't let up about it since you've been gone," Carly said, rolling her eyes.

"Um…well, sorry guys. There were a lot of people there. We really did try and find you all," was all Michael could think to say.

"Yeah well you owe us one, buddy. You just better bring your A game at the three on three tournament, then we may just forgive you," Dave said, as he and Perminder both took a seat on the front steps.

"You can count on me, buddy. The way two play you'll need me," Michael said, pointing at both Perminder and Dave.

"Well, I don't care about any stupid basketball. There are much more important things to talk about besides that," Monica said under her breath. She then sharply turned her head toward Carly, causing her long dark hair to whip out in the direction of the boys. "Carly, did you see what Samantha Chu wore last night?" she continued. Michael, Dave, and Perminder simply shook their heads and laughed.

As the five friends sat and enjoyed the summer sunshine, a big black stretch limousine pulled up in front of them. They all stopped talking and looked at it with avid curiosity. It was definitely not the kind of car that would normally be seen in this neighborhood. Heads began peaking out of many different windows and doorways around the street. The limousine driver got out and went to the back door without even a glance in their direction. Then Dylan Thompson, one of their very own, stepped out from the car, wearing a grey, three-piece suit. He shot his old friends that cocky grin of his. Michael' eyes went wide with delighted surprise at seeing Dylan Thompson. That look quickly soured though as Vince Novak got out of the long black car right behind Dylan.

Dylan smiled and nodded to the five of them. Vince seemed to be oblivious to his own brother sitting little more than ten feet away. Dylan shook hands with Vince before giving another polite smile to Michael and his friends and got back into his limo and the driver closed the door behind him. As soon as the door closed Vince finally turned towards Michael and his friends.

"You said you were busy earlier, but I had no idea you meant busy with Dylan Thompson," Michael said, his voice going high. Vince stepped away from the curb as the limo started up and pulled away.

"Yeah, well there are a lot of things you don't know about what I do," Vince replied.

"Well. I don't doubt that, but you hanging out with Dylan?"

"So, what's the deal, man? You gonna be working with Dylan or something?" asked Dave, clearly curious.

"Or something. Well, you guys have fun holding down those steps. See ya losers." Vince said, as he turned abruptly and started walking away.

"Wow, I never thought I would be jealous of Vince, but here we are and I am jealous," said Monica, still batting her eyes at the limo which was by now barely visible.

Michael looked towards Carly whose brow was furrowed and clearly as unimpressed as Michael by the scene that had just unfolded in front of them.

"For once I gotta agree with Monica. Mike, you gotta find out what that was all about, man," said Perminder.

"Oh, I plan to," Michael responded coolly. He kept pivoting his head between the distant limo and his brother walking away, unable to believe what he had just seen or know what any of it meant.

Chapter 7: Enter the Titan

As dusk once again began to blanket Delta City, Michael and Carly returned to the rooftop. Breaking away from their friends had been easier than Michael had thought. Once Dylan had left in his limousine, and Vince had gone everyone seemed disinterested and bored, so Carly made an excuse for her and Michael to go upstairs to have dinner with her parents. No one seemed to object. In fact, Dave was already preparing to leave, with Perminder quick at his heels. Michael had been afraid to enter the building at first not knowing what her dad would say, but Carly assured him he was working late and not home.

"Besides," she had said. "He's cooled down now. He was just freaked out cause I didn't come home until dawn. I think you should be more concerned about Dylan and your brother than my dad." They stood at the foot of the building staircase, Carly trying to drag Michael up it.

"Easy for you to say, I'm the one your dad blamed for you not coming home. Now just don't say I told you so about Dylan."

"OK, fine, but I did though. Trust me my dad's over it. My mom loves you, and she stood up for you. You saw how scared she was. Even still I think we managed to convince him that he was a little over the top."

"Carly, he compared me to Vince. I think he hates me now." Michael caved briefly taking two steps up toward Carly.

"Big surprise, he doesn't like Vince, but he does like you. Now, I agree it was not right for him to compare to your brother like that, but we'll just have to show him that you're better than that." Carly managed to pull Michael up two more steps.

"Well, I hope we can, because otherwise I don't think he'll let us see each other."

Carly stopped abruptly and scowled at Michael. Her brow furrowed and her lips pursed tight.

"He did not say that, did he?"

"Uh…" Michael did not want to start something even bigger out of any of this. At that moment he wasn't sure who scared him more, Carly or her father. "I'm just saying that if you show up late for curfew or anything else I'll probably get blamed."

"Well, I'll just have to stop breaking curfew then, won't I?" Carly broke into a sly grin let go of Michael's hand and bolted up the stairs without looking back. Michael had hesitated a moment then took off after her

Now, alone on the rooftop again, they stood in a warm embrace. Michael was already holding the ring in his hand. It had been safely tucked into his back jeans' pocket all day. For some reason he could not bring himself to wear it in public.

"So when are you supposed to do this exactly?" asked Carly.

"Well," said Michael, "I wasn't given an exact time, just night time. So I guess since it's dark, now's as good a time as any."

Michael slid the ring onto his finger. As he did, Carly began to back away from him. Her body tensed as she readied herself for the lightning blast. Before he said anything he simply stood there staring at her. No word needed to be spoken; all Michael needed was the warm smile Carly sent his way. As soon as she was out of the way, Michael said the magic words.

"Exaudio Fortis!"

Once he spoke them, a brilliant bolt of blue lightning came crashing down. Michael seemed to become engulfed in its brilliant light. He could feel the energy and power flow through his body. Invisible sonic waves seemed to pulse out from around him. This time Michael had been prepared, leaving him more aware of the changes he was undergoing. His heart raced and the hairs over his body seemed to tingle and stand on end. All the exciting sensations he had felt the night before were now flooding back. He felt good knowing that he hadn't dreamed it all. As the smoke cleared, Titan was again standing where Michael had stood.

"That is so cool," said Titan, as he once again assessed his transformation.

"Michael, I don't think I will ever get used to that. I find it very hard to believe that doesn't hurt you in any way," said Carly, lowering her hands away from her face.

"It's Titan now. I'm not Michael when I wear the gear."

"Oh, whatever. Sorry I didn't mean to offend you," Carly said, rolling her eyes.

"Well anyway, don't worry, I'm okay," Titan replied.

Titan, are you ready to begin?

Azure's voice came from everywhere once again. It surrounded Titan.

"Yes, I'm ready," Titan said.

"Is that...Are you talking to... um...are you talking to him again? That voice?" asked Carly.

"Yeah, it's him. I need to go now, but don't worry I'm sure I'll be back before you know it. I'll be just fine. You should probably wait inside tonight though," said Titan.

"No way, I'm going to wait right here until I see you back on this rooftop safe and sound. Don't worry I'll go downstairs make an appearance and then just slip out and come back up here. Just because you're a superhero now doesn't mean that you can tell me what to do."

"You can't just stay up here every time I have to go out."

"Don't worry about me, tough guy. Just get going, will ya?" said Carly, suddenly back to her confident self again.

We must get going, Titan. We shall begin in the area we started off in last night. You may take us there when you are ready.

"Okay, Azure, I'm ready," said Titan. Then, he turned to Carly. "Well, here I go. Wish me luck!"

"Good luck!" Her voice sounded sure but her face looked anything but. Her eyes remained wide with fear and she nibbled nervously at her lower lip.

Titan stepped towards the edge of the building facing downtown. Before he went to leave, he took one last look at Carly. It would be that last image of her that he would carry with him to comfort and calm himself as he spent his first night officially as Titan. He smiled at her, and waved goodbye, trying to reassure her, hoping she would get used to all of this. Carly was the only link he had between his old life and his new one. He needed her full support. He just didn't know yet what it would take to gain that.

He looked out towards the downtown skyline, and set his sights on a building topped with an antenna with a flashing white light. In a flash, he hunched down and then launched into the air. He was off and sailing through the night sky, feeling the exhilaration of the wind howling past him, and with the city speeding past below him. His bandana and belt billowed wildly behind him. All the incredible sensations from the night before came flooding back. He had to remind himself to breathe. He angled his body and sliced neatly through the air, sailing higher and higher. The closer he came to downtown the more relaxed he felt. He even let his arms spread out wide, soaring like an eagle. It felt to Titan as though he were already an old pro as his target started to come into view. He was headed to the Empress Building once again; he agreed with Azure, what better way to survey the city than from its highest point.

He landed on the roof top, and was surprised to find that it was the best landing he had done yet. He even managed to stay on his feet, coming to a jogging halt. He looked around and saw that there were dark clouds around this part of town and it was already starting to rain. He wasn't sure exactly what he was supposed to be doing, as Azure was being silent. He leaned forward on the building's ledge and focused his eyes on the scurrying of tiny antlike people below. It was still early in the night and the city bustled with activity. He focused his ears on the muffled sounds that were drifting up from street level.

"I don't get it. What is it I'm supposed to be doing exactly?" Titan asked confused.

You need to focus, Titan. You must focus your mind. Now close your eyes and focus on what you are here for. Focus on the sounds the city and its people make all around you. Then you should know what to do next.

Titan could have sworn that he was trying to focus on the city's sounds, but he didn't protest and did as Azure told him. He closed his eyes, squatted down and tried to clear his mind. He allowed the night sounds of the city to enter his head. Before, he heard everything simultaneously, and it all came up to him as a bunch of muffled noise. Now suddenly he was able to distinguish individual sounds. Car engines revving, footsteps on the concrete, doors slamming. He found he could even hear sounds of people on the streets below that he would never have to be able to have done. It all came up to him like sonar.

Then he heard a sound that jarred him. It was the sound of a woman screaming and Titan knew it wasn't for joy. He heard her high-heeled feet pound on the pavement, and her words shot up at him again and again. "No, please!! Help!" Then he heard the heavy footfalls of two more people trailing her. Titan could almost feel their anger. They were attacking her. He leapt up instantly and flew towards the scream. He instinctively drew his staff from its sheath in midair.

What did you find, Titan?

"I heard a woman screaming," Titan said breathlessly. "She's being attacked and it's coming from this way," he said pointing down to an alley.

Very good, Titan, now go…

Titan reached the alley. He had flown through the air once again, knowing this time it was not practice. He was now putting his skills to use for the very first time. He landed on a rooftop where he heard the sounds and quickly looked down, scanning the area. He saw a young woman scrambling backwards clutching her purse tightly as two big thugs came towards her with knives, clearly relishing her fear. They splashed through fresh puddles created by the rain that now gave everything a new polished look. The alley was a dead end, and both men stood between the girl and safety. Titan tightened his grip on his staff and went to help her.

Now use caution, Titan. These men are armed. Remember to keep your staff between them and yourself. You are outnumbered but they are weaker than you. And of course, keep in mind the safety of the intended victim here.

"Oh don't worry. I intend to teach these knuckleheads how to treat a lady."

Titan swooped down, landing behind the two men with a thud. They stopped where they were, and quickly turned to see Titan crouched there.

"What is this here?" one thug said. "It's not Halloween yet, kid. So why don't you go play dress up somewhere else?"

"Yeah beat it," said the other. "Can't ya see we're entertainin' here?" He waved his knife in the direction of the young woman.

"Oh," said Titan. "Well then, why don't you come over here and entertain me?"

"Oh, is that how you want it, sunshine?" one of the men said through laughter. "I usually don't go after punk little kids. Okay we'll teach ya a lesson here, then we'll deal with the girl."

Titan suddenly felt butterflies in his stomach. The falling rain embraced him in a warm cloak. Jumping practice and crushing cinderblocks was one thing, but this was a whole other matter. Now that he was in the alley standing only a few feet from the attackers, his perspective was a little different. He felt all of his confidence drain out of him. He knew he had no choice now; he had to put an end to these two thugs.

As Titan started to come at the two men he tripped on a scrap of metal that littered the alleyway. He stumbled, splashing through a giant puddle, but was able to catch himself before falling over completely. Instead he fell awkwardly into the brick wall of the building which broke his fall. Titan's face immediately flushed with embarrassment. How was he going to tell Carly that his first glorious moment as a super hero was stumbling into a corner?

The men were both laughing hysterically. Stumbling, they came at Titan with knives drawn and ready. Titan regrouped, stepped to the middle of the alley and waited for them to attack. The two of them spread out, preparing to take Titan from two angles. From the corner of his eye, Titan saw that the young girl was seeking refuge behind a stack of crates piled beside a dumpster.

"I'm 'bout ta make you regret dressing up ta play hero, kid. I'm gonna enjoy takin' you apart," one mugger said, as they both approached Titan.

For a moment there was a silent standoff as the two thieves circled Titan, preparing to strike. Then the first thug made a lazy swipe at Titan with his blade, but he was able to dodge it with ease. The second took a swing with much the same result. They were nowhere near as fast and agile as Titan, and they soon became frustrated, each taking several more swings, and not even coming close to him. With several pointed jabs of his staff, Titan was able to not only do some damage but keep the thugs at bay as well. One was sporting a bloody lip and the other had the beginning of a black eye. Both were no longer smiling. As Titan had them running in circles he shot his staff out again, this time much lower.

The first thug got his feet tangled around it, falling face first into the alley. He quickly clambered back to his feet. The thugs knew the tables had turned. It seemed that it was they who were defending themselves from Titan.

Their attacks became clumsier. Titan toyed with them like a cat with a captured mouse. He always gained distance before the blades ever got near him. Eventually the men tired of swiping at thin air.

Do not get too arrogant, Titan. Subdue them as quickly as you can. Do not toy with them.

Hearing Azure's words, Titan decided it was time to end this. One of them came at Titan again with a lazy swipe of his blade. Titan easily batted him aside and dropped his elbow on his back. He went down with a hard crash, practically flying through the air and into some trash cans against the wall. It was the first time he'd ever had to strike an enemy and he wasn't exactly sure how hard to hit. When Titan saw the guy flinch but not get up, he figured it was just hard enough. The second one was about to make another move on Titan. He suddenly stopped dead in his tracks at the sight of his buddy lying unconscious just five feet away.

"Please don't hurt me, man," he pleaded, dropping to his knees in front of Titan.

Titan grabbed the man by the shirt with one hand and tossed him over by his partner. He sailed through the air like a paper cup and flopped down just two feet from the other thug. Titan grabbed an old cord that he saw hanging out of a dumpster and tied the two men back to back. The one would-be mugger was still out of it, while the other continued to beg for mercy.

"Please, man, we weren't gonna do anything to her, I swear!" said the thug, no longer resisting. Titan ignored him and turned to the young woman cowering in a corner.

"Are you all right?" Titan asked the woman.

"Yes, I think so," she said. She slowly made her way from the corner and came toward Titan. "Thanks to you."

"If you can, get to a phone right away and call the police," Titan told her. "I don't think you need to worry about them anymore."

"Okay I will," said the woman, now grinning broadly, "And thanks again. You saved my life. I don't know how I can repay you."

"Don't worry. The fact that you're safe is thanks enough," said Titan.

Titan then leapt quickly into the air and back to the rooftop. He decided for now that it was best to put some distance between himself and the scene.

"Wow, can you believe that! I was all like 'the fact you're safe is thanks enough.' I hope that didn't sound too corny," Titan said, as he sailed across the rooftops. "I mean overall, that was amazing if I do say so myself. Not to mention easy. Was that easy? I thought that seemed easy."

Overall you did very well, Titan. There are some minor points of detail you will need to manage, however. You need to control your strength, as well as how to end these battles a little more quickly. You must show no arrogance. It can become your greatest weakness.

"Sure, sure," said Titan with excitement. "So what's next?"

With the thrill of his first battle still upon him, Titan tried to regain his focus and find where he was needed next. With his adrenaline still running high he found it difficult to contain himself and once again focus his thoughts. His mind kept replaying the fight over and over again. He wondered how he would describe it to Carly and what she would think. He was also starting to wonder what his friends would think as they heard about Titan's exploits the following day. Already he was wondering what all the news coverage would be the next day, and if he would get mentioned at all.

Eventually he was able to refocus and just as he did, the steady patter of rain was once again shattered like glass. From five blocks away came the sound of an alarm. The shrill alarm bell bounced over buildings and cut like a knife through the blanketing rain. Titan immediately turned and made his way towards it without even the slightest word from Azure. He moved swiftly, bounding across the rooftops of Delta City, the sound becoming increasingly loud. Its piercing blare sent goose bumps up and down his arms. Titan had the feeling that he was getting into something a little bigger than a couple of purse snatchers. The louder the alarm got, the faster his heart seemed to pound.

You must stay alert, Titan. This sounds as though it could pose a greater threat to yourself and others.

Titan landed in an alley just beside where the alarm was coming from. The rain was coming down in sheets now. On the street at the edge of the alley he saw a van with its back doors open. His instinct immediately sent off an alarm of his own. As he went to take his first step towards the van, he saw a man in a ski mask run to the back and toss an armload of bulging sacs inside. He was quickly followed by another man, then yet another. From a mugging to a robbery in progress, Titan was beginning to think that he had picked the right night to start his superhero career.

Instead of walking to the end of the alley, Titan jumped over the corner of the building and landed in the street right in front of the van. He found himself looking at a bank and three men grabbing money from the vault inside and taking it out through the broken front window to their van. The bars that used to come down at night to block the front window lay severed along the sidewalk amidst the shattered glass. Up against the wall sat a large case with saws and power tools spilling out. At first, the men were so busy that they didn't see Titan as he quietly landed. They didn't see that he was now standing in the street just feet away.

Titan was not quite sure what to do now that he had found himself in this situation. Helping a girl in trouble was one thing, but stopping an armed robbery was another. As empowered as he felt only moments ago, he now felt quite unqualified. He started to wonder if he would ever be able to approach these situations and not feel the jitters. As Michael Novak, he never would have attempted to actually intervene. He would have just called the police. Now, as Titan, he knew that no such option was available.

"What the...?" said one of the masked men, as he caught a glimpse of Titan.

Titan you must remember to act swiftly and with great care. These men are much more dangerous than your enemies from before. Go! Now!

Forcing himself to forget his fears, Titan knew that he had to stop these men before they got away. He dealt a swift kick to the chest of the man that had spotted him. The sacs the man had been carrying dropped, spilling scattered bills into the air. He crashed into the side of the van with a dull thud, leaving a huge dent in its side. Just then he looked up into the van's side mirror to see another man in a ski mask waiting behind the wheel. As the driver's eyes locked on the mirror, Titan knew instantly who it was. He would have recognized those eyes anywhere. The other two thieves, catching sight of their partner hitting the ground, dropped the armloads of money they were carrying and turned to Titan. As the sacks hit the ground they burst open, the contents instantly soaking in the rain.

Before Titan could move toward the driver's side door the other two men were on him. The distraction of the driver nearly cost Titan dearly as the two assailants started to throw wild punches at him. Luckily the blows slid off him with hardly any effect. Suddenly the van started up, its taillights quickly coming to life. Titan dropped another kick at one thief, and sent him sprawling. The other thief tried to run up and throw a clumsy punch, which Titan easily managed to duck. Then the van's tires started spin out in the slick wet road surface as it made its getaway. Needing to turn his attention back to the van he belted the other thief with a vicious uppercut and the man dropped to the ground hard and didn't move again.

As the last thief hit the ground, Titan found himself simply watching as the van gained speed as it careened down the vacant street. He was not about to let it get away so easily however. Titan quickly aimed his staff at the moving van. It would mark the first time that he would use his lightning strike against anyone. It would not be easy to hit a moving target, but he felt ready. From a distance he could hear the sounds of approaching police sirens. Time was running out. Titan simply had to see the face under that mask, he needed confirmation. He steadied his arm. Just as the van was set to turn the corner and vanish from sight he fired.

In a brilliant flash the blast collided with the rear passenger tire of the van, blowing it to pieces, and sending big chunks of rubber into the air. The force of the shot rocked the van hard, causing it to lose control and swerve wildly as it made the turn. With the van out of sight, Titan heard the crash as it collided with an unseen obstacle. He deftly leapt over the building to the opposing street. Once there he found the van's front end smashed in as it rested at the base of the light post it had crashed into and knocked over. The sound of the sirens continued to draw closer. He stepped over the post and went to the van. He ran to the driver's side door, which hung ajar, and pulled it back, hoping to find the driver and the answer to his fears inside. As he peered in through the darkness, he could find no one. Behind him he heard footfalls through puddles in the alleyway. He whirled and turned only to see a long shadow bound across the alley walls, then into darkness and out of sight. The sirens were practically on top of him now, their lights illuminating the entire street.

Before Azure could even start to tell him that he needed to get out of there he was off to the safety of the rooftops again. He nestled into the shadowy crevices of a nearby building six stories up. He watched as the police arrested the three thieves left behind, and put them in handcuffs and into the back of the squad car. He could hear them arguing below, as one of them tried to tell an officer he saw a guy in a mask jump into the sky. Satisfied, Titan turned and again focused his attention on a city that needed him.

You did well, Titan, even if one of them did escape. They did not manage to get away with anything they had intended.

"Yeah, thanks." His mind was wondering, and Azure's words barely registered.

He tried his best to ignore the memory of the familiar eyes staring back at him in the van. If it was in fact who he thought it was his whole world was about to get turned upside down. It would greatly affect not only his new life as Titan but his personal life as Michael Novak. There was little he could do about it now however; he would have to deal with all that later. Still, only one name and face kept running through his mind.

"Vince," he whispered. "Please be somewhere else right now."

What was that, Titan?

"Oh, nothing. It was nothing," Titan said, slightly startled by Azure. He certainly did not want to share with Azure the fact that he may have just encountered his own brother taking part in a bank robbery.

"Shouldn't we go after the driver of the van?" Titan asked, not really sure if he wanted the answer.

It is not necessary at this time. There is little harm he can cause now.

"Yeah I suppose you're right," said Titan.

That was much better, Titan. You dealt with the situation swiftly and made sure no further damage was done. You are progressing very well.

"Thanks," Titan said, not knowing what else to say. This is definitely going to take some getting used to, Titan thought. Having a guide or teacher he could talk to but not see was still so strange to him. Now he would also have to repress this new revelation about Vince. He would simply have to try and deal with him later, perhaps as Michael. For now he would simply hope that his eyes had been playing tricks on him.

Titan sat perched on a building ledge trying to regain his breath. In no time, he had stopped two crimes in progress and apprehended five criminals. So much of this still felt surreal. Seeing the crime that had infected the city was eye-opening. Even those close to him might be involved, and he had had no idea the whole time. He knew the hard times that had hit the old neighborhood, but to see the full scope of it was scary. He was beginning to realize just how badly Titan was needed.

Have you found where we are to go next, Titan?

"Uh, no. not yet. Just taking a breather here."

The hour grows late. We must keep going.

"Alright, alright, let's keep on going then," groaned Titan.

He failed to see the urgency, but he did not want to disappoint Azure on his first night out. He saw no point in arguing over the need for a break, he really didn't think he could win that argument.

Trying to stay low and as out of sight as possible, Titan went bounding over rooftops and ledges. He was running on auto pilot, focusing more on the sounds of the city than anything. This time he seemed to go for quite a while, hearing nothing really out of the ordinary. Things seemed to have calmed down. Either that or he was just missing something, and he figured Azure would let him know if that were the case.

"Is this how it's always going to be? Me coming out every night and seeing what crime I can find?" asked Titan, as he continued moving.

Not at all. This is simply the best way to train you to use your powers. However, you will always have to be ready for evil to strike at any moment whether you are prepared or not. Of course patrolling as we are tonight is always a good way to maintain order in the criminal world.

Suddenly, Titan became aware of a faint echoed voice that sounded like it was coming out of a loudspeaker. He began to move in its direction. As he went, he began to pick out words that were coming through.

"We have the place surrounded. Come out with your hands up," was all Titan heard over the police megaphone. It was all he needed to hear.

Just as Titan neared, the voice on the megaphone stopped. In its place was the loud crack of gunfire that pierced the night air. The sound reminded him of the police chase that had brought him the ring only one night before. His muscles tensed, and his heart skipped a beat at the thought of it. Instinctively he drew his staff, preparing for action. Blue electricity sparked and flowed from its end.

Azure had told him he was nearly invulnerable; he feared that might be tested tonight. The very idea of entering the middle of a gun fight frightened him. He had already thought of it as something he would likely have to face, but he never thought it would be on his first night out. Gunfire was still only something he was familiar with through TV and movies. Titan tried to restrain himself from recoiling after each gun blast. He knew that the limits of his courage were about to be fully tested.

A big neon GLOBOTEK sign called out from across the street at him from atop the building. The GLOBOTEK building stood three stories higher than the one he was currently on. He knew that building was where he needed to be. The gunfire continued. The small crack of pistol fire was now joined by the loud boom of shotguns, and the rat-tat-tat of machine guns. As Titan tensed and readied his legs to spring forward he saw a man in the top story window aiming a shotgun down into the street below. As his feet hit the building's edge, he dove straight at the shooter pushing away all his fears. A big electric blue and yellow blur shot across the street. Several officers below stopped shooting to look up, baffled, as Titan shot past overhead. He cut like a knife through the lightly falling rain.

Titan hit the window head on with such force that the shooter was knocked clear across the room, along with his staff. The shooter was out cold, his head stuck in the wall plaster. Getting back up, Titan grabbed the shotgun and snapped it viciously over his knee, breaking it to pieces. He then went over and picked up his staff, prepared to fight.

We know not how many foes you will need to face here or where they may hide. Be wary and move swiftly, Titan.

"I'm on it," Titan said with authority.

Titan was five stories up and could hear gunfire continue directly below him with no way of telling exactly where it was coming from.

You must end this now before innocent people below are injured.

"I said, I'm on it," said Titan, feeling nagged. As if he couldn't tell that this was urgent enough.

With both hands, Titan raised his staff above his head. As it sizzled and sparked he brought it down onto the floor hard, just as he shot off a blast of lightning. Immediately the floor began to buckle and give as the area all around Titan was charred and destroyed. A three foot hole appeared at his feet. Then it gave, spilling Titan to the floor below. The lightning blast he had shot went through the first floor and into the second as well. As Titan hit from above, the whole room seemed to buckle under the force of the fall.

As the dust settled, Titan sat crouched, regaining his bearings. He had landed right in the middle of two more shooters. The one to his left rounded immediately, leveling his gun at him. Almost on instinct Titan shot a lightning blast, hitting the shooter's gun out of his hands. Out of the corner of his eye he saw movement. He fired his right leg back, catching the other shooter in the midsection and knocking him to the floor. With every motion the floor buckled and bounced as though they were at sea. Suddenly the first shooter was trying to take a swing at Titan while his attention was diverted. He caught the man's arm, twisted it back easily, then flipped the thief overhead, causing him to land hard in the middle of the room.

At last the floor gave and all three were dropped below in a tangle of plaster, wood and metal. When they hit the floor below, that floor cracked and creaked, then gave way in the blink of an eye. The three of them crashed down on the second floor mezzanine. The two shooters were still out cold. Through the main atrium however, Titan saw six others fully conscious and looking up at him bewildered. Unlike the other criminals he had encountered this evening, these guys all seemed very professional. They were all dressed in black military style clothing and gear. They carried a bunch of high tech equipment that Titan had never seen before. They didn't seem to be looting the place, so Titan had no idea what they had been up to before the police crashed their party.

"Well," Titan said to Azure. "Only one way to find out what's going on and that's to go down there and ask."

Their weapons are beyond those I am used to. You will need to stay in motion to avoid attack and draw them in to you.

Giving himself a quick dust off and tightening his grip on his staff, Titan leapt over the railing with ease and landed right in the center of the lobby.

They were on him right away. He hardly had time to breathe. Wild kicks and punches came at him furiously. Luckily Titan was able to easily dodge or swat most of them down. Only a few landed, hitting him in the side or head. Titan thought the blows felt as though someone was throwing marshmallows at him. He caught one of the men with the end of his staff under the arm and was able to fling him onto two others. Then one jumped onto Titan's back, trying to pull his staff back, choking him. Titan was able to push down on the staff while lunging down himself, sending the man flying through the air. The thug crash landed on a bank of computers by the security desk, attempted to get up once, then lay still.

Titan prepared quickly as the last two paced around him. The room was dimly lit and made Titan's yellow uniform stand out more. Both criminals gazed intently at him approaching slowly, as though looking for the chink in his armor. Titan stood poised and ready for their attack. Then he noticed their stares break. They looked quickly at each other, as though speaking in their own private language. Titan didn't like the look of where this was going. He jumped up and flipped over them both as they charged. They were able to catch themselves in just enough time so that they only bumped into each other. They both turned to look for Titan, yet all they saw was his staff speeding toward their heads just before knocking them out.

Well done, Titan.

"Yeah, thanks. But where were you with the advice on that one?" asked Titan, standing over his victims.

I saw that you had the situation well in hand.

"Thanks, I guess. I did kinda kick some butt there, didn't I?" Titan boasted.

You did well, but it is best not to get too cocky.

Suddenly the whole lobby flooded with bright lights, nearly blinding him. Vaguely, through the floodlights, Titan saw the silhouettes of the SWAT team move towards the main door. The megaphone was on, but Titan was paying no attention. He didn't need to. The police had heard all the commotion, and were now storming the building.

I believe it is time we vacate the premises.

"I couldn't agree more," said Titan.

Just as Titan was jumping out through the hole in the roof, he heard the shattering of glass as the SWAT team charged into the lobby. By the time they had reached the criminals, Titan was jumping up to the third floor. He leapt the nine feet distances with incredible ease. Once he reached the fifth floor and looked down he could see the police flashlight beams reaching back through the floor holes, searching for him. He stepped back, edged towards the broken window, and stepped out onto the ledge.

Titan paused momentarily and looked down at the frenetic activity. The rain had nearly stopped, now only coming down in a fine mist. Suddenly one of the police spotlights fell on him. Titan held up his arm to shield his eyes. He had to get out of there, and quickly.

"You, on the ledge! There is no way out! Throw down your weapon! Don't move any further, and officers will be there to get you," came the voice from the megaphone.

"Uh, what do I do here? These are the good guys. Do I stay to get congratulated or what?" asked Titan.

"Throw down your weapon now. If you fail to comply we will open fire!" blared the voice.

I don't believe they wish to congratulate you. I think it best if we vacate the area now.

"You're the boss," said Titan.

He turned and ran along the length of the building ledge. Halfway across the building he heard the crack of gunfire from below. Small explosions seemed to be going off on the walls, sending out puffs of dust and tiny fragments of concrete. The spotlight could not keep up with

Titan, and all of the gunfire missed him. At last, his foot touched the far edge of the ledge and he launched himself up into the air. He continued leapfrogging over and along buildings until he thought he was well away from the scene. Then he flopped down, heart pounding, wedged amid the vents and ducts of a downtown skyscraper.

"Well that was something new," said Titan.

You swiftly put an end to the situation, no doubt saving lives in the process. You did well.

"Yeah, thanks. Although I never expected the police to wind up chasing me in all of this," said Titan.

It is unfortunate, but at this point expected.

"Expected? By who? I sure wasn't expecting it."

You must put yourself in their shoes. They do not know who you are, or that you had stopped the criminals. You must have faith. In due time they will know you are on their side.

"Yeah, I guess you're right. I did make pretty short work of those guys. I suppose the police will come around," said Titan, more to himself than anyone. He stood and sheathed his staff. "So, off again I suppose."

You have done very well, Titan, but I think we are finished for tonight.

Titan looked around and saw that the dark night sky was lightening as the sun was starting to rise, parting through the remaining dark clouds.

"I guess you're right. But I don't feel tired or anything. We can keep going if you want to. I'm ready."

Titan really didn't want to stop; although he did want to get back to share it all with Carly. He was feeling electricity course through his whole body. He had felt joy in doing all they had tonight. As he saw more and more of the dark underbelly of the city he called home, he felt a deep urge to continue. He felt the need to keep fighting against the criminals and make this city as great as he felt it should be.

Your enthusiasm is good, but this is only your first night and you are far from finishing your lessons. We will retire for now and we will continue later when we are needed again. There will be other times.

He made his way to the rooftop where Carly was waiting for him. He vaulted easily over rooftops and ledges. Passing over the trendy west end to the far less exotic east side, he began to wonder if this was what it was like for Dylan Thompson every time he came back to the old neighborhood. It had been the single most exciting night of his life, and he really did feel like he could go on. He also knew he needed to get back to Carly. He had been gone hours, and he knew she would be on the rooftop waiting.

Titan landed gingerly on Carly's roof. He found her curled up again on the bus bench wrapped in a blanket and fast asleep. She had set up a big umbrella to keep the rain off. They usually used it to shield themselves from the sun.

"Extermino Fortis!" he said after landing, and turned back into Michael. He slipped the ring in his back jeans pocket and peered down at Carly lovingly. As he gazed at her, he thought of the criminals he had faced tonight. The idea of keeping Carly safe from any lowlife only strengthened his conviction to his duty as Titan.

Michael gently stroked her hand. Carly barely even twitched. Carefully he bent down and scooped her up into his arms and carried her back into the apartment. Michael tiptoed into the Edwards' apartment, trying not to wake Carly or her parents. He didn't even want to know what her father would have to say about this, but he felt it was his duty to do so. Still wrapped in the blanket, Michael gently placed her on her bed. He kissed her cheek and gently brushed her hair back from her face before tiptoeing out of her room. Feeling like something of a cat burglar himself, he slipped back out the front door, locking it as he left.

As he walked home he couldn't help noticing how rejuvenated he felt, as he kept reliving the events of the night in his mind. He should have been exhausted but he wasn't. Then it hit him, he hadn't called his grandpa all night again. He had no idea how he was going to explain why for the second night in a row he had not managed to call and let him know he was alright. The rest of the walk home Michael resolved to do a little better planning while he was out as Titan. He would just have to bring his cell phone or something. He was beginning to find that being a superhero had many more responsibilities and challenges than he had ever imagined.

Chapter 8: Chief Ross and Vicki Earnhardt

Police Chief Thomas Ross stood solemnly in front of the scene at the GLOBOTEK building, taking it all in. Ross was a tall, slender black man in his late forties, wearing his usual suit with a beige trench coat. He stood surveying the aftermath, talking to no one, taking mental notes. His men were currently rounding up the remaining perpetrators, combing the scene for evidence and assessing the damage. It was the third, and he hoped last, such incident he would face that night.

Three times, three different crimes had been attempted. It seemed that the same masked vigilante had stopped all three. From all reports this masked man had swooped in and stopped the crime and apprehended the suspects each time. Yet the most amazing part seemed to be how this would-be hero stopped these crimes. Ross heard stories of fantastic strength and gravity defying feats and even flashes of lightning. This supposed vigilante had been wearing a yellow and blue costume with a bandana over his face. He had even given himself a symbol, a big lightning bolt T across his chest. For now he chalked it all up to exaggeration and the stuff of urban legend. A city clasped in fear was desperate for any sign of hope. Chief Ross would make no assumption until he had some hard evidence.

Ross had been Chief of Police for five years, and had been with the city's police force for another fifteen years. He had watched helplessly as his beloved city had sunk into a pit of crime, decay and corruption. A night full of crimes had become the norm in Delta City. The masked man who had intervened and put an end to them was not. Villain or vigilante, Ross would have to bring him in. The sun was already starting to rise and he was tired. He knew as soon as the mayor caught wind of these events, Ross would have to answer for them.

What could he say? He enjoyed seeing these thugs caught and behind bars as much as the next person. What he didn't like, however, was the idea of a citizen running around playing superhero. It was too dangerous and could spawn copycats, and then he would have one really big unstoppable mess on his hands. The part that baffled him most was that from all the reports there was only ever one man at the scene. But from what he saw of the scenes, no ordinary citizen could have just waltzed in and singlehandedly apprehended all those criminals. Still, that was just what appeared to have happened. A part of him wanted to catch the masked man just so he could find out how he had done all this. Chief Ross was determined to get to the bottom of it all.

"Chief, they have everyone all loaded. They're gonna take 'em back to the precinct for questioning now," said a detective, sidling close to Chief Ross.

"Sure, Frank. Although I'm sure it won't get us anywhere; they're Mr. Midnight's boys," replied Ross morosely.

"I'll follow 'em and oversee the questioning myself, Chief," said Detective Frank Langara.

"Thanks, Frank, I appreciate it. Who knows, we just might get lucky," replied Ross.

"Anything on this new guy, Chief? Any idea whose side he's playin' for? What I mean is do ya think this is some concerned citizen or a rival gang attack?" asked Frank.

"I don't know, Frank. It just doesn't make sense. I don't think he's on Midnight's side, so that would point to him being on someone else's side. Yet Midnight has crushed all his competition, so that points to someone new. Maybe this guy works on his own. Either that or we simply have a rogue vigilante trying to be on our side. So to answer your question, I honestly have no idea, but don't worry, when I figure it out you'll be the first one to know," said Ross.

"It's all pretty strange, isn't it? I mean, about the stories of this masked guy? All the stuff they say he can do?"

"It's strange alright, but I bet it all has a perfectly good explanation behind it," Chief Ross answered.

"Yeah you're probably right, Chief," said Frank.

"Frank, I'm sure this guy will show up again, and next time I know we'll catch him before he gets himself or someone else seriously hurt."

Frank walked away leaving Chief Ross in a shower of police lights and fluorescent lamp glow pondering the scene, and the rest of the night's events.

Chief Ross looked up, dismayed to see the reporter for *The Courier*, Vicki Earnhardt. She was standing right at the front of the line of police tape, waving down Chief Ross, trying for a comment. She stood front and center around a dozen other TV and newspaper reporters. Vicki was of average height with long brown hair, and was strikingly beautiful. She also had brains to match her beauty. Ross wasn't so much surprised to see her as he was surprised that it took her so long to show up. He didn't dislike Vicki. The problem was that she often seemed a step ahead of his own department. Knowing things she shouldn't, she often managed to embarrass him and his men. Still she was an excellent reporter and could even be a valuable tool at times for the police to use in solving cases. At other times, such as this, her prying eye was the last thing he wanted at his crime scene.

"Chief can I get a quick comment?" asked Vicki.

"Vicki I'm sorry, but as I already told everyone else here, there is nothing I can tell you about this crime at this time," said Chief Ross as he passed by the police tape.

"Well can you at least verify for me that the same masked man that was seen here was also seen at least two other major crime scenes tonight?" Vicki said, as the other reporters looked on, hanging their heads and scribbling furiously in notepads.

"Ms. Earnhardt," Ross said stopping in his tracks, "that has not been confirmed. Please try and keep rumor and speculation out of this investigation."

"So, it isn't denied yet either, is that right, Chief? I have several eyewitness reports." Vicki asked.

Ross sighed deeply, and rolled his eyes. "What we have here is a robbery that didn't pan out for the bad guys. Which, you should find a comforting change. It seems they turned on themselves."

"So then, are you denying the existence of this masked man? He was reportedly seen by at least a half dozen witnesses over three crimes scenes across the city tonight," said Vicki flatly.

Chief Ross did not reply. He knew with the little he had said to her that he had already said too much. Vicki Earnhardt was the kind of reporter that could fish out as much information from his non answers as she could from his actual ones. She had caught Ross with his foot in his mouth more than once when he first became chief. The less said to her the better. As chief he had learned when to walk away.

With the crime scene under control Ross got into his car, fired the engine to life and put the scene behind him. He was anxious to get back to his office and figure out what he would tell city hall. Ross knew that this vigilante business would not escape the mayor's radar. He found it always best if he had a written statement waiting to answer any of city hall's predictable questions.

Vicki Earnheart had all her notes in order for the next day's edition of *The Courier*. She had arrived late at this scene because she was coming from the last robbery. She had been busy getting direct quotes from various witnesses. All said they saw a masked man, performing amazing feats. It sounded to Vicki as if they were embellishing quite a bit. These people were making it sound like this guy could practically bend steel and fly. She could tell from the look Chief Ross had given her that he too had all the same information on this masked vigilante.

"So you got any more info on this masked guy?" asked a short fat man from *The Daily Dispatch*.

"Why don't you do your own reporting, Merv," said Vicki, turning his way.

"Come on we're colleagues," said Merv.

"The day I ever get some new information from you, I'll look at helping you out," snipped Vicki.

"Ah, come on," said Merv as Vicki started walking away.

From all reports, this crime fighter sounded scarier than Mr. Midnight. Witnesses described him as big, strong and mean. Yet from most witnesses, it wasn't fear she read on their faces but hope. Hope that their city was being taken back at last. It sounded a bit too idealistic for her, but definitely worth checking into. Maybe some more witness interviews would be required. Or maybe, she thought, this would just be a one trick pony never heard from again. She only hoped that if it were real, he would put an end to the city's escalating crime rate.

Maybe this is just what this city needs to get it going again and out from under the thumb of Mr. Midnight, Vicki thought. Chief Ross seemed to be one of the only bright lights left in the city. Yet even he could only hope to do so much. She wasn't sure yet what she believed about this vigilante, but she did know one thing, and that was that either way this would make a great story for the paper. She only hoped she could get it done and submitted in time for that day's edition. This vigilante sounded too good to be true.

Chapter 9: Sunset Showdown

The next morning Michael felt better than he had in ages. He had snuck in undetected and just had time for a quick forty minutes of sleep. Grandpa Dale had been asleep and did not stir as Michael had crept to his room. As Michael passed Vince's room it was closed as usual. He was tempted to try the handle and open the door to see if his brother was there. Yet, there or not, it would not answer the questions he now had. Instead he had simply crawled into bed for some much earned rest. When his alarm had gone off less than an hour after his head had hit the pillow he had shot out of bed, as though he had slept all night rather than having spent it leaping all over the city fighting crime.

He hopped in the shower, trying to prepare himself for a day of normalcy. He was excited yet nervous to find out what the news and the papers were saying about his exploits, but he had wanted to wait until he got to Carly's so they could read the paper together. He started to dress quickly so he could have breakfast with his grandpa before going back to Carly's. He knew he would need to make up once again for forgetting to call in. While grabbing a pair of socks, a familiar old photograph caught his gaze from the bottom of his drawer, and froze him in place.

The picture was clearly old and had been handled quite a bit. The corners and edges had all been worn and slightly bent. It showed infant Michael and young Vince sitting on a picnic blanket in a grassy park. Behind the boys were their smiling and proud parents. His mother was slender and beautiful, with long curly brown hair. Vince had his father's build, but otherwise showed quite a bit of resemblance. Clearly, much of Michael's looks had come from his parents. He seemed to have his mother's eyes and cheekbones, and his father's nose, chin, and even the same messy tangle of brown hair. It was the only picture Michael had of the four of them as a family. He fished the ring out of his pocket and looked at it. He wished he could tell them about it, and see what they would say. His father had been known as a pillar of the community in his day. He wondered what advice his dad would offer.

Kevin Novak had been one of the few who had stood up to the corruption of local politics and policing. Beyond his work at city hall, he had worked with local Neighborhood Watch and other community groups. Crime seemed to always stay just out of reach of the east side neighborhoods he worked in. His mother worked in the bank, but was just as active in a variety of neighborhood causes as his father. Yet once they died, the people here seemed to lose their voice, and strength. Michael only hoped that through Titan he could give some of that back to them.

Michael wished more than anything that his memory of them was stronger and clearer than it was. It was all he had, and most days it was more than enough. He tucked the photo back into his drawer, threw on the cleanest shirt he could find and went to the kitchen for some breakfast. He may have felt rested, but he was still starving.

"Good morning," Michael said as he entered the kitchen.

"Well hello there, stranger," Grandpa Dale replied in a low voice, seated at the table. Vince only scowled at him while buttering toast by the sink. Michael did his best to avoid eye contact with Vince.

"What's up?" Michael asked, already pouring cereal into a bowl.

"Well, I was going to ask you that same thing. I figured you must have news since you didn't call again last night," Grandpa Dale said.

"I know, and I'm so sorry, Grandpa. I really didn't intend for that. I was gonna stay over at Perminder's, but I ended up coming home real late instead."

"Well, son, I know you're going through a big time in your life, but you are still only fourteen. I don't want you just running all over town all through the night. I'm sorry but if it happens again I will have to ground you."

"Okay. I am really sorry Grandpa that I left you worrying again all night." Michael hated the smug look spread across Vince's face as this exchange went on. All Michal was trying to focus on, however, was how much more difficult it would be to sneak out as Titan when his grandpa would be keeping a closer watch on him no doubt.

"Now that that's out of the way there is some good news you just missed this morning," Grandpa Dale said to Michael. "Vince just got a new job."

"Oh really. What's that Vince?" Michael asked, more for his grandpa's benefit. He really didn't want to venture his guess about what he thought that this new job might be out loud. Michael, feeling defiant however, cast a scowl of his own at Vince. He was becoming surer by the instant that it was Vince he had seen last night. Vince was no doubt working his way into some super villain gig, he figured.

"Oh it's just this thing doin' deliveries for a place downtown. It's with your old buddy Dylan. I got to talkin' to him when he was here yesterday," Vince replied. His scowl now turned into a full snarl aimed at Michael. For good measure, Vince brought up his right hand, made it into a fist and began caressing it with his left.

This silent fighting had being going on between them for many years. Grandpa Dale was seldom able to pick up on it. It was one of the only things the old man did not sense. Occasionally Vince would get careless and do something like crack his knuckles, and then Grandpa Dale would turn his head. He rarely got mad and could usually silence the boys with a simple look.

Carly's warnings regarding Dylan came back to him then. Maybe, Michael thought, Dylan wasn't the most well intentioned guy if he was really willing to hire Vince for anything. Maybe it was Dylan that Vince was working for last night. He hoped he was just being paranoid.

"Ah, my two boys growing up," Grandpa Dale beamed. "Changing the subject a little, did either of you two hear about those disturbances last night? I only caught a little of it on the radio."

Michael's heart froze. Once again he found it hard to look at his grandpa. Deep down he was a little frightened of what Grandpa Dale might have to say about Titan prowling around Delta City. He still wanted to share all that was going on, and was starting to feel guilty for keeping it secret from him. It was the only time in his life that he had withheld anything from his grandpa and he hated the feeling. He thought that his grandpa knew that he was keeping something from him. Grandpa Dale had always shown a knack for knowing everything, and Michael had always been horrible at keeping secrets.

"No, what is it?" Vince said breaking the silence.

"Oh, sounded like someone in a mask and costume involved with the police," Grandpa Dale said.

"No. I didn't hear anything about that." Vince was talking and chewing at the same time. Michael could see big wads of chewed toast floating around in his mouth. He also noticed that Vince had turned a shade paler at Grandpa Dale's mention of Titan.

"Apparently someone took to violence to fight some criminals on their own. Got dressed up and everything according to the news. I just don't know what's become of this city," said Grandpa Dale.

Michael sat at the table, unable to speak. A million thoughts swirled through his head. Michael clearly thought he had seen true disappointment in Grandpa Dale's face when he had mentioned Titan. Michael couldn't bear the thought. He wanted his Grandpa to say more of what he had heard, but was afraid. He was also monitoring Vince for any change in tone or emotion, searching for any sign for whether it had been his brother at that bank last night.

"Well I gotta run, Grandpa," Vince said, patting the old man on the shoulder as he went by. "Later, runt," he said to Michael.

"What? Where are you going?" Michael asked Vince. He found himself unsure of how to handle the idea of the secrets that Vince might be hiding.

"I'm meeting up with some people. What's it to you?" Vince snapped back.

"Well...well I was just curious is all," Michael found himself stammering, not knowing what to say.

"Now boys, can you please just get along?" Grandpa Dale pleaded.

"Sorry, Grandpa. Anyways I gotta get going. See ya." Vince hurried out the back door, closing it with a bang.

"Well, what are your plans today?" Grandpa Dale asked, after Vince had left.

"I was gonna go over to Carly's, hang out with the guys maybe," said Michael, unable to tell him that he needed to go over all things Titan with Carly.

"Listen, Grandpa. I do have some news actually."

"What is it, son? Sounds like something is troubling you," Grandpa Dale replied.

"Well, I am going down to enroll for my classes this week."

A broad smile crossed Dale Novak's face. "Michael that's wonderful. I truly am proud of you, my boy. It's important for you to get a good start so you can get into a good college. I always thought you'd be the one to go to college. Get a degree, become a real professional. Not that Vince isn't capable; I just don't think he's cut out for the college life. But you, you always have had the drive your brother lacks."

"Thanks, Grandpa, but don't get too excited. You haven't seen any marks yet," joked Michael.

"Nonsense, I know you'll do fine. So, can I expect you for dinner? You can bring Carly of course," he said.

Michael let out a silent sigh of relief. Nothing could have sounded better, and he told his Grandpa as much. After having a nice breakfast with him, Michael went to Carly's house to tell her all about his exploits of the night before. The neighborhood seemed to be getting up slowly that morning, as he hardly passed anyone on the way. Yet there was so much on his mind Michael barely noticed.

Michael was bursting at the seams to tell Carly about the night before. He was actually surprised that she hadn't even called his cell yet. He started to panic that maybe her father had found out she hadn't been in her room all night again. He didn't want to even think about what that could mean. As he got to her building he buzzed the door to get in and he bounded up the steps to her door. Michael knocked, waiting patiently, smiling like a fool. When Carly opened the door all he saw was a look of panic on her face. Without a word she grabbed his hand and led him up to the rooftop. Once there, she passed the morning's copy of *The Courier* into his hands. Michael's heart sank as he read the headline and ensuing article.

'HERO OR VILLAIN?' the headline read. The rest of the article by Vicki Earnhardt went on to tell of the three incidents the night before and the appearance of some "masked vigilante" that had taken the law into his own hands. How he might be dangerous to the public, and even begged the question of whether the masked man was any better than the criminals he seemed to stop. It went on to list many of the major problems that gripped the city. Then, the article questioned whether the masked man was an answer to any of them or simply adding to the long list of problems.

Michael sank to the bench Carly had been sleeping on the night before. All the good feelings he had been having all morning washed away. He thought Titan would be seen as the hero of Delta city, and here he was being labeled as a possible criminal by the media. He looked up at Carly who was standing by watching and waiting for him to finish the article.

"Oh man. At least tell me your dad didn't find out you were out again last night did he?"

"No he's fine. I told you don't worry about him. What happened last night, Michael?" Carly asked finally.

"I don't understand," Michael said after a brief pause. "After the crimes I put a stop to, the good I did last night, they want to just cast me into the same category as all those criminals?" Michael hung his head, not knowing what else to say, think, or feel.

"Michael I'm sure it's not as bad as you think. Now will you please fill me in a little on what happened?" Carly asked in a pleading tone.

Finally Michael told her everything that took place from the moment he had stepped foot off her roof. He told her about the foiled mugging, she only giggled slightly when he explained how he tripped into the wall, the failed bank heist, and at last about the incident at Globotek. He told her about how he had searched the city with Azure looking for crimes that were happening. He even told her about his fears regarding Vince. As Michael recounted his tale, she simply sat and listened, spellbound. When he was finally finished, Carly just sat a moment and let it all sink in.

"Well, Michael," she said at last. "I think there's only one thing you can do to fix what people may be thinking of Titan right now. You need to keep doing exactly what you did last night. You need to prove to this city that Titan is here to help."

"Yeah, I suppose you're right. This just isn't how I expected things to go," he moaned.

"What, you thought you would get thrown up on everyone's shoulders, cheered for and celebrated?" said Carly.

"Well, maybe not celebrated," he shrugged.

"Michael this city hasn't had much to believe in recently. You may not win them all over right away, but if you continue to fight for them they'll see the good you do. Besides, nothing good ever comes easy," said Carly.

"What should I do about Vince?"

"That one's a little tougher. Not sure what to tell you there," Carly replied.

"Carly, you're supposed to have all the answers! You're way better at all this thinking stuff."

"Well, what did you expect me to say? You're not even sure that you saw him last night. The way I see it, you have two options. Option one is to keep this quiet and just keep a watchful eye on Vince to see if he slips up at all. Option two is you confront him somehow and ask if he was there."

"Well, I definitely think option one is easier," said Michael.

"Hey, I can't solve all your problems, now can I?" she asked with a laugh.

"Well, I can always hope can't I?"

"Well, I did happen to do a net search on Titan and Azure last night when I went back in to see my parents."

"What? That's fantastic. What did you find?" Michael couldn't believe he hadn't thought of that yet.

"Not too much actually. I did however find some similarities between many of the mythological heroes from the time that azure told you he was training all these past Titan's. When I downloaded some pictures that were apparently done closer to their times all the heroes seemed to have been dressed in a specific uniform as well. Not quite like yours, but still something that would set them apart from the average citizen of the day. They all also seemed to have had a specific weapon like a sword or a shield and many were painted with a very distinctive ring on their finger. Of course if being Titan was as much a secret then as it seem to be now then it kind of makes sense that all we get is the people of the day interpreting all these amazing feast they were witnessing. Just like I'm sure people will see and read about hundreds of years from now with you."

"Carly, you're amazing," Michael said, clearly amazed at her investigating skills.

Suddenly Perminder burst through the rooftop door with an excited look on his face. Panting heavily from running he said, "Here...you guys... are...I've been looking...everywhere...for you." He was leaning on the door frame, exhausted.

"Perminder, after all these years, this should be like the first place you would look for us," Carly said.

"Yeah...I suppose," Perminder replied.

"What's up? Must be big to get you running all over the neighborhood," Michael said.

"Hardy har, funny man," Perminder replied sarcastically, still slightly out of breath. "Come on, you guys gotta come in and see what's goin on down at the docks right now," he said, turning towards the stairs and gesturing for Michael and Carly to follow.

The three of them came into Carly's living room where her parents were already gathered around the TV watching the breaking story. As the three of them sat down Michael couldn't help but notice the apprehensive look Mr. Edwards gave him. On the screen they saw about a dozen police cars parked around a docked ship. On the ship's deck were men armed with pistols and shotguns, and they were all tucked behind different objects firing at the policemen who were all taking cover behind their squad cars. The TV reporters indicated the men had been trying to smuggle in illegal goods and the police had been waiting for them as the boat docked. Once it was secured, the police had come out to apprehend the men. After a tense standoff, shots were fired. The men on the boat were cornered, but were refusing to surrender without a fight. The reports were unclear what the men had been trying to bring in.

"Whoa," said Perminder. "They weren't shooting like this before. First the police chase here, now a Wild West shootout. Can you believe this? Well at least I never have to worry about this old town gettin' dull on me."

"Perminder, you bite your tongue," said Mrs. Edwards. "I mean, honestly, what is this world coming to?" she seemed to be asking no one in particular.

As everyone was busy staring at the violent scene on the TV, Carly shot Michael a look. Michael nodded slightly.

"Um ... I'm sorry but I've gotta run," Michael said, suddenly jumping to his feet and heading for the door. "I forgot I have some errands I have to run for my grandpa. I'll catch you guys later, okay," he said to Perminder and Carly.

Perminder didn't even take his eyes from the TV. He just gave Michael a wave of his hand saying, "you're gonna miss the show, man."

"I'll just catch the highlights on the news later," Michael replied.

Carly was on her feet and walking him to the door.

"Good luck, and be careful," Carly said to him as she opened the door.

Michael gave her a confident, knowing smile and gave her a light kiss.

"Don't worry. This'll be my time to shine. Hey, you may even get to see me in action this time," he said.

"Just go knock 'em dead," Carly replied, even managing a smile.

Michael turned up the stairs to the roof. He burst through the door, the sun glaring in his eyes. He was full of energy, excitement and nervousness. This, Michael thought, was sure to be his first true test as Titan. It was his best opportunity yet to win over the public. With everyone watching, no one would question his intent after this. Last night, under the cover of night, was nothing but practice really. Now, however it was the middle of the day. The police were all around, and the whole city would be glued to their TVs. If it made Perminder run all the way over, you'd bet it would do the same to most everyone else.

Fumbling through his pockets, Michael grabbed the ring, brought it out and slipped it on. While he held it firmly he said the magic words.

"Exaudio Fortis!"

The lightning struck in a brilliant flash and, as the smoke cleared, Michael looked around at himself and again marveled at his transformation to Titan.

"Azure, are you there?" Michael asked. "We have to get to the docks. There's trouble."

I am always here with you, Titan, as long as I remain your guide. You must go there immediately. Land just outside of where the incident is happening so we may assess our situation.

"Okay. Any other parting words of advice?" said Michael.

I can say no more until we arrive at the docks and I may assess the scene further.

"Right, let's go then."

With a running start, Titan took to the ledge and was off. He touched down on a rooftop several blocks away, then after a few running steps was off again. He was hopping up like a grasshopper, bounding a good fifty feet into the air between each jump. Titan followed this process all the way to the docks. He was not yet confident enough to try one leap to such a vague area so far away.

As he was leaping through Delta City, Titan tried his best to prepare himself for what he had to do. Despite the incredible powers he now possessed, he still felt butterflies swirling in his stomach. He thought back to the night before, and how he had handled those situations and hoped that they would help today. Although that all seemed like an ancient memory. He only hoped it would all come back to him. As he began to approach the docks, Titan could already hear gunshots, and the sound of sirens, as well as someone talking into a megaphone.

Titan landed at the top of a four story building close to the docks. He squatted down on the rooftop and looked over the ledge to assess the situation. Flashbacks of Globotek went through his mind. He saw a group of men scattered on the decks of a large cargo ship. It was much different than his view from TV. It was like watching a baseball game on TV and then going and seeing the real thing live. The men all seemed to be taking refuge behind the large crates that were scattered all over the ship's deck. From behind the crates they were shooting at the police who were just on the dock around the ship. The police were ducking behind squad cars and attempting to fire back. There seemed to be more police surrounding the ship than Titan had ever seen at one time in his life. There were more than there had been at the crash where he found the ring, or at Globotek.

He also saw that the megaphone was coming from the front of one of the squad cars. There, Titan saw a slender middle-aged black man, who he knew from TV and newspapers to be the chief of police, Thomas Ross. He seemed to put himself fearlessly in harm's way. He was close to the ship without much cover. He was barking orders over the megaphone at the policemen as well as trying to reason with the men on the ship.

Luckily, Titan also saw that all media and spectators had been pushed well back and out of the way.

Do you see how many men are on that ship?

"Yes, eighteen of them from my count, and they're all armed."

Leap into the midst of this battle and waste no time in neutralizing your opponents here. Use the element of surprise to your advantage. Now go. Do not hesitate. You mustn't remain in any one spot for long once you reach the ship.

Titan stood, and he hesitated for only a moment to take in a large breath. "Well, here goes nothing," he said. Then he dove straight over the huge group of police, stretched out as a yellow and blue blur, and landed onto the middle of the ship's deck. The pop and bang of gunfire was shrill and loud. Titan sat crouched amid numerous crates on the ship deck. There was a buzz of activity everywhere.

He had no idea where to start. There were men scrambling all over the ship, and they all had guns. He had faced guns the night before, but had reacted mostly on instinct. His stomach was doing somersaults as he thought about what to do now. All he knew was that he better move fast. Luckily he did not have to wait long to figure it out as two men came at Titan from behind. He easily heard them approach. In a flash he shot his staff out, and with several quick jabs sent both to the ground, out cold. As his nerves settled he looked about to fully assess the ship.

Titan saw three others huddling behind a crate to his left. They were still focused on the police below, and had yet to notice him. He went right for them, taking out one of the men with a swift punch. Before the other two could even realize what was going on, Titan dealt them a combination of vicious blows. At the last second, the third tried in vain to dodge the swift kicks and punches. With bone crunching force, Titan took them all down.

Titan, behind you!

He could already sense another of them had caught sight of him. He back-flipped over the thug and kicked him hard in the back, sending him flying face first through the air and crashing into another crate. With all the commotion, soon all the men on the ship were becoming aware that they were being attacked on deck and were turning their attention to Titan. Bullets started whizzing by, bouncing off surrounding crates and the ship, and narrowly missing Titan. Some thugs tried to take Titan down on their own, coming in cautiously, throwing calculated punches. He swatted them all aside like bugs.

Bullets passed by him, never connecting. He was leaping from one spot to another all over the deck. He stopped only long enough to take down another of the men. Titan was in constant motion, and just too fast for them. They just kept coming, however. To Titan's dismay, he spotted three more men emerge from beneath the ship's deck. He realized that for every one of these men he brought down, another came up from below.

"Where do these guys keep coming from?" Titan asked aloud.

The odds were beginning to stack against him. He knew that if things kept up like this at some point one of those bullets was going to bounce off him. He had no desire to test his invulnerability. He had to find a way to gain control of this situation quickly or people would be hurt.

"STOP! Hold your fire!" Chief Ross bellowed into his megaphone from below, as he turned, addressing his men while waving his hands wildly. "No one fires unless I say. Stay covered and be ready. We are taking down this vigilante with them."

Titan seemed to be so busy dodging their gunfire that he was unable to attack any of the men on the ship. From down below he could hear the Chief yell into his megaphone, then shortly after it seemed that the fire from the police had stopped, at least for now.

Titan, you must attack, go on the offensive. If you cannot have time to fire yourself then you must use the gunfire of these men against themselves. Force them into a careless attack.

As he contemplated those words, he kept moving around the ship, throwing punches and dodging blows equally. Using his staff to vault over a stack of crates, he kicked two thugs in the head that were coming up from inside the ship. At first Titan had no clue what Azure was talking about. He wished that he would just say what he meant instead of giving him riddles. Then, as a bullet ripped past his arm and punched a hole through a wall of the ship, it came to him.

Titan jumped into the middle of a group of crates, and then quickly leapt away. Sure enough, bullet holes littered the area where Titan had just been. The holes followed and chased him like his shadow. A couple of bullets whizzed close by, too close. He could hear the hiss they made as they flew past him. A few times he could feel the searing heat as the bullets narrowly missed him. He knew he couldn't just keep this up forever. Then it happened. Several bullets had ripped through some electrical panels on the ship's deck close to the bridge. Flames shot out from the shattered electrical boxes. Suddenly, sparks and flames shot outward as the panel exploded. Everyone ducked, including Titan. Then a low rumble came from within the ship as the fire spread.

Within seconds of the flames sprouting to life, a much bigger explosion rocked the ship's deck. A whole stack of crates blew apart, sending their contents flying. All the men who had been shooting at Titan in a blind frenzy were knocked to the ground. In some way, that one explosion seemed to set the whole situation right again. Titan looked around and saw some of the gunmen crawling and stumbling around dazed, but otherwise they appeared fine. The contents of the crates were strewn all over the deck, everything from electronic parts to a variety of weapons.

Slowly the men began to scurry. Some tried to fire at Titan or the police in a futile last stand, while others tried to save the contents of the crates. Just then a second explosion burst forth from deeper within the ship. Titan noticed a police helicopter circling the ship. He had not noticed it until now as it came down closer for a better look. Perched high at the back of the ship, Titan also saw that several police officers were making their way up the stern gangplank despite the explosions and fire that had begun to engulf the ship.

It seemed that one of the gunmen also saw this and quickly dove into a pile of debris that had spilled out of a crate. He pulled out some sort of ray gun. Before Titan could react he had aimed and fired it at one of the officers. A strange sonic ray shot out of it and hit the policeman in the chest. The policeman instantly went rigid and fell face first in the middle of the gangplank. He remained in a frozen solid state as he lay there. With a sinister grin plastered across his face the gunman began to take

aim again. The gunman fired another quick shot at the lead officer on the gangplank, getting the same result as the first shot. As Titan dodged bullets, fire, and armed men, another shooter appeared with the same strange ray gun. With the two of them firing, three more officers fell, all frozen.

Titan, you must save those officers from further harm.

"On it."

Titan quickly flew down and knocked the ray gun away from the first gunman with one end of his staff, then with the other end caught the man in the jaw, dropping him to the ground. The second gunman turned on him, but before he could finish taking aim Titan dealt him a vicious uppercut that sent the shooter to the ground. He could only hope that the policeman would be alright. He wondered what the strange weapon could possibly have been. He thought of trying to snag one to examine later. As gunfire narrowly missed him, he realized that he would have to leave it for the authorities to look into later.

Suddenly Titan saw that small fires and explosions had sprung up all over the ship. None of the gunmen seemed overly concerned about him anymore. They had no choice but to jump overboard or attempt the plank with the police waiting. He then noticed a couple policemen had actually made it onboard and were attempting to round up the gunmen. None of them were putting up much of a fight anymore. Between Titan and all the explosions, most of the fight had gone out of them.

Titan saw that his work was done and at the suggestion of Azure turned to leave the ship. Just as he was about to take off he looked down at the chaos below. Lights were flashing, people were yelling, and fire trucks were starting to move in. Then he caught Chief Ross' gaze. Ross' eyes were suddenly fixed on Titan. Just as he was about to jump from the ship, he saw Ross give orders to some of his men with his finger pointed straight up at Titan. As his feet left the ship and he was flying through the air, he caught a glimpse of the police helicopter. It made a sharp turn and headed his way.

Chapter 10: Hot Pursuit

As Titan was high in the air, the helicopter was right on his tail. He could hear someone on a megaphone ordering him to stop. He looked back. The helicopter was about fifty meters off and slightly above him. Below, a couple of the police cruisers had left the scene at the ship and were headed his way with lights flashing and sirens wailing.

It appears that the authorities here still do not believe that you are on their side.

"Well, I'm not sure what I'm supposed to do about it exactly," Titan said, landing on the edge of a skyscraper and then sprinting across its roof before taking flight again.

You must not stop now.

"Oh, I wasn't planning on it, believe me.*"*

You must use your powers to lose them, and hope that before long they will be willing to let you help them in apprehending criminals, and not chase you like you are one yourself.

"First let's worry about losing them, shall we?" Titan asked, as he leapt through the air.

As soon as Titan touched down on the next roof he began to sprint across it as fast as he could. Already he could feel the wind from the helicopter flying in low behind him. He momentarily feared that the long ends of his bandana might get tangled up in the helicopter's blades. All he could think of was the humiliation of his Titan career getting cut so drastically short. He pushed himself as fast as he could go. He leapt from building to building in a zigzag pattern trying to put some distance between himself and the helicopter. The policeman on the megaphone was still commanding him to stop. Titan bounded easily over to the next building, keeping his brisk pace. Suddenly the helicopter swung out, whirled around and idled itself right in front of him at the end of the building.

Without hesitation, Titan ran at the hovering helicopter. The pilot at the controls showed no emotion and held his position. Det. Frank Langara, sitting in the passenger seat, simply stared as Titan challenged them, with his eyes wide and mouth hung open. At the last moment Titan hit the ground and slid right under the helicopter's nose like a base runner stealing third. He passed so close that he could have easily reached up and touched the metal belly. He was going so fast that he slid right off the edge of the building.

He went over the edge, clawing and grasping for anything that he could grab onto. The vertigo hit him hard. Falling was very different from one of his normal landings. He managed to slide down the face of the building, clinging desperately to every edge he could find. After falling two stories, he dug his feet into the building's concrete side and pushed. He flung himself across the street to the adjacent high-rise. He hit the building feet first and instantly shot himself back in the air diagonally across the street again. Titan now stood on the rooftop gazing across at the helicopter which hadn't moved since he slid under it one building over. He looked around quickly at where to go next to finish his escape. Then the helicopter pulled up, and turned left toward him again.

This time when he took flight he did so with all his might. He went as high as he could and as fast as he could. When his feet left the ground he was no more than fifteen meters from the helicopter. It was by far the hardest he had ever shot himself into the air. With the sheer force of the jump, he felt like he was strapped to the side of a space shuttle during liftoff. The city began to fall away from him until he could no longer make out any defining characteristics.

Titan instinctively held his breath as he shot into the air. After what felt like minutes, he stopped rising. He was suddenly plummeting back down towards the city like a torpedo. He could barely open his eyes against the rushing wind. As the city began to quickly rise up towards him, Titan tried to catch his breath. Suddenly his two story drop a moment ago seemed like child's play. From high above, the only place he could see through his squinted eyes that could provide refuge was Campbell Park at the edge of the city. He turned and angled his body toward the lush green expanse of the park. He shot through the canopy of trees in the middle of the park like a meteor, and crashed into the creek that ran across the width of the park. A giant cloud of water, dirt, grass, and rocks shot into the air from the impact.

Well, you certainly made that dramatic.

Azure's attempt with sarcasm showed the first signs of emotion from the guide. Azure went on as Titan got shakily to his feet in the waist deep water.

A jump like that may have lost them. And it could have cost you as well if you had not fallen into this stream. It should now be clear to you that you must be careful as long as the police see you as a criminal. And in the meantime we must come up with a clear way of showing them that you will be helpful to this city, and not part of its criminal element.

The few people who had been around had turned and ran from fear of what may have crashed into their park. Titan could see the watermarks from his impact on trees several meters away. The entire width of the creek where he had landed suddenly seemed a little wider than the rest.

"Well, I've got nothing. So if you have any ideas I'm all ears. Hey, I'm just glad that these powers kept me from turning into human pizza," said Titan, scanning the area to see where he should go from here.

I am certain that a solution will present itself in due time.

"At least we lost that helicopter. There's no way they could follow us after that jump."

Titan looked up as he heard the rhythmic whir of the helicopter hovering overhead. In the distance, he could also hear the approach of police cars. Dripping wet, he climbed up the bank of the creek. He felt trapped, yet unlike the ship he could not attack the police who were now closing in on him. He also couldn't allow himself to be captured. He did the only thing he could think to do; he ran.

"How could they have found me so fast?" asked Titan.

You didn't exactly make a quiet entrance into this park.

Titan crouched low behind some bushes once he got about one hundred yards away. He watched as the helicopter touched down in a clearing close by. The helicopter blades caused the grass to ripple and flow like a lake in a storm. Tree branches swayed to the point of breaking against the high wind. Suddenly, the sliding side door of the helicopter opened and a plainclothes detective got out. He had sunglasses and a mustache and a beige trenchcoat that billowed against the wind of the helicopter blades. In his right hand was his pistol held out at waist height. Two armed SWAT officers flanked him on either side as they began to fan out across the open field.

"Well, we're going to have to make a quiet exit somehow," said Titan.

Agreed. I believe it would be best if we stay undercover, and go undetected.

The sound of the police cruisers increased from the other direction and Titan knew he had only a short time to get away. Titan saw the lights from cruisers cut in from the park access roads at different directions. He could also hear the sound of another helicopter surveying from above the foliage of the park. He was boxed in with no escape in sight. It wouldn't be safe to just leap out of the thick forest foliage with a helicopter hovering somewhere overhead. If he transformed now someone was likely to see him do so. Titan knew his only choice was to find a place to hide and wait for the heat to die down.

Detective Frank Langara motioned for the two officers to his left to fan out farther and head down a small pathway. He then motioned the other officers to fan out farther on the other side. Frank cautiously continued through the center of the park and towards an area of thick trees and bushes.

"Remember, I would much rather we bring this man in alive and unharmed. He does have unknown weapons and capabilities, however. So be alert and stay safe out there, people," Frank said into the radio he grabbed from his belt.

As Frank approached the wooded area he had lost sight of the SWAT officers and could only see the lights of two of the squad cars that were patrolling the park. His hand was sweating profusely as he clenched his gun. He began to walk very slow as he approached the cluster of dense bushes. Once he was several feet away he saw the bushes rustle, and stopped abruptly. His gun began to tremble in his hand slightly as he released the safety and prepared to fire. He lowered his gun at the bushes with one deft hand and then brought the radio back to his mouth with the other.

"All officers report to…" Frank began to speak into the radio.

He let out a loud sigh of relief as a small raccoon scurried out from the bushes and headed back into the wooded area, and away from him.

Doubled over with his hands resting on his knees, Frank could only chuckle at the sight of it. He re-holstered the radio and gun, and pulled his cell phone out and dialed.

"Talk to me, Frank," said Chief Ross into his cell phone.

"Sir, we've been down here for a bit now and haven't seen hide nor hair of him. We have the park blanketed. If he was still here we would have found him by now. A guy like that doesn't blend in easy," replied Frank, heading back towards the helicopter.

"Alright, Frank. I think it's safe to say we've lost him. Come on back, and we'll finish cleaning up the scene here. I do want some men left to monitor all entrances to that park, and we'll leave the other copter up in case he gets spotted in flying through the air again," Chief Ross said.

"10-4, Chief. We're heading back. I already have a couple units back at the park entrance, and will leave them in place just in case this guy shows up again," said Frank.

"Good work. See you when you get here," Ross said, before closing his cell and dropping it back into his coat pocket.

Frank radioed the other officers to regroup back at the clearing so they could depart. They were all seated back inside within minutes, and the helicopter began to make its ascent. The police helicopter made one final lap of the park, and then turned sharply and headed across the downtown skyline towards the docks. A giant column of smoke still rose high in the air from the smoldering ship wreckage.

I think it is safe for us to come out now.

"Yeah, I suppose so," said Titan.

Titan poked his head out from under the four lanes of the Foreman Bridge that connected Campbell Park to the city. It had been some time since he had heard any helicopters or police sirens. Night had now begun descend on Delta City. He hesitantly made his way back down to the bank of the park. There were no police officers or cruisers in sight. The coast seemed all clear.

"Well, I guess I'll be walking home from here," said Titan.

I do believe that is best.

"You know, I didn't see my superhero career going quite like this," said Titan, as he carefully climbed the bank from the base of the bridge to the park.

These things seldom do go as planned. It's how we choose to handle them when they go wrong that counts.

"I suppose. The good news from all this is that all the bad guys were caught and I wasn't arrested in the process. I guess I'll just have to work on my public image a little," said Titan.

We will work on your image at a later time. You have done well today. Do not be bothered by how this ended.

"Thanks, Azure. I'll talk to ya the next time there's trouble."

Titan returned to cover beneath the bridge, held out his ring, and said the magic words. He felt the power flow out of him and return to the ring. Michael stepped onto the main path of the park and jogged across the pedestrian walkway of the bridge. As he got back towards the hustle of downtown he realized he was a good two hours' walk back to Carly's apartment or his grandpa's. Dark gray clouds had swooped in since Michael had taken refuge and it looked like rain was on its way. Not the kind of walk Michael felt up to with the way his day had gone so far. He fished through all his pockets and managed to get just enough change for the bus.

Michael found the next stop four blocks away. A large overweight man and an elderly couple occupied the bench under the bus shelter, so Michael had to stand out in the rain which had just begun to drizzle down. After waiting fifteen minutes, a bus arrived going Michael's direction. The ride back was agonizing. The bus was quite crowded and Michael had to stand holding onto the safety bar. The whole ride he couldn't help but think that Perminder and Mrs. Edwards had been watching the entire time. He was very nervous to hear what they would think of Delta City's new hero. Or its new wanted criminal depending on their point of view, of course. All he really wanted to do was sit and relax with his girlfriend and buddies, safe with the notion that he could talk to Carly all about it.

Thirty minutes later Michael got off the bus two blocks from Carly's apartment. He was walking, deep in thought, as he replayed the day's events in his mind. The whole thing had been a victory overall, even if it had all ended with him being chased by the police. He was also overwhelmed at how exhilarating the entire experience had been. Using his powers like that was still something he was not quite accustomed to, and it had been absolutely thrilling. He could still picture the looks on the faces of all those criminals as they got a close up look at what Titan could do, and he could still feel the wind on his face as he soared through the air.

Just then a glass door opened right in front of Michael, and he crashed right into it face first. As Michael snapped back to reality he looked through the glass to see Vince on the other side. They were in front of The Burger Shack. Vince had been holding a couple of fountain sodas', and they had spilled all over him as Michael had walked into the door knocking it back at him.

"Look what you did, you little jerk," Vince snapped.

"Vince, I'm sorry. Look, I didn't see you, honest."

"Oh, you're gonna be sorry all right."

Michael had already begun to backpedal, trying to get as far away from Vince as he could. Just as Vince went to lunge at Michael a foot shot out between Vince's legs, sending him sprawling to the sidewalk. Michael was shocked to look over and see Dave, who had sidled up unnoticed to trip Vince before he could get his hands on Michael. Dave quickly stepped to Michael's side as Vince roared in anger while lying face first on the ground.

"You're so dead! Both of you are dead once I get my hands on you," Vince yelled, looking up at the two of them.

"Um…I think maybe we should hightail it outta here, buddy," Dave said to a still dumbfounded Michael.

Michael said nothing in reply. There wasn't anyone to say it to. As Michael turned he saw that Dave was already running at full speed, and now almost half a block away. Michael quickly followed as Vince was getting to his feet. Vince may have been much bigger than both boys, but thankfully for them he was not blessed with any sort of speed. With Dave in the lead they were able to quickly put some distance between themselves and the rampaging Vince behind them.

They wove through the busy afternoon pedestrian traffic of the neighborhood seamlessly. Michael looked back only briefly to ensure they were plenty far out of Vince's grasp. It may not have had the same thrill as fighting bad guys or evading the police as Titan, but there was still a great amount of satisfaction in getting one over on his older brother, with a little help from a friend.

"Thanks, man. I owe you big time for that save," Michael said, as the two had slowed to a jog. They had both doubled back and were taking the long way to Carly's, causing them to run three more blocks than if they had tried to go around Vince.

"Hey, no prob, man. What was I gonna do? Just let my buddy get slaughtered on the sidewalk like that. It's just lucky for you that I happened to be coming from that way when I was."

"Yeah tell me about it. I'm sorry you had to get on Vince's radar though. That could seriously ruin your summer," Michael said, as they got to the front of Carly's building.

"That's okay. I'm sure Vince will forget about it soon enough, and get distracted with something, or should I say someone, else."

Michael hit the buzzer and opened the door as it buzzed them in, and the two of them went inside. They took the stairs slowly as they were now winded and tired.

"Where were you coming from anyway? Perminder called me to come over and see this thing on TV at the docks. I just assumed that you'd already be there."

Michael was now stunned, and had no idea what he could say to Dave that would sound believable. He hated the idea of lying again to his friend, especially after he just saved him from the clutches of his evil brother.

"Oh, I was here. I just had some stuff I had to take care of." It was vague, but seemed to work.

When they got to the apartment Monica was now also there. Carly's father had left, but her mom still remained. As Michael walked in, he lingered a moment, hoping that Carly would come in to the front entrance to greet him. He was bursting to tell her about everything. Luckily, Dave had gone right into the living room with the others to check out the footage on TV. After a brief moment Carly appeared at the doorway. She stayed by the door with a worried look on her face and nibbled nervously at her lower lip. Suddenly she lunged at Michael, locking him in a full embrace. Then just as suddenly she pulled away and started smacking his arms and chest.

"Oh, Michael! You had me so scared. Don't you ever do that to me again," she exclaimed.

"Okay, okay. I promise I'll try," Michael said, unable to contain his laughter.

"It's not funny." She seemed unable to contain a smile of her own.

"Well, you don't know the half of it. Seriously, I'm fine though. You can stop worrying," he tried to reassure.

"That's easier said than done. We saw the whole thing. My mother was freaking out. I don't think we can talk now, but you better tell me the rest later," said Carly, suddenly back to her usual tone.

"What did everyone else think?" Michael asked.

"Um well, let's just say that Perminder's a big fan," said Carly, leading him back into the living room.

"Dude, please tell me you've been watching all this," Perminder said, when he saw Michael walk into the room.

"Oh yeah," Michael said coyly. "I was watchin' some of it at my grandpa's when I dropped his things off. Crazy stuff, isn't it?"

"God, I love this town!" exclaimed Dave, glued to the TV.

"You would," sneered Monica, bored and already flipping through a magazine.

As Michael sat on the couch beside Carly, he looked to the TV just as it showed the beginning of a news conference with the Mayor stepping to a podium with Chief Ross at his side. City hall loomed large behind the two men. The mayhem was evidently contained, and the clean up was well under way. First Chief Ross came to the mike, and answered some questions about the shootout. He answered questions about the criminals and their activity, saying it was an illegal smuggling operation that had been under investigation for some months. He informed the crowd that most of the ship and its cargo were lost to the fire. Ross was refusing to answer any questions about Titan. Naturally that was all the media wanted to know about. What about the powers of the masked man? Where did he come from? Who was he? Was he on the police payroll? Was he as young as he looked? One question came after the other. Ross looked more comfortable dealing with the bad guys on the ship. The Mayor then came to the mike and took over.

"Let me make this perfectly clear," said Mayor Winfield. "The city knows nothing about this masked man. He is as much a criminal here today as those men who were caught on that boat. He caused millions of dollars in damages to our docks and has been terrorizing Delta City for the past two days. This kind of glory seeking vigilantism will not be tolerated in this city. And with the help of Chief Ross, my administration will do everything we can to bring him to justice no matter what powers he seems to possess."

Michael looked away in anger. Until now he had simply been frustrated that his motives as a hero were being questioned, but now the mayor himself was labeling him a criminal. He had put his life on the line. Had even stood in front of bullets, and yet here was the mayor of the city saying he was a no good criminal. The only thing that seemed to lift his spirits at all was seeing that Dave and Perminder seemed to think that Titan was absolutely awesome.

"I mean seriously, did you see what that guy could do?" Dave said in wonder.

"That was so sweet, and he seemed like he could have been our age," Perminder said with equal awe.

"Well I don't care what that mayor says," said Mrs. Edwards. "This city could use a hero. Besides I never voted for the man anyway."

Michael felt a good boost of confidence at this and his anger lessened. He glanced over at Carly. At least she was beaming proudly at him. She cast her eyes around the room, gesturing to Michael to take in the praise the people he cared about were giving him. He had to admit to himself that it did feel good. He wondered what his grandpa thought of all these events. He was sure that he was at home listening to it all on his radio. He knew he should go and see him. The thoughts were making him feel very neglectful. He became scared his grandpa might somehow share the views of someone like the mayor. He just wished that he knew why the police were treating him as a threat, and only hoped that he would be able to persuade them that he was there to help, and soon.

"I'll be right back," said Michael, getting up from the couch.

"You just got here," said Perminder, still not looking up from the TV.

122

"Oh. I uh forgot something, and I just have to call my grandpa quickly," said Michael.

Michael went to the kitchen pulled out his cell and dialed his grandpa. It rang for a long time, which was nothing unusual with his grandfather. Being blind, Dale Novak usually took longer than most to get to the phone. As though he thought if you really wanted to talk to him you wouldn't mind waiting a few extra seconds.

"Hello," came his grandpa from the other end.

"Hi, Grandpa. It's just me, Michael. I just wanted to let you know that I'm at Carly's still." Michael hesitated a moment, then went on. "We've all just been watching the footage of the attack at the docks. Have you heard about any of it?"

"Oh yes. I've been listening to it all afternoon. It's just horrible," said Grandpa Dale.

"Yeah I know, isn't it?" Michael could think of nothing else to say. He simply didn't have the courage to ask whether he meant the men on the ship or Titan.

"I just don't know what's becoming of this city anymore," Grandpa Dale said.

"Well I'll be home in a little while," was all Michael could think to say.

"Okay, son. I'll see you then. Take care now."

When Michael returned to the living room, the questioning on the TV had switched from talk about Titan to the weird guns the crooks had pulled against the police. None of the strange weapons had been recovered. Chief Ross was once again at the podium. Mayor Winfield was in the background looking poised to jump in again at any moment. In the top right corner of the screen they kept showing highlights of the action from a few hours before. Everyone was watching the shooting, the fire, and Titan repeatedly while the press conference was going on.

"We have no confirmation as to the type of weapon that was used against several officers. All we can say is that the officers were left temporarily incapacitated, but are currently in stable condition," said Chief Ross, looking wearier by the second.

"Is it true that these men were reportedly working for Mr. Midnight's crime syndicate?" asked a young female reporter in the front row.

Michael and Carly both shot each other worried looks. Michael fighting crime as Titan was one thing, but taking on Mr. Midnight directly was another.

"At this time that is nothing more than rumor," Chief Ross said, sticking to the old police media line regarding Mr. Midnight.

"Ah, who cares? With this new guy around, Mr. Midnight doesn't stand a chance. Am I right?" said Dave, looking around the room for a show of support.

"I sure hope so, Dave," said Michael, looking gravely into the TV.

Chapter 11: No More Hero

The view at dusk from the office of Mr. Midnight would almost be beautiful if it weren't for the cold feel of the office itself, and its two main occupants. It had a stunning view of the downtown skyline of Delta City. Even with the early summer sunshine coming through the office windows, the room still managed to feel dark and gloomy. Mr. Midnight sat solemnly at his desk, with his chief bodyguard Kaizen standing at his side. The three men currently sitting in front of Mr. Midnight's desk surely paid no attention to the view before them; they were far too concerned as to what would happen to them during this meeting. The three men were the top captains and leaders of Mr. Midnight's organization; therefore they were responsible for its successes and also its failures. The day's shipment coming in at the dock had gone badly, to say the least. They all knew they would have to take the blame for it and suffer the consequences. It's what those consequences might be that was the most frightening.

The three men sat nervously awaiting their fate. Mr. Midnight sat still looking down at that day's newspaper folded out on his desk in front of him, the sun reflecting brightly off his golden mask. The paper told the whole story of the police involvement as well as the masked man that showed up and only made matters worse, if that were possible. As Mr. Midnight was looking down at the paper, Kaizen simply stood rigidly at his side, the sun reflecting off her face plate making it as golden as Mr. Midnight's. She was glaring at all three men at once, as though she were letting them know that if it were up to her they would all be in for something quite unpleasant. Rumors had already gone around on how hard Kaizen was on the last guy to let down Mr. Midnight. Her reputation preceded her.

"Well gentlemen," Mr. Midnight began at last, "an entire shipment of goods is arriving at our docks and who is there waiting for that ship?" Mr. Midnight paused and looked around as though daring one of them to speak. He then continued. "The police! Now I want no excuses. I only want you to find out why, and fix the problem so that it never happens again. Some of those items were very necessary for the completion of my motion inhibitor. We have policemen on our payroll so that things like this can't happen."

"Boss, we're trying to find out how the shipment got leaked to the cops. And when we find the person responsible, he is gonna pay. Until then all we can do is damage control," said Phil, an older slender man sitting at the far right.

"Well forgive me if my confidence in your ability to control this is not overwhelming," Mr. Midnight replied.

Phil went quiet instantly and said no more. Mr. Midnight then stood and began to pace in front of the big office window, as the three men continued to sit nervously, fidgeting slightly, wanting this meeting to be over. Finally Mr. Midnight turned and headed toward the office double doors. He pushed them open and continued to walk toward the elevator. The three men sat in stunned silence. As soon as Mr. Midnight began speaking again they all clamored to get through the door and follow with Kaizen closely behind as fast as they could.

"What I do want to know from you three is, who is this masked man who came and ruined everything?" Mr. Midnight continued entering the elevator as the doors slid open. "Because of him, none of our cargo is salvageable. Not to mention that the ship is completely destroyed and the number of men we now have in jail instead of on the street earning money. This is the second time that I have heard of him. This is the second time that he has interfered with my business. First Globotek, now this. Why is he showing up and why do I know nothing about him?"

The three of them looked around at one another, none of them wanting to be the one to speak up. Finally the fat balding man named Tony standing in the middle spoke up. "Well boss, the truth is we have no idea who this guy is, where he came from, or how he's able to do those things that he does. But believe me, boss, we're working on it."

"Is that supposed to make me feel better?" Mr. Midnight asked indignantly. The elevator dinged ominously as the floors counted downward.

"Boss, all we know for sure right now is that this is definitely the same guy who botched the Globotek heist," said Alexander, a thick, broad-shouldered man standing in the far left corner.

"Is this supposed to be comforting somehow? This is nothing I don't know already," hissed Mr. Midnight, coldly facing the elevator panel.

"Um, no sir. I was just saying that we're gettin' some leads on this guy," said Alexander, lying. "At least we're trying to get some leads," he added after feeling the weight of Kaizen's glare fall across his broad shoulders.

"Boss, if I may?" said Phil, and after a nod from Mr. Midnight he continued. "With the power of this guy, and the incredible abilities he possesses, maybe the best move isn't getting rid of him. Maybe we extend him a hand and make him an ally. Seeing as perhaps it would be far more valuable to have him working for us rather than try and fight him or stop him."

Mr. Midnight flew through the elevator door as they slid open. Phil, Alexander, and Tony attempted to keep pace with Kaizen again at their heels. The faced a long dark hallway with closed doors every ten feet or so. A handful of small domed lights buzzed and barely lit the passageway. Mr. Midnight walked in silence until he came to one of the closed doors then turned and faced them all. Screams of pain and agony could be clearly heard coming from the other side. Mr. Midnight was breathing hard now through his mask, showing the signs of mounting frustration.

"Extend my hand to him shall I? Out of the question! I am a man who prefers to understand everything around him. I like to know everything about any given situation my organization must enter. This is how I was able to create a certain business monopoly in this city. This man I do not understand. The way I have always seen it, if there is something in your way you can't understand, simply remove it with whatever means necessary. And in this you have all failed. Twice this man has foiled us. There will not be a third," he said flatly.

Mr. Midnight turned toward the wall beside the door and kaizen wrapped her fist on the door as though on cue. Instantly the upper part of the wall came down exposing a window with a full view into the room.

The room was bright white and had trays and tables all about much like a hospital surgery room. Two men in surgical masks and gowns scurried about the room. In the middle was a table with a man strapped to it. As the wall lowered one of the men hit a pedal with his foot and the table holding the man began to rise to meet Mr. Midnight's gaze. Once the man was in view all three men beside Mr. Midnight recognized the face looking back at them from events of the previous couple days. There was an intercom by the door and Kaizen pushed and held the talk button.

"Please! Please make it stop!" the man screamed as he saw Mr. Midnight before him. His face and body were covered in bruises and cuts, and he was drenched with sweat days old. "Please! I'm so sorry. I won't disappoint you again."

"That is the first correct thing I have heard you say in two whole days," said Mr. Midnight coldly into the intercom. He then nodded and the two men in masks closed in around the man and the table began to lower again. As the wall began to go back up blocking the view from the hallway the screams intensified much worse than they had before. After seeing all this, all three men hung their heads in shame and began to tremble noticeably as they awaited their punishment.

Mr. Midnight simply stood facing the wall with his back to them. He did it as though he was thinking up some suitable punishment for them all. Then at last he turned to speak to them and to their surprise it was not punishment that he doled out.

"We are on the brink of a new criminal age in Delta City. The motion inhibitors we are developing will fully bring us there. Do you gentlemen know exactly what the motion inhibitors will be able to do for us in this city?" Mr. Midnight said, sounding even more tired and frustrated. "Just to refresh all your memories, they will let us freeze anyone who gets in our way for up to ninety minutes." All three nodded in sync. "Do you all know what that means, what that is?" Mr. Midnight paused and scanned all three men before continuing. "That is absolute control, gentlemen. That's ninety minutes of pure uninterrupted mayhem. Ninety minutes before the person shot with one will be able to do anything to even try to stop us. Why kill people when you can completely control them with fear. And those ninety minutes are just the beginning. It starts with the city, then the country, after that the entire world market is ours.

"We will have the mass inhibitor finally ready for phase one in a few days time. This will allow us to freeze the entire city, making all of Delta City our playground, and with no one able to stop us. Except now this masked man has entered our playing field. He is a variable I do not like. He simply must be removed. And you all are proving to be completely incompetent, and your incompetency is threatening all our plans. There must be no more hero running around in any little costume interfering. Do you all understand?"

No one spoke up. They stood with their heads down. Mr. Midnight swept his gaze at all three men, daring them to look up and challenge him. Kaizen continued to stare them down unflinchingly in her statuesque pose as well. The light of her implanted eye gave her face an eerie glow.

"This city will remain mine," continued Mr. Midnight, no longer sounding frustrated but relishing every word. "So, I now have to bring in outside help to deal with this little masked avenger problem. I see now it's time to turn up the heat. Now go out and... BRING ME INFERNO!"

Chapter 12: Reality Check

"So now, Mr. Novak, tell me, what exactly are your plans?" asked Mrs. Samuels, the short rotund woman from the East Side High councilor's office.

"Um, I want to enroll for my classes in the fall semester," answered Michael, who thought that should have been painfully obvious already.

"Yes, well I did assume that. You do know that you have left things rather late, Mr. Novak, don't you? Most students began their booking classes some time ago." She continued to stare over her thick glasses at Michael's transcripts.

"I'm sorry, I realize that, and I'm sorry. I'm willing to take whatever classes you still have available," said Michael.

"Whatever alright, I'd say," snorted Mrs. Samuels, pushing her glasses back up the bridge of her nose with one pudgy finger.

The little office Michael was in was very small and cramped with a great number of stacked books on the floor next to the desk and filing cabinet behind Mrs. Samuels. Jutting out of many of the books were loose pieces of paper which only seemed to add to the clutter. Mrs. Samuels' desk was littered with papers and bits of trash making it look like a trailer park after a tornado. Michael seriously wondered when this woman would do away with all this paper and go green and join the rest of the twenty-first century and upload these files to the archaic computer that occupied the corner of her desk. He thought of Carly and how she would be appalled by the waste of paper. The office walls must have been built around the desk, as it seemed far too big for such a tiny office.

Michael had decided the day before to take Carly's advice and stop wasting time. He had found himself with a rare day off and decided to use it to stop stalling and get his fall class schedule organized. He didn't have much of a plan. He figured he would just show up, with his transcript in hand and an eager attitude. He had waited over an hour before he was even able to sit down with Mrs. Samuels. He had found the school to be very cold and hollow. It wasn't the warm and inviting place of higher learning he had imagined.

"I do remember your brother, Vince. He started his high school career in a similar fashion, and that did not end well," Mrs. Samuels said, referring to Vince dropping out in the middle of his senior year last year.

"That's my brother. I'm nothing like him."

"I certainly hope that to be the case."

They sat a moment in awkward silence and Mrs. Samuels seemed to be appraising Michael over her thick glasses. Michael did not know what else he could say that would further separate him from his brother. That was just another negative about being the little brother of Vincent Novak. Vince always managed to leave quite the trail of destruction wherever he went that Michael inevitably had to follow.

"Now, you really never answered my original question. What are your goals? What do you want to do after you get a diploma from our school? In short, Mr. Novak, what do you wish to become?" pressed Mrs. Samuels.

"Well I never really thought about it all that much," replied Michael in a meek tone.

"How could you never have thought about matters of such importance?" she said. She began to shuffle some papers about on her desk at a rapid pace before continuing. "I suppose we can start you off with the basics: Math, English, the sciences. You can make your choices from there, limited as they may become. Now, what courses are you most comfortable with?"

"Well, I suppose I was al…" Michael began before Mrs. Samuels cut him off.

"Oh well, it really doesn't matter I suppose. It's not like you'll have much to choose from anyhow," she said indignantly. "These are the four I can fit you into this September: Math, Physics, Biology, and Social Studies."

Mrs. Samuels placed the sheet with the tentative timetable down in front of Michael. He snapped from his reverie and began to go over the list.

"Um, do I really have to take two science classes in one semester?" Michael asked.

"Considering the lateness of your admission I do not think that you are in any position to ask for flexibility. If you wanted options you would have started this process much earlier. I have filled all the freshmen classes with any open seats," declared Mrs. Samuels. She dropped her pudgy index finger on the sheet and began to drag it back toward herself. "Of course I could take you out of some of these. You would get fewer credits and then have to make them up over the next two and half years, including summers of course."

"No, no! I'm sure this will be fine." Michael snatched the sheet from beneath Mrs. Samuels's finger.

"I do think that would be best, Mr. Novak," she said, clearly out of patience. As he scurried out the door, Michael felt sorry for the next student to go into that little office.

As Michael walked down the hall he noticed a poster on the wall calling for football try outs that would be starting three weeks before classes went in. Michael read over it carefully and cringed when he saw that the practices would interfere with some of his shifts at the store. He knew it would take some convincing to get Mr. Caruthers to accommodate it, but he knew he had to try.

Feeling overwhelmed with his first high school experience, Michael ran down the front steps, hit the sidewalk and never looked back. As he walked he began to wonder whether all of the faculty would end up having the same demeanor as Mrs. Samuels.

Suddenly Michael felt his cell vibrate in his jeans pocket.

"Hello," Michael answered.

"Mike, it's Dave. I just wanted to remind you that our basketball game is at two. You gonna make it?"

"I'll be there. Don't worry. I'm almost back in the neighborhood now. I just need to stop at work quick and then I'll be there," said Michael.

"Back? Where were you?" asked Dave.

"I'll tell you and Perminder both all about it when I get to the tournament."

Ten minutes later Michael walked into Caruthers Grocery with butterflies in his stomach for the first time since his grandpa had sent him down to have an interview with Mr. Caruthers. He had never really denied Michael anything before, but then again Michael had never asked for anything like this. He glanced in through the front window and saw that the store was currently empty. There was just the old shopkeeper himself perched on his stool behind the till reading the paper. He braced himself for the possible confrontation and marched into the store.

"Michael, what are you doing here today? You have the day off," asked Mr. Caruthers.

"I just got back from the school, and they gave me my class schedule."

"Oh, that's nice. It doesn't interfere with your shifts here too much I hope. Especially on Thursdays, that's the delivery truck day as you well know," stated Mr. Caruthers, seated on a stool behind the front counter. Michael began to feel as though the old man could tell what was coming.

"Actually, Mr. Caruthers, school's fine, but football does affect Thursdays." He explained the practice schedule to Mr. Caruthers. Michael then took a deep breath and launched into the speech he had mentally prepared on the walk over. "Mr. Caruthers, this is very important to me. I have a good chance of making this team. If I don't play freshman year than I will probably have to give up on it altogether. Please, there must be a way we can work around my Thursday shift here."

"Now, Michael you know full well that the delivery truck comes in Thursday mornings." He paused momentarily, and in that moment Michael thought he sensed a slight weakening. "So, what time does this practice end?" asked Mr. Caruthers.

"At five o'clock," replied Michael.

"I'm sorry, Michael. One of the reasons you first got work here was so you could help me with the Thursday delivery truck. You know perfectly well that the truck gets here at three thirty. I need you here from then until at least six as it is."

"Please, Mr. Caruthers. There has to be something you can do," said Michael, surprising even himself with this show of conviction.

Mr. Caruthers let out a deep sigh and began to stroke his chin in concentration. Michael knew that usually when his boss set his mind to something, such as Michael working on Thursdays, that that was usually it. He also knew that when he was about to come out with some great new proclamation that it all started by Mr. Caruthers stroking his chin and staring up into the ceiling.

"Well, I suppose that I could talk to old Tom and see if he could come by earlier. If I know Tom's route like I think I do, then he might be able to get here for his first stop without causing himself much of a headache. That means that you would have to be here for five thirty in the morning to unload the truck. Then I'm sure you could get to your classes on time and not have to come back in the afternoon."

Michael's jaw dropped open and his eyes went wide. He knew that even with that time he could just make it to school. Plus, he had no idea how he could balance his role as Titan into that day as well. He also knew however that he would be hard pressed to get a better deal at that moment from Mr. Caruthers.

"Okay, Mr. Caruthers. That sounds great," Michael said, sounding less than enthused. Michael left the store and began to walk to the basketball court. He was starting to feel that most facets of his life since finding the ring were quickly spinning out of control, and growing much more complicated. At least with the ring he knew what was going on, even if he had a hard time believing it. Right then he didn't know whether to feel happy or upset. Confused seemed to be the only way to sum the whole day up so far. Michael looked down at his watch, saw the time and began to sprint to the court. He thought briefly about pulling out the ring and making one jump to the tournament, and then quickly thought better of it. The temptation to use the ring for such small personal gain was becoming quite tempting, but still he resisted.

As Michael arrived at the basketball court, already drenched with sweat and badly out of breath, he saw Carly waiting with his shorts and tank top. She was with Monica. Perminder and Dave were warming up on the court.

"We thought we were gonna have to forfeit," said Dave, walking towards the stands as he saw Michael approach.

"No...worries...I'm here," said Michael, through gasping breaths.

"Hurry and change, then we can start," said Dave in cool tone, as he turned to rejoin Perminder on the court.

"They gave the boys two minutes to produce a player or they were gonna have to forfeit the game," said Monica.

"So he wasn't just kidding around," said Michael, as he took the clothes from Carly. Both the girls gave him sympathetic looks. It made him wonder just what Dave was saying about him before he had arrived.

Michael ran to the washroom and changed as fast as he could. He wasn't sure how the time had gotten away from him so quickly, and he wasn't sure if he was really up to playing after that run from Caruthers Grocery. He also knew he couldn't let down his friends. He only hoped he had enough energy left to play well.

"Players ready!" the referee signaled, and then threw the ball straight up into the air.

Perminder, being the tallest, stood as center. He easily managed to get to the ball first and tipped it back to Michael. Dribbling, Michael took two steps back to survey his opponents. He moved forward wearily. He looked quickly to his left and saw Dave ready to take a pass. Michael threw the ball toward Dave just as one of the opposing players ran up and intercepted it. Just past half court the other player was easily able to go in for the lay up.

"Mike, come on man, you gotta get with it here," said Dave, as he came to take the ball.

"It's okay, Mike, we can get it back," said Perminder, sounding a little more optimistic.

Up until that moment, basketball had been one of Michael's least concerns. He had a city that hated and feared him as Titan. There was his brother, who might just be robbing banks. Then there was high school to prepare for, and a boss who was a little less than understanding. Yet he knew that this tournament was important to both his friends. They had been preparing for it for weeks. Michael had put the whole thing to the back of his mind, but now the tournament was here, and he couldn't let his friends down.

Michael did his best to focus on the game at hand. The only bit of outside world that Michael let in was Carly who cheered loudly in the bleachers. He pushed aside exhaustion and tried to focus on assists, setting up either Dave or Perminder. With each successful pass he made he felt it pushed the memory of his first intercepted pass farther from everyone's mind. With Perminder's height they were able to have full advantage of the rebound front as well. The tallest person on the other team was only Michael's height, leaving Perminder a full head taller than anyone else on the court. Michael also saw that practicing had paid off for Dave as his shooting had never been better. Michael was starting to even think that they could win the whole tournament.

Finally the last whistle blew and it left Michael, Dave, and Perminder winners by ten points. Michael high-fived his teammates and they all gave their opponents the consoling handshake. Carly and Monica were standing by the edge of the court waiting to greet the three boys. Michael immediately went toward Carly. He was exhausted. He had no idea how he would be able to go through with another game. Then he saw Vince, in shorts and tank top, heading toward the court.

"Hey, little brother," said Vince, as he approached. Whenever he spoke to Michael Vince always managed to sound condescending.

"Vince you're playing in this tournament too?" asked Michael, unaware that Vince had any interest in sports. Michael thought that the only sport Vince enjoyed was pestering and antagonizing anyone smaller than himself.

"You bet I am, and right after we beat this team looks like we play you kids in the semi final," said Vince, as an evil grin crept over his face.

"I'm surprised you got anyone to have you on a team at all," said Carly from over Michael's shoulder.

"Well, that's them warming up now," said Vince, pointing toward the back half of the court.

Michael turned and saw two huge gorilla like guys shooting the ball. One of them was at least as tall as Perminder, but had a good fifty extra pounds of muscle on him. The other was just shorter than Michael, but was one of the biggest guys Michael had ever seen. He was very stocky. Without so much as another word, Vince walked over and joined his team on the court.

"We have to play them?" asked Perminder, after taking a big gulp of water from a bottle he grabbed from his bag.

"Well, it's been nice knowing you guys," Monica piped in as she watched Vince's team lumber around the court. All three boys turned and stared at her unbelievingly, but Monica seemed not to notice.

The five of them sat and watched as Vince's team creamed their competition. The other team was literally half their size. The biggest hulk on Vince's team was Jamal Thurston. Michael had heard plenty of rumors about the guy and none of them any good. He was the kind of guy the police just ran away from. The other was Tyler Jennings. Tyler made Jamal seem like an altar boy. Michael had heard Tyler had been sent to juvenile detention for aggravated assault. Michael and the guys had known them only vaguely as neighborhood bullies. If there was a fire in the neighborhood you could be sure that Tyler and Jamal were probably close by holding matches. The other side had superior players, but Vince's team was able to bully and push them all over the court with ease. Many fouls went unnoticed as Vince and his teammates strategically placed themselves out of sight from the referee so he was unable to make any calls. Seeing Vince's dirty plays was nothing surprising for Michael. In fact he would expect nothing less.

When the game ended and Vince's team named the winners, the other team just seemed happy to have the experience over with. Michael watched as all three players walked away bruised and battered. He looked over just in time to see Vince wave at him mockingly and mouth the words, "you're next."

"Well I guess it's our turn," said Dave as he stood and made his way to the court.

"Anybody have any plans? I say we just play dead and wait for it to all be over," said Perminder. He followed Dave to the court. Both looked to Michael like a couple of condemned men on their way to the electric chair.

"I'll be right there guys," Michael said.

"Okay, but no skipping out. We know where you live," said Perminder half jokingly, as Michael smiled and walked towards the public washrooms.

Michael dragged his weary body over to the water fountain next to the washrooms and began to gulp water. Then he stumbled into the men's washroom. Michael was relieved that it was empty. He made his way to the sink and began to splash water over his face and the back of his neck. He had been hoping to confront Vince ever since the attempted bank robbery. Vince and his thug friends on a basketball court were another matter. Looking at his haggard face in the mirror, Michael was struck by a great idea.

Michael bent down and pulled the top of his sock down. The ring tumbled out onto the cement floor. Earlier he had taken the ring out of his jeans pocket and slipped it into his sock. He hadn't felt comfortable leaving it anywhere else. He knew he needed to have it on his person at all times for safekeeping, and there were few options in his basketball gear.

Holding the ring in his hand and looking into its blue center, all Michael could think about was the energy boost he got after he let the power drain away from him. He knew right at that moment if he could have that same feeling he would be able to have the strength to face his brother on the court. Michael walked over and turned the lock at the washroom door to secure privacy. He had no idea what Azure would have to say to him about it, but he was willing to risk it. Michael knew that Vince would not let up one bit on Michael and his friends. After seeing the way they trounced the previous team, he was taking no chances.

"Exaudio Fortis," Michael said with trepidation. This was the first time he had used the ring for personal gain and he couldn't help but feel guilty. It was also the first time he had transformed indoors. The flash and noise were deafening. Michael stood still a moment and waited to see if anybody noticed, but no one did.

Titan, is there an emergency I am unaware of?

Azure's voice startled him slightly. He tried to think of something to say, but nothing came to mind. He had yet to be reprimanded by Azure, and had little desire to start now.

"Sorry, Azure. False alarm," he said, feeling the incredible power quickly course through his whole body. "Extermino Fortis," he added before Azure could go on.

Once again he stood in the middle of the washroom floor as plain old Michael Novak. He knew somehow that Azure would know what Michael was doing with the ring and he would have to explain himself. None of it mattered now however. Michael felt completely refreshed and energized. As he unlocked the door and reentered the afternoon sunshine he started to think about what Azure had told him about being chosen and the special qualities he seemed to possess. Could there not be any little perks, since the ring was set to demand so much from him? He knew deep down that there was no legitimate excuse for using the ring for his own personal advantage. He knew he would find out the price of using the ring's energy soon enough.

"What was going on in there?" asked Perminder as Michael came out on to the basketball court.

"What are you talking about?" replied Michael.

"All the light I saw from the washroom you were in," said Perminder.

"Uh…oh that," said Michael, struggling to think of an excuse. "A light bulb blew while I was in there. Man, freaked me out too."

"Okay guys forget that," Dave said, as the referee was coming to center court behind him. "Let's get it together. We can beat these guys."

Michael looked over at Vince and his two teammates as they lumbered around center court. He liked Dave's optimism, but was unable to share in it. As Michael looked over at Perminder he saw that Perminder didn't seem to share in it either.

"Oh, I'm sure there will be a beating all right," said Perminder under his breath, as he took his place at center.

"Hey, little brother. I hope you and your boys are ready for this," Vince said to Michael as he stood in front of him.

Michael only glared at his older brother, as Vince smiled his wolfish smile. As Michael stared over at the size difference of Vince's teammates he felt his knees buckle despite the energy burst the ring had given him. The referee blew his whistle and tossed the ball straight up at center court. Jamal, the hulking center, charged at the ball and Perminder, taking him down like a bowling pin. Jamal casually walked down with the ball and dunked it with ferocious authority, then turned back with a broad, gloating smile.

Michael, Dave, and Perminder all looked around at each other in disbelief. All three were confused as they waited for a foul call, yet the ref simply stood at the end of the court with ball in hand waiting for one of the boys to take it. Suddenly Michael found himself wishing he could just play the whole game as Titan. It appeared, Michael thought, to be the only way that they were going to get anything resembling closely to fair game.

Dave took the ball and passed it in to Michael who stood dribbling while he surveyed the layout and positioning of the court. Perminder and Dave were covered almost instantly making any pass next to impossible without an interception. Michael took several steps toward the basket when Vince came out of nowhere to guard him. With his stance wide and arms outstretched he stopped Michael in his tracks.

"Don't double dribble now. Come on lil' bro who ya gonna pass to huh?" Vince taunted. He would randomly and wildly swoop his arm in and try and take the ball from Michael.

Finally Perminder broke free and Michael was able to make a quick pass to him. With a pass to Dave for an easy layup, the game was tied at two. Michael grinned and pumped his fist in the air. He quickly looked over at Vince, who was gritting his teeth. Michael was not about to let the power of the ring go to waste. As Vince went to pass the ball in bound to Tyler, Michael ran in, and made the steal and charged right in for the layup. Vince was quick to jump out in front, and Michael was able to quickly pivot to the left and still make the easy jumper. Michael wasn't watching to make sure his shot made it; he was looking over for a reaction from Vince. Vince's look of outrage was enough to make Michael smile.

"Whoa, buddy, were did those moves come from?" asked Dave, as he moved up court to join Michael.

"I don't know, man. I just thought we should try and play a little aggressively ourselves," said Michael, as he back-pedaled down the court trying to maintain some defense.

Michael was able to make another steal on Jamal, but was blocked on his way back down the court and his pass to Perminder was intercepted by Tyler. It did nothing to slow Michael down however. He was in constant motion all over the court, making it hard for anyone to properly defend him. Perminder and Dave both seemed impressed, and encouraged to improve their own level of play as well. Michael's energetic and high-powered play seemed to keep his team in contention, at least for the start of the game.

The game stayed close for the first quarter. Then Vince and his team started to play rough and began to run the lead up by ten points to start the second half. There was plenty of bumping and flying elbows to keep

Michael and his friends on edge. It was also enough to bring the tempo of the game back to where Vince's team seemed a little more comfortable. All the rough play was going unnoticed by the ref who seemed to want to have no part of Vince and his teammates. All three members of Michael's team were nursing bumps and bruises all over their bodies by half time.

"Okay, guys, what's the plan going to be here? Are we gonna go and give it our all here? 'Cause I don't plan on just turnin' tail and runnin'. I don't know about either of you two," asked Dave in his most diplomatic manner. The three of them sat huddled over at the side court for the intermission.

"I'm with you, Dave. I couldn't give Vince the satisfaction," said Michael, as he rubbed his ribs where Vince had rammed him with his elbow just before halftime.

The rough play had definitely taken its toll. Michael was finding himself getting tired again and his body now aching. Michael was getting used to dodging criminals and did not like having to take this punishment from his bully of an older brother or his friends. Yet he knew he couldn't leave his best friends to deal with it.

"Guys, I think if we just keep away from them and stick to shots from outside the line we can take these guys," said Perminder, as he brushed at a fresh scrape on his knee. He chugged water and tried to regain his breath, he seemed to have found renewed confidence. "Come on, let's do it, and just don't get anywhere near these psychos."

As the referee blew his whistle all six players took their positions at center court. As the ref launched the ball into the air, Perminder jumped up and away from Jamal just giving himself enough to lay his fingers on the ball and tip it to Michael. Michael ran down the court with Vince trailing him, but he was up with his shot away before Vince could reach him. The shot arced and came down right through the basket for three points.

Michael, Dave, and Perminder kept up their perimeter onslaught for much of the third quarter. Their mutual fear of a continued beating seemed to rejuvenate all three as they moved more quickly than they had the whole first half. Vince's team was left frustrated, and always just out of reach of the other players. They started missing passes and trying to take the same long shots as Michael and the others, but they clearly lacked the skill. Many of those shots missed badly. By the start of the fourth quarter the game was tied again, at forty eight.

"Okay, guys, just one more quarter. We can so do this," Dave yelled to Michael and Perminder.

Dave took the ball from side court and passed it far up through the middle court and over to Perminder who was easily able to out maneuver Jamal and Tyler for the easy layup and go ahead two points. It was then that Michael noticed how sluggish Jamal, Tyler and Vince had become. By trying to run around them Michael and his friends had managed to wear the three of them down.

As the quarter wore on the game stayed close. Vince and his teammates might have been fatigued but they still had plenty of fight left in them. On several occasions, Perminder and Dave both found themselves getting too close to Vince's team, and once Perminder got clotheslined hard, which the ref claimed not to have seen. Also, Dave was blatantly tripped by Tyler while running up court. The result was Dave doing a face plant and coming up with a bloody chin. Finally, the game came down to its last minute of play with Vince's team up by two points with a score of sixty to sixty-two.

Michael was now starting to feel sluggish and worn down himself. All the energy he had gained from the ring was gone. His body ached and he wasn't sure if he could do one more minute against Vince. Just as Michael had thought, Vince did not let up on him one bit. Frequently Michael wanted to go against everything he represented as Titan and just turn and deck on Vince. He wanted to show him a few of the new moves he had learned while fighting real villains. He secretly wished he could just turn into Titan right there on the basketball court and teach all three of them a lesson.

Michael knew though that the way to hurt Vince right at this moment was to walk off this court the victor. As usual he would be the bigger brother in ways that Vince could never fathom. Michael was ready for this. With what he had already learned and experienced as Titan, he felt it had helped prepare him for a showdown with his older brother. He was trying to forget all about the last few days, the bank robbery, and just focus on all his years of torment at Vince's hands. Without a mask or powers he was determined to stand up to Vince and come out on top.

Michael took the inbound pass from Dave, and charged up the court dribbling the ball. Michael could hear Vince's heavy breathing bearing down on him as he made his way down the court. Just as Michael hit the three point line, he made a sharp left with a quick cross over dribble. He was then able to dodge Vince and pull up for a three point shot. The ball arched high into the air. Michael felt as though it was stuck as it hung in mid-air. Everything around him seemed to come to a complete standstill. Finally, it dropped through for three points with a deafening roar as the mesh grazed across the ball.

As everyone in the stands cheered, Michael looked over and saw Carly beaming at him. Monica hardly seemed aware that a game was going on at all as she was studying her fingernails. Michael also noticed to the far side of the bleachers a familiar figure in a fancy three piece suit clapping. He had no idea what would bring Dylan Thompson to an event like this, but he was glad to show up Vince in front of him.

"That's not going to be enough, li'l bro. Now you've forced my hand. I'm gonna have to jam that ball right down your throat," seethed Vince. He gave Michael a light shove as he went by to take the ball for the inbound pass.

"We'll see," replied Michael.

Vince briskly passed the ball inbound to Tyler. Tyler faced no opposition from Perminder or Dave as he moved up the court. Michael knew better. Tyler and Jamal could do all they wanted for all Michael cared. He knew they would pass to Vince, their best player, as the clock ticked down the last few seconds. Michael moved cross court in anticipation of intercepting Vince as he took Tyler's pass.

Michael stood straight with his arms across his chest; his mind's eye floated back to images of criminal's blows bouncing off him like flies. This would be it, Michael knew. He would finally put Vince in his place and teach him a lesson. Vince took two lumbering steps to the basket. As he saw Michael blocking his path, his eyes lit up like a tiger. It did not go as Michael had planned. The collision was like a freight train running into a moped. Michael was knocked completely head over heels. His head crashed hard against the concrete court. As his world was going up and over in a blur he was just able to make out Vince's final layup going in and his teams final celebration as the ref blew his whistle to signal the end of the game.

It had all come down to Vince against Michael, and he had lost. As he watched Vince and his team celebrate, his temperature rose. He was angry with Vince, but also at himself. He had acted childishly, he thought. He had wanted to confront Vince since the night of the bank robbery, and had not had the courage. So instead he had tried to confront him on the basketball court and had lost. He didn't know how he was going to be able to show his face around the house for the next few months. Vince was no doubt going to have an infinite amount of taunts ready to hurl at him. Still he had misused the ring and its power, and in the end wasted it. He had acted poorly, and knew it. Plus he had let down his friends.

"It's okay, buddy. You did the best you could. I mean, you didn't have a chance against him anyway. None of us did," Perminder said as he tried to help Michael to his feet.

Michael snapped his arm back with his lips pursed tightly and his eyes squinted. He saw the look of shock on Perminder's face and wished he could take it back, but being taken out by his brother like that stung. Michael dropped his head and stormed toward the bleachers before Dave could come over and join them.

"Michael, I'm sorry you lost, but you really shouldn't treat Perminder that way," Carly said, having witnessed the episode.

Michael glanced back over his shoulder as Perminder and Dave slowly dragged themselves over toward the bleachers. Both of them were limping and clearly in some pain. They had fought it out against Vince and his team just as much as he had. Of course Carly was right and he knew it.

"I know. I'm just so mad at myself," said Michael.

"Well tell them," Carly said, pointing behind him.

Michael turned to see Perminder and Dave both approach with complete looks of defeat on their faces.

"Sorry, guys. I'm sorry I let you both down," said Michael, head still hung so low he could almost hit his knees with his chin.

Neither Dave nor Perminder said a word. They simply stood and nodded their understanding.

"Geesh, guys. I'll never understand them," Monica said under her breath.

"Where'd Vince go?," Michael asked, finally bringing his head up to scan the crowd.

"You don't want to know," replied Carly.

Before Carly finished her sentence, Michael spotted Dylan. He saw him over by the parking lot, laughing heartily as he joked with Vince. Jamal and Tyler stood a few paces back; Tyler was holding the winners' trophy. Michael was stung again at how Dylan could be so friendly with Vince after watching Vince rip through him. Then, Dylan reached out and shook Vince's hand. Michael was stunned. Suddenly everything seemed to become clearer. Could Carly have been right all along? Was Dylan really up to no good? If it really was Vince at that bank, was he there working for Dylan? As Michael turned away, Dylan caught sight of him, Dave, and Perminder waved slightly and then headed to his fancy sports car. Suddenly Michael's body and mind had taken more of a beating than during anything he had faced as Titan. All Michael wanted to do at that moment was go home and sleep forever.

"Well does anyone want to go drown our sorrows down at the Burger Pit? 'Cause I'm starving," said Perminder as he gathered his bag and prepared to leave.

"Yeah, sounds good to me. You're all coming too right?" said Dave, as he looked back at the rest of the group.

"Sure," the three of them said in unison.

No one spoke during the walk to the Burger Pit. All three walked head down with gloomy looks. Michael and Carly walked hand in hand. Occasionally they would gaze at each other. Michael said nothing, but he could tell she understood what was going on in his head. Once they all arrived and ordered the atmosphere seemed to change. Moods began to lighten, and much of what Michael loved best about his friends began to emerge.

"Hey cheer up, Mike, it's not the end of the world, man," said Perminder as he stole a fry from Michael's basket.

Dave and Perminder had started joking around, but Michael found it very hard to let go of the memory of Vince bulldozing him. He was picking away uncharacteristically at his burger and fries in silence, idly listening to the conversations taking place around him.

"I know you're right. I just wish we hadn't lost to Vince," said Michael finally.

"Ah well, we kept it closer than any other team. That's something to be proud about," Dave piped in.

"You guys did great, and played a fair game. Vince's team can't say that," Carly said, trying to cheer them all up.

"Yeah, that ref was blind too," said Monica, surprising everyone by proving that she actually had been watching the game.

Monica blushed slightly as they all laughed. Being able to laugh at all felt good to Michael. So, he decided to stop feeling bad for himself for the rest of the day and enjoy it with what mattered most, his friends.

Chapter 13: Digging Deep

Vicki Earnhardt sat in her office staring at her blank computer screen, seemingly unable to write. Writing was something that had always come easily to her, judging by the countless accolades and awards that graced her office walls. She could always be counted on to be able to take the facts of a given situation, and write them so that anyone who read her article would come away with a clear, concise idea of the whole story.

Now the biggest story of any journalist's career had fallen on the city and she was currently sitting with a blank screen. This super powered vigilante that had just shown up, protecting the innocent and capturing the guilty. So far she had simple articles detailing some of the events, but the paper and the public were demanding more. She had yet to do an entire investigative article on him. For the past two days she had been chasing leads and interviews. She had even been there firsthand at the incident at the docks yesterday. Yet she was still completely blocked.

She had started the story the day before, by attempting to interview those who had witnessed the vigilante. The first person who seemed to have had any contact with him was Marjorie Banks. She was being mugged in an alley when the vigilante had shown up and intervened.

"It was the single scariest experience of my whole life," Marjorie had told Vicki.

"You mean because of this masked man? What was it, his powers, the fact his face was mostly hidden?" Vicki had asked.

"Oh no nothing like that. I mean it was scary right up until he showed up. Once he took down those creeps I knew that everything would be just fine. He was just magnificent, and strong and fast too," said Marjorie beaming.

Vicki had been scribbling furiously on her notepad as Marjorie recounted her experience. She went on to tell Vicki how she had just been trying to take a shortcut through an alley to get home. She had known it was stupid, but was late and in a hurry. That was when two creeps jumped her and were about to rob her, and god only knew what else. Then out of nowhere she had seen this flash of yellow. Marjorie had shut her eyes tightly as she spoke, as though she was trying her best to relive every moment. She told Vicki how the two would be thieves had tried to fight the masked man, but it was absolutely useless. The next thing she knew the two thieves were gone, just like that. Then she was left standing face to face with the man who had saved her.

"He was just amazing," Marjorie said, dreamy eyed.

"So, at no time did you feel threatened or in danger from him?" Vicki asked.

"From him? Are you kidding? He had just saved me. Plus he was real nice and kinda cute, even if he did look a little young. The last thing I felt was in danger."

Next Vicki went to the bank where a robbery had been foiled by this masked avenger. The bank no longer showed any signs of an attempted robbery. On the night of the attempted crime, Vicki had arrived at the scene shortly after the police. Since then all windows had been replaced, all garbage and debris had been taken away. It was back to business as usual. That is until Vicki made it into the bank manager's office.

"I don't know who did more damage to us, those thieves or that guy in the mask," the manager blared.

"Aren't you at least grateful that he was able to stop those men from robbing your bank? Doesn't that count for something?" Vicki asked.

"The police would've caught them I'm quite sure, even if this vigilante hadn't stuck his nose in," said the bank manager.

"But police didn't arrive on the scene until after the vigilante had left," retorted Vicki.

"Look, this is a fine place of business. We're hardly a blip on the radar. Mostly people know we're here but pay us no mind. Now we've had a super powered guy in a cape swoop in and stop a robbery. We're like a bloody tourist attraction now, and none of the gawkers are doing any banking in a place that was nearly robbed," hollered the manager as he pointed at the large windows where gawkers and picture takers were mingling.

The bank was on Grandview Avenue in midtown; which was a posh shopping district that was not used to this kind of scandal. A robbery in itself would be one thing; people forget those more quickly. Something like this tended to linger in peoples' minds.

"I wish that the police hadn't confiscated the surveillance video. Then I could show just what this guy was all about, what a menace he really is. I wouldn't even be surprised if this guy was in on it. Hey, we didn't even recoup all of our money that night. So you tell me who took it?"

"I wish I could, sir, I wish I could," Vicki replied before leaving.

Vicki spent the rest of the day checking out all the locations that the vigilante had reportedly been spotted. She tried to talk to anyone who might have witnessed him parading across rooftops or alleyways. She even asked average people in the streets what they thought about this so called super powered citizen taking the law into his own hands. The city seemed completely polarized. Some citizens she spoke to feared the vigilante and some supported him. At the time it appeared the beginnings of a great story.

"You sure you're not gonna use our real names or anything right?" asked the young police officer in front of her, his equally young partner nodding in agreement.

"Absolutely, you will both only be named as members of our city's police department. I assure you," Vicki told them.

She had had a hard enough time finding any officers willing to talk to her, on or off the record. She was ready to tell them whatever they wanted to hear. She had made contact with over a dozen officers throughout the city. She had managed to find eight who had been at the docks to witness the superhero, but only these two would talk to her with anonymity. She had met them at the end of their shift in a little diner downtown.

"Okay good. You have no idea how much trouble we would be in if our superiors found out we were talking to the media about this mess," replied the officer.

"So, what exactly do you want to know?" the other officer asked.

"First, you called this a mess. What do you mean by that?" asked Vicki.

"Oh, it's just that this guy has created quite a stir down at headquarters. The mayor's been driving the Chief nuts with trying to catch the guy," the officer replied.

"Are you getting anywhere with catching him?" asked Vicki, as she scribbled in her notebook.

"Well, at this time there are no serious leads," the officer replied, starting to flush a little.

There was an awkward pause as the officers looked down at their shoes silently while Vicki made notes. As her pen stopped she looked up to see them shifting nervously in the booth and trying hard to not look at her.

"Well, I would like to know if either of you has witnessed anything of this vigilante. My readers want to know what the Delta City police department's official stand is on this masked superpower going around town doing your jobs," Vicki said.

"Hey, this guy is not doing our jobs. He's breaking the law and we intend to catch him," the second officer snapped.

"Of course, I would expect as much," Vicki said. "So I take it then that the DCPD is against this vigilante and doing everything in its power to bring him to justice."

"Look, we get it. Crime levels are up in the city. People no longer feel as safe here. So this costumed guy shows up, he can do some amazing things, and he manages to stop a few bad guys. Some people begin to cheer for him, but these people need to understand that this is not the way to get things done. His 'acts of heroism' do not need to be rewarded or cheered for. He's being no better than the crooks he catches by breaking the law the way he is," the second officer said.

"Yet many are saying that things are getting done. Crimes are being stopped in progress, criminals are getting caught red handed," Vicki responded.

"Again, this guy is breaking the law. The DCPD will catch him. The last thing we need is more people to get the idea they can run around in costumes trying to be just like this guy," the first officer said.

The two young officers resumed their silence, staring down at the ground. Their intentions had been good. They had been asked to come out and talk about the incredible things they had seen, and what they thought about this masked man. Now they seemcd to be thinking that they might have gotten in over their heads by accepting this interview with Vicki Earnheart.

"Look, I think we have established that the department's stance on the vigilante is to apprehend him," Vicki said trying to change the tone. "Were either of you on hand to witness either the incident at Globotek, or the scene at the freight ship yesterday?"

"Yeah, I was at both," the first officer said.

"Would you care to tell me what you saw?" asked Vicki.

"Well, I didn't get to see a whole lot at Globotek. By the time we got in there things were pretty much over. I do remember being down on the street, and looking up and seeing this streak of yellow and blue go flying across the street and crash through one of the upper floor windows. It was so fast; I can remember it so clearly, you know? It's kinda like my mind took a snapshot as he shot over the street. It was like a cannon ball was fired from across the rooftop.

"Next thing I know the shootout we were facing started to quiet down, and then it stopped all together. Then there were several bright flashes that came through the windows, a whole lotta commotion started going on in there. The Chief started mobilizing SWAT to go in. Then, the whole thing seemed to be over. I heard from some guys on SWAT that they had spotted a guy in a costume on the ground floor but they never came close to catching him. By the time I got to go in the building, the only thing I actually saw were these holes that went through the roof to the bottom floor. It was like a rocket had shot right through the inside of the building," explained the first officer.

"What about the incident at the docks? Were you both there to witness that?" asked Vicki.

"Yeah we were both there. And we saw the same thing that everybody else saw on TV," said the second officer.

"Of course, but what my readers need is to know what it was like for someone that was actually there. They need to feel what it was like being that close. Down on the ground, what was happening that maybe people didn't see?" asked Vicki.

"It's kinda hard to explain. It was almost like watching a movie," said the first officer.

"What was it like seeing something like that though? Watching him, getting that close of a look at those abilities? Do you both truly believe that this person has some kind of superpowers? Or do believe as some have suggested that he is from another world?" Vicki asked.

"All I know is what I saw. And I know what I saw was completely real, and it was like nothing I have ever seen," replied the second officer.

With her pile of notes, Vicki sat at her desk prepared to write. She still didn't have a clear direction on the story, but it could easily end up being the single greatest story of her career. She was starting to run ideas over some fresh note paper. She had been writing away furiously when her boss had dropped a bomb on her that she was currently blaming for her writer's block.

"Vicki could I speak to you a moment please?" her boss had said, leaning up against her office door frame.

"Sure, Charles, but make it quick. I'm trying to get this story in by deadline," Vicki replied.

"Well actually, your story is what I need to talk to you about," Charles said. Charles Wilson had peppery grey hair, and thick black framed glasses. He had started growing a little thicker around the midsection in the last ten years, when he had become the editor-in-chief of The Courier, and had left field reporting for good.

Vicki stopped leafing through her notes and stared at him wide eyed. Her reporter's instinct kicked in. You didn't need to be an ace reporter to know that something big and bad was coming.

"What about my story, Charles?" Vicki asked.

"Well I know, heck we all know around here, that you've been running around the city trying to cover this vigilante story," Charles said.

The articles Vicki had written already had been a hit. Ever since then, Charles had been clamoring for another, but this time one with some real substance. She had no idea what the problem could be.

"Well, isn't that my job, to cover big stories like this for your paper? Big stories that will sell papers for you like crazy," Vicki said, already sounding defensive.

"Yes Vicki, yes it is. But I've just had the mayor in my office giving me the third degree about what we print about this vigilante. He was furious that your first article on him questioned whether he was a criminal or not. The mayor does not want the public to even question such a thing. He wants this masked man labeled a criminal. He wants us to never publish anything that could be possibly indicate otherwise," Charles said, clearly tired and frustrated.

Vicki sat stunned into silence for a moment. She had never liked the mayor, and her articles reflected that, as they were especially hard on him. Yet she had never had her boss question her judgment before. Charles had always given her the benefit of the doubt.

"I can't believe this. We're sitting on the biggest news story this city has probably ever had, and you want me to play by the mayor's rules. Do you think that The Herald will play nice like this? Charles this story has the city divided. Just the fact that this vigilante can do the things he does is amazing. Let alone that he seems to do them for a city that wants him hunted down. We're a newspaper, Charles, members of the media. The mayor has no business and no power in this matter. We have the freedom of the press and free speech on our side," Vicki said.

"Look, we do not need city hall and the police department breathing down our necks making our jobs harder than they are. Crime is already running rampant through this city. We don't need to be cheerleading for any criminal out there. We cannot have it, no matter how well intentioned that criminal may seem, or we may hope him to be. From now on all stories regarding the vigilante will pass through me before they get printed. Just for your information, The Herald and Local News 4, are all feeling the same pressure from city hall. "

"Fine, but I thought you had more backbone than that. Maybe our next story should be about how the mayor now runs The Courier," Vicki replied with a sneer.

Charles flushed red with anger, his frustration finally boiling over. He turned sharply and charged across the floor. Staff who saw him coming quickly ran out of the way. Charles didn't even seem to notice as he forced a young staffer to tumble backwards dropping a big stack of papers that scattered everywhere.

"I want the vigilante story on my desk by the end of today. If it's not suitable for print I will edit it myself to make it suitable," Charles yelled back over his shoulder as he stormed through the doorway to the elevators.

That was over three hours before and Vicki still sat facing a blank computer screen. Most of the Courier staff had left for the day. She knew she would miss the deadline for the next day's edition, but she was also willing to bet that Charles would wait and run with her story when it was ready no matter what he had said earlier. Being the most decorated and acclaimed reporter on the payroll still counted for something. Her next move would be critical. She had never seen Charles so worked up before. Having him question her and being expected to give in to the demands of city hall, rattled Vicki into her first writer's block in years. She stood up for what she thought was right. City hall trying to dictate what the paper could print was wrong.

She closed her computer for the night. In the end, making Charles wait another day to print an actual story on the vigilante would help in making a silent protest against censorship. She needed to take her time in choosing the proper direction for her article. For now The Courier would just have to run brief blurbs on the events. The city would get her article soon enough.

Chapter 14: Inferno

"Novak wake up!" hollered Mr. Caruthers from across the store.

"Sorry, Mr. Caruthers. I was just getting this pricing and stocking done," Michael answered, a little defensively.

"Well, see to it that there's more stocking and less lollygagging being done. I'm paying you to work, not sit around," Mr. Caruthers snapped back.

Michael quickly busied himself back to pricing cans of corn and putting them on the shelf. He had been working very hard all morning trying to keep his mind occupied. Unfortunately, Mr. Caruthers had taken notice of him in the one moment when he had paused to take a quick daydreaming breather. It was as though any lack of activity in the store popped up on the old shopkeeper's radar. Michael was just thankful that the store was currently empty. He continued to work, dutifully keeping an eye on Mr. Caruthers. Once he headed into the back of the store, Michael leaned up against the wall, and began to rub the sides of his head.

His career as Titan had been less than stellar so far. As Titan he had managed to help destroy millions in public property in less than a week. He had the city's mayor starting a hate campaign against him, and he had managed to get Titan marked a wanted man by the police department. He had even tried using the ring's power to gain advantage in a simple basketball game against his own brother. He was starting to expect Azure to pop up any minute and tell him that the ring and all its power were being taken from him as he was now deemed unworthy.

His personal life was also coming apart at the seams. He had managed to get signed up for his high school class schedule and football tryouts, but that only seemed to cause more trouble. He had no idea how he was going to manage being at work so early in the morning. He had managed to avoid disappointing Carly's father, but how long could that last? Since the basketball game, he had seen or heard very little from Dave or Perminder. Dave hadn't called him since they had lost, and Perminder, who was rather sensitive, still seemed sore over Michael snapping at him after the game. The two times he had seen Perminder, he had barely said three words to Michael. Vince however hadn't seemed happier since he had steamrolled over Michael on his way to his team's victory. Vince had kept the trophy in plain view at home at all times just to rub it in. Vince seemed to be relishing being able to remind Michael who the bigger, badder, stronger brother was. Sadly, Michael still sported the bruises that proved Vince right.

Michael hated having to keep Titan a secret from his grandpa. It forced him to lie to him. So far the lies had been relatively small, but how long before they became much larger in scope? He had to lie about where he was going, what he was doing. He had no idea where it would end. He even found himself starting to avoid his grandpa so that he wouldn't be forced into a position where he had to lie to him. He hated that most of all; it made him feel like Vince. He was beginning to resent Azure and the ring.

Michael no longer knew which side of his life he felt more secure in. Whenever he thought of Titan all he could hear was police helicopters as they bore down on him. Then, whenever he managed to block out Titan and focus on his own life, he felt like he was trapped in Mrs. Samuels' cramped little office again. It was as though all the people in his life sat behind her desk passing judgment on him for all his failures. He knew he needed to regain control, but how?

The only time he actually felt good was the time he spent with Carly. During his time with her he still managed to feel like the superhero he was supposed to be. He never had to lie to her about anything. He never had to try and live up to some image he thought she held of him. Being the only person who knew about Titan, he could talk to her about his fears and worries. Her love and support made him feel invincible. Yet, it seemed at that moment like any time with her was very far away indeed.

All Michael wanted at that moment was to focus on his job and try to avoid Mr. Caruthers' wrath before he punched out for the day. Then he could slip out and meet Carly for dinner at his grandpa's. All that meant was four more hours of not breaking anything, mispricing anything, not spilling anything, or making any messes. A rare feat for Michael on any given day at the store, but he figured the extra attention he would have to pay would just make the day go by that much faster.

"Hi there, handsome," came Carly's voice floating up from behind him, startling him as he was pricing a flat of soda.

"Oh, hey there. I'm so glad to see you! This is turning into the longest day," said Michael, relieved to be able to see her face beaming at him.

"Don't worry. It's after noon; you'll be outta here before you know it. I think Perminder and Dave are dying for you to be done too. It's kinda sad watching the two of them try and figure out what to do without you," Carly replied.

"I'm not sure if either of them are too keen on me right at the moment. I've barely spoken to them since the basketball tournament," Michael said.

"Michael, as long as I've known all of you guys none of you have ever stayed mad at each other for long over anything, especially over some stupid basketball game. Besides I'm sure that they are well aware that the game was much harder on you after what happened with Vince. I'm sure they're over it by now," Carly replied.

"Yeah, I guess you're right. I'll have to track them down as soon as my shift is over." "Good. I hate seeing all three of you moping around the neighborhood. Sheesh, if guys would just learn to talk to each other," Carly said, as she rolled her eyes.

"What have you been up to?" asked Michael, suddenly desperate to change topics. He was also finding himself craving any news of the world outside the store.

"Not much. Just dropped in to say hi," she said. "Monica and I are just going downtown for a day of shopping and fun, and I wanted to see you before we went."

"Oh that's nice," Michael said. "Glad someone around here gets to have some fun." Michael regretted saying it as soon as it came out, wishing he could take back some of the sarcasm that had slipped in inadvertently.

"What?"

"Nothing, it just seems unfair," he now found himself unable to stop. "Even after I'm out there putting my butt on the line, I have to spend my entire day in here just to make a little money. I don't get any play time of my own. No time for myself." He couldn't stop himself now.

"Michael, what's the matter with you? Just listen to how selfish you sound right now. Do you think you're the only one hard done by? Do you think you're the only one who's made sacrifices?"

"That's not what I meant. But really, it'd be nice if I could just take some time and go off with my friends for a while," said Michael defensively, his cheerful mood suddenly gone.

"What, am I supposed to just sit at home and feel sorry for poor burdened little Michael?" Carly asked. She seemed to be straining to keep her voice at a low register.

"Carly, you know what I meant by..." Michael began, but there was no stopping her now. Michael had only seen her with that angry flare in her eye a few times before.

"Do you think this has been the easiest week for me? Do you have any idea what it's been like worrying about you? I can't even defend you when I hear the horrible things said about you on the news or in the paper, or when I hear people on the street make some nasty comment about Titan," said Carly in a whisper. They both kept peering over to make sure that Mr. Caruthers or a customer wouldn't hear them.

"Hey I'm just saying, it's nice you can go out and have fun, as you try to cope with my problems," said Michael sarcastically. He felt like he was only able to watch and listen to what came out of his own mouth next.

"I can't believe you, Michael Novak," said Carly, looking hurt and angry.

"Look . . ." Michael tried, before she cut him off again.

"Sorry, I gotta go now. I'm meeting Monica in a couple minutes. Why don't you call me when you decide to grow up." Before Michael could even try to apologize, Carly turned away.

"Oh Carly come on. Don't do this," Michael begged, as she reached the door. The overhead bell rang as she went through without slowing down.

"Novak. Back to work. I'm not paying you to fraternize," came Mr. Caruthers's voice from the back of the store.

Michael hung his head, and turned back to stocking shelves. The last thing he needed today was to get into a fight, and with Carly of all people. He had no idea why he had chosen to vent his problems and frustrations the way he had. He just wished he could explain his fears since discovering he was no longer like anyone else, nor would he ever be again.

Anywhere Michael went and whatever he did there would always be Titan separating him from all the other so called normal kids. Carly could still go out anywhere with friends without the worry of duty calling. All because he had been chosen to accept the call of Titan. He could never just take off with the guys at a whim and with no worries, because at anytime the city might need Titan. The thought of the carefree days being forever behind him did nothing to lighten Michael's mood.

Michael carried on working, yet he remained distracted, continuing to make small mistakes. Thankfully he was able to catch most of his mistakes before Mr. Caruthers noticed.

"No running, you kids! This is a place of business, not a playground," bellowed Mr. Caruthers, just as three third graders barreled into the store. The smile vanished from their faces as they went to the candy section. Michael smiled vaguely, remembering doing the same thing when he would come here at their age.

Most people didn't like Mr. Caruthers all that much. They just thought of him as nothing more than a grumpy, miserable old man, and they weren't all that far off. However, Mr. Caruthers had given Michael a job when no one else in the neighborhood would. It was the first time Michael had felt chosen for anything. Many neighborhood kids had already been turned down from work at the store; the old man had decided to hire Michael. That did not mean however that Michael was above his heavy scrutiny. Michael usually took it all in stride. Today however Michael just wanted to try to avoid him as much as possible and get through the day. He couldn't avoid him forever though as the store just wasn't big enough.

"Novak!" Mr. Caruthers beckoned from across the store. "That's enough daydreaming out of you. I'm paying you to work, not stare off into space." He waited for Michael to get closer before continuing. "Now here's a list of things for Mrs. Simpson. Round them up and go deliver them to her, and no dawdling. I'm not paying you to dawdle."

"Sure, no problem. I'll get right on it," Michael said.

He turned and started collecting the various items on the list. He hardly had to glance at the list, since he had been delivering Mrs. Simpson's groceries for the last couple years and the items on it rarely changed. He moved about as quickly as possible, looking forward to a reason to get out of the store. Michael set out into the fresh early summer air carrying the two bags of groceries, the fresh air rejuvenating him. He had every intention of making the walk to Mrs. Simpson's place last as long as he possibly could without drawing the wrath of Mr. Caruthers. Michael tried his best to block his fight with Carly from his mind. He could not believe that he had snapped at her the way he had, and he had no idea how he was going to make it up to her.

For the first time that day as he soaked up the summer sun, he felt as though he were finally able to think straight, and was determined to take the time to try and sort out his life's problems. As his grandpa always told him, there was no sense sitting and sulking when you could just take action. At last he came to the small square one story house that belonged to Mrs. Simpson.

"Why, Michael, my dear boy, hello there, and I see you've brought my groceries," exclaimed Mrs. Simpson as though he would be coming for any other reason. "Please come in and put them on the kitchen table. I'll get to them in a moment. I just want to see what happens to this maniac on the TV," she said as she turned and headed for the living room.

"What is it that's happening?" Michael asked, setting down the two bags of groceries and scooping up the money Mrs. Simpson had left for him. He was assuming that she'd tell him about some soap opera that she'd been watching. Michael had made many deliveries to Mrs. Simpson, and knew that she was widowed and alone. She always tipped if Michael stayed and chatted with her.

"Why haven't you seen?" she replied. "Some lunatic is wreaking havoc downtown, setting everything on fire."

Michael stepped into the living room and from there he could see the TV over Mrs. Simpson who was sitting in an old armchair that was about five feet from the set. Michael was shocked by what he saw. Right in the middle of downtown was a man clad head to toe in some kind of orange and red armored suit. His right arm extended into the barrel of a massive flamethrower. He had a large case on his back that Michael could only assume was for fuel. He wore a helmet with glass eye plates and breathing apparatus like a gas mask in the front with a slight tint to the eye glass that all made it rather difficult to make out the man's face. From behind the man, Michael saw several small fires had started; the police and fire department were trying their best to put them out, as well as remove any innocent bystanders. Unfortunately, they were not having much luck. Whenever any rescue worker would get near a bystander or a blaze, the madman would fire a long arc of flame in their direction.

Then Michael saw something that scared him more than anything else. Off to one side huddled into a front corner of a building was a trapped group of civilians and among them in the front of the crowd was Carly. She was in front, her arms tightly wrapped around Monica.

Michael's heart sank. As soon as he saw her, he could practically feel the ring pulsating in his back pocket, screaming for him to take hold of it and transform. Until now he had never imagined any of his loved ones in danger like this. Their lives were in the hands of some lunatic, with only Titan to save them.

Michael left without another word to Mrs. Simpson. In a flash, he was in the alley behind her house with the ring in his hand. His heart was racing and a nervous sweat broke out across his forehead. He paused only to make sure that no one was around to spot him. He slid the ring on and held out his fisted hand.

"Exaudio Fortis!" Michael exclaimed, as the lightning blast engulfed him. Before the smoke had cleared, Titan was running at full speed to the mouth of the alley.

Whoosh! A thick cloud of dust was kicked up as fences and garbage cans rattled in place. Titan's coiled legs had fired like pistons, launching him into the air towards downtown. His hands trembled slightly with nervousness. All he could see was the TV image of the arsonist in his mind's eye. Then he was gone, soaring through the sky.

As he made his approach to downtown, he frantically scanned the skyline, trying to spot Carly's location, under the marquee of the Park Avenue Cinema. The dense downtown skyline suddenly stood out. Panic set in as he found he could no longer place it. Trying to find one small building among hundreds of others suddenly seemed next to impossible.

Suddenly spotting long thin tentacles of black smoke reaching up to the sky, he turned his body, directing himself straight for the cinema.

"Azure, are you there?" Michael asked in flight. "Did you see that guy with the flamethrower downtown?"

Yes I am aware of it.

"Then you know that Carly's there too," Titan said, his voice thinning and wary with nervousness.

Yes I know. But you mustn't think only of her for now. It will cloud your judgment; many more will need your help also.

Titan knew that would be a lot easier said than done, but said nothing.

As he landed on a rooftop across the street from the cinema, the scenario appeared much worse than on TV. The arsonist was standing in the middle of the intersection randomly shooting out long blasts of flame from his arm cannon. Signs of havoc reigned all around him. Various storefronts had been blown in; glass and debris littered the sidewalks and streets. Jagged chunks of glass stood out like teeth from the window frames, long tongues of flame rolled around and leapt several feet into the air. Two cars parked on the street were now ablaze and charred. Fire trucks and police cars blocked off the access to the streets, hoping to contain the carnage.

Titan scanned through the fire, smoke and chaos, trying to find Carly. In a tight group directly under the cinema marquee, Titan saw a frightened group of people, including Carly and Monica. All exits were blocked as fires blazed around them. Only the arsonist stood between them and safety.

You are about to embark on your most difficult test to date, Titan. You would do well to take note now of your surroundings. Divert his attacks away from everyone. Then be ready, find his weakness and exploit it.

Anxious to get Carly and Monica to safety, Titan didn't have much time to take in Azure's words of wisdom as he landed in the middle of the street about twenty feet away from the arsonist. His flamethrower stopped abruptly as Titan landed. As he turned to face him Titan got his first look at his new adversary. The arsonist gave Titan an appraising look as he cocked his head back and forth. He did not appear the least bit intimidated by the arrival of Titan.

"Ah, and you must be our new masked avenger. I was wondering how long it was going to take you to arrive, and I gotta say you're much smaller than I thought you'd be," said the arsonist, his flamethrower halted. Close up, Titan could just make out his sadistic grin through the tinted face mask.

"Yeah, thanks. I get that a lot," Titan replied.

"Well allow me to introduce myself. I am Inferno, and Mr. Midnight has sent me to give you a little message."

"You're working for Mr. Midnight?" asked Titan.

"Yeah, right now I work for Mr. Midnight. I work for whoever is the highest bidder. And he paid a lot to have me come down here and pass on his message to you," said Inferno.

"Please, do tell. I'm dying with anticipation," snapped Titan.

"It's simple, one even you may pick up on. Stay out of his business! You see he wants you exterminated 'cause you've been messin' around in his affairs. No one messes with Mr. Midnight and lives to tell about it. Now having said that, unfortunately even though you've just arrived, I'm afraid you must go," grunted Inferno.

Titan remained still, completely stunned. Inferno had been waiting just for him, setting the bait strictly to lure him in. So many questions leapt into Titan's mind. Was Carly bait as well or was her being here strictly coincidence? He knew he had little time to think of those things now.

"As long as Mr. Midnight's business is crime and corruption, then it's my business too.

So I'm not going anywhere," said Titan.

"Oh we'll see. Of course the only problem for you is I never fail," said Inferno in a deadly whisper.

Inferno raised his right arm and shot out a large line of fire straight toward him. Titan leapt up and flipped sideways out of the way. The blast had sailed just past him and vaporized an empty bus stop. Shards of glass and debris flew everywhere. Titan had acted just in time, but still felt the intense heat that emanated from the blast.

Before Titan could even catch his breath, Inferno began launching a furious fireball attack at him. Titan could hear the whirring engine of Inferno's arm cannon as it assaulted him. Fireballs rained down all around him. They crashed like giant explosive pieces of hail that sprayed debris in a big cloud around their impact zone. As Titan did his best to dodge the fireballs, bits of brick and glass bounced off his arms, chest, and back. Many of the fireballs missed him and shattered parts of surrounding buildings.

As the barrage stopped Titan faced Inferno, he heard the screeching sound of grinding metal come from above. As he looked up, he noticed that one of Inferno's fireballs had struck the bracing of a big neon sign above a store front next to the cinema, and it was teetering dangerously. The sign was roughly five feet high and three feet across, and easily weighed a few hundred pounds. Titan could only imagine the damage that sign would do if it came down onto the street. As he looked down he saw that if it came the way it was leaning it would fall on to the sidewalk where Carly and the other bystanders were huddled. It clung to the brick wall by a lone bracket.

Titan you must make sure these bystanders remain safe from that falling object.

"Yeah, I got it!"

Just as Inferno let loose with a scorching blast of fire, Titan leapt into the air missing the blast as he attempted to intercept the falling sign. As fire licked at Titan the sign gave, but he was able to catch it and keep his footing just in front of the cinema marquee. It felt light as he held it over his head; just inches away from the frightened crowd. He wished he could look over and make sure that Carly was all right, but he didn't dare chance it.

"I knew you held a soft spot for these pathetic cowards," Inferno snarled as he approached.

Titan said nothing. With the lives of all these people at stake he knew he had to be focused to take on Inferno, and still keep everyone safe. He recognized the buzz and hum that was coming from the arm cannon and dropped the sign down like a shield just as another deadly blast of heat came at him and the crowd. The blast hit the sign head on and rocked Titan slightly back on his heels. As it eased, Titan peeked around and saw that everyone was safe. He spotted Carly and Monica tucked in the corner, practically out of sight.

"That's enough, Inferno!" Titan hollered, as he hurled the blackened sign towards Inferno.

Inferno leapt to safety as the sign crashed at his feet. He fired two fireballs at Titan as he leapt into the air. Staff in hand Titan batted them both aside like giant softballs. Inferno's attention was again solely on Titan so the crowd was relatively safe again.

"Sorry pal," Titan said perched on the roof of an abandoned car. He re-sheathed his staff. "I think it's time for you to cool down."

"Oh really, cool down will I?" Inferno seethed. "We'll see about that."

Inferno was disgusted that Titan could not be easily defeated. He fired again, and this time a giant fireball of radiant orange and red flew directly at Titan. He leapt backwards out of its path. He was just barely in the air when the fireball hit the car he had been on. The car exploded in a giant ball of molten metal and plastic as it shot into the air. The sheer force of the explosion sent Titan crashing back against the building behind him. The heat was so intense that Titan had to shield his face with his hands. The blast rattled the building, causing many of its windows to shatter and sending a sprinkling of glass to rain down over him.

Instinctively, once Titan had recovered from the blast, he looked across at Carly. He looked just in time to see her push an old bald man out of the way as a piece of flaming car tire came crashing down where they had been standing. As they lay crumpled on the ground, the old man gave Carly an appreciative smile. His glasses had been knocked off and he looked quite disheveled, yet he was grateful to her for saving him. Monica had rushed to Carly's side, quickly helping her up.

Curious onlookers and reporters who had been busily gawking and taking pictures to document the mayhem were forced to stop and head for cover when the car had exploded. Vicki Earnhardt had been among the many onlookers at the scene. It was only luck really that she was there at all. She had been having lunch with a friend down the street when Inferno had arrived and started to torch the city. She had been one of the first on the scene. The reporter in her had instinctively taken over.

From a little notebook that she always kept in her purse, she immediately began to take notes from a safe distance.

Luckily all of Inferno's attention was now focused upon Titan. He seemed to have completely forgotten about the innocent people he had trapped. His prey was now Titan and Titan alone. The police seemed to have noticed this, and were now using it to their advantage. Through the wreckage of the explosion, the police were able to finally reach Carly and the others. As two policemen moved stealthily towards the trapped group, Inferno never even looked their way. They managed to evacuate the group of civilians and take them beyond the police tape to safety. Titan felt a heavy weight lift from his heart as he saw Carly safe from Inferno's wrath, with Monica and the rest right behind her.

As Titan looked over at her, their eyes locked, and he saw fear for him etched on her face. He hated to see her so worried. He wished desperately that their last words together had not been in anger. He felt unable to look away from her until he knew that she was indeed out of harm's way. He was afraid of what Inferno might do if he saw him looking at Carly with such concern. So he tried his best to keep his glances at her short and abrupt. Then, at last, she was gone and out of sight, and to safety.

Chief Ross looked on hesitantly from the sidelines. He stood poised at the edge of the police tape that blocked off the scene. Cell phone in one hand megaphone in the other, he seemed to be simultaneously talking into both. The Chief was trying his best to direct everything that was going on outside the perimeter of the police tape. The Chief's first minutes on the scene were frantic. In a short time he managed to bring the situation under control, and was making his first attempt at taking down Inferno when Titan arrived. Ross had made his men stand down as he reassessed the situation after Titan had shown up. With the innocent civilians evacuated he seemed to think they would be able to hold back a couple more minutes before his men moved in on both of them.

Titan knew he had to act fast and put an end to Inferno. He could almost hear Azure telling him this as he thought it. Titan was trying to regroup when he saw that Inferno was getting ready to attack him again. Inferno stood slightly crouched. He used his non-cannon arm to steady and hold his cannon about fifteen feet from Titan. The mechanisms in the cannon were buzzing and whirring loudly with sparks shooting out through vents along its sides. There was no doubt for Titan; Inferno was coming in for the kill.

Titan pulled out his staff and used it to vault over Inferno just as a massive blast shot out at where Titan had been and collided into the side of a wall, blowing it to smithereens. Inferno let out a loud roar of frustration as brick, steel and big clouds of dust rained down all around him. Titan landed back in the middle of the street with his staff clutched tightly in his hands. Inferno shook off the dust and debris from the building, screamed in anger, and slowly turned to face him.

Azure's words began to ring in his ears. Azure had told him to find Inferno's weakness and exploit it. Pride definitely seemed to be one of those. Titan could see that the madder Inferno got, the more reckless he became. It seemed to Titan that Inferno was ready to blow in more ways than one. He knew he had to get in close and get his hands on Inferno to end this whole mess. So far, he couldn't seem to get close, at least not without getting flame broiled. Whatever else there was, Titan knew he needed to find it, and fast.

"I can see why Mr. Midnight wants you gone so badly. You are quite the nuisance," Inferno growled. "At first I was just going to destroy you quickly, you little maggot. But now I think I'll take my time and make you suffer."

"You know," said Titan rising slightly. "I sense a lot of hostility in you. I think you may need therapy."

"That's right you little twerp, keep yapping. It's only gonna make it all the more satisfying when I fry your face off. You see I always complete my mission. I never fail. So your days are numbered," bellowed Inferno.

Inferno dropped low and charged, launching a barrage of fireballs in a giant arc towards Titan. Titan flipped up, twisting and arching his body in an attempt to dodge the assault, but there were simply too many. One collided in an explosion of flame and sparks right in the center of his chest. Titan dropped to the ground, stunned and aching with a hard thud, feeling like his chest was in a vice. He rolled over and tried to regain his bearings. As he lay face down in the center of the street he could hear Inferno's footsteps over the shards of glass and chunks of concrete. As his world swirled and tilted in his eyes he looked and noticed the dark shapes of police sharp shooters taking position on the rooftops above. Time was running out. Suddenly a long dark shadow passed directly over him.

"Well ya little punk, don't have much to say for yourself anymore do ya?" Inferno asked, standing right over Titan. "What? No more snappy little comebacks?"

Inferno gave Titan a quick kick to the midsection, causing him to let out a grunt. Titan arched his back and rolled to his side to protect himself from another blow.

"Come on, you little pus bucket. I want to hear you beg for mercy. I want to hear you scream." Titan was hunched over facing the ground; Inferno couldn't seem to get any reaction at all. This only made him angrier. He dealt Titan another swift kick to the midsection.

"Ha, I told Mr. Midnight that you weren't gonna be so tough. Okay, you're done," said Inferno triumphantly.

Inferno hooked his foot into Titan's hip and flipped him onto his back. To Inferno's surprise Titan had a wide smirk across his face. He held his staff tucked in to his body with tiny blue sparks coming from its end.

"I dropped in here right out of the sky, and I can pick up a car with one hand. Did you really think that one little fireball from you would take me down?" asked Titan, full of confidence. "You didn't do very well in school, did you?"

Titan gave Inferno a quick kick to the stomach slightly lifting him off his feet. Then he aimed his staff and shot him with a lightning blast that connected into Inferno's chest armor. Inferno flew back six feet into the air. He arched back, doing a full back flip and landing face first on the street. For a moment Inferno lay motionless; then slowly he managed to prop himself up on one hand. His face shield was now cracked and a large piece of glass had fallen out just over his left eye. Blood trickled out of the corner of his mouth. Titan remained where he had been, poised and ready to strike again.

"Oh, you think you're pretty clever, do ya?" asked Inferno through giant gasps for breath. "You're gonna pay for that one."

"Inferno, stop! You're hurt. If you keep on this will only get worse for you," warned Titan.

"I will never give up. Only cowards give up," said Inferno, still trying in vain to get to his feet.

"Why are you doing this? Why are you putting all these people's lives at risk?" Titan asked, pointing to the crowds gathered at the police barrier. "Is this really all just for Mr. Midnight, just because he wants me dead?"

"I gave my word that I would see you destroyed. Inferno lives by his word."

"Well I gave my word too. I gave my word to protect the people of this city. Protect them from the likes of you," said Titan.

With a loud primal roar, Inferno stood up on shaky legs and fired three wild fireballs toward Titan. Titan leapt high, dodging the attack easily. He vaulted clear over Inferno, going past him by several feet. As he landed he came down, swinging his staff hard. It connected with a nearby fire hydrant, knocking the valve clear off, sending out a torrential gush of water. Standing only a few feet away Inferno was hit square in the knees by the blast of water. It swept him off his shaky feet, and dumped him into the middle of the street.

Titan sheathed his staff, moving forward with caution. Drenched and dripping with water, Inferno had crawled up on all fours panting heavily and near exhaustion. Weary and wobbling badly, he managed to get up on one knee. Peering through the hole in his visor he sighted Titan, carefully bringing his cannon level to him. Suddenly it appeared far too heavy; it dipped and swayed dripping water down its muzzle. Before he could utter a shot Titan was on him and seized Inferno's deadly arm.

"No, no you can't," said Inferno breathlessly.

"This ends now, Inferno," said Titan. Squeezing his hand closed, he crushed the cannon. When he released it there was nothing left but scrap metal. "Today you lose."

"Oh, I wouldn't say that just yet," snarled Inferno.

Slowly Inferno staggered to his feet while reaching behind his back. In a flash he had pulled out a pistol from the base of his fuel tank. Titan ducked just as the trigger was pulled, sending out a long thin tendril of blue and orange flame directly over his head. Titan dealt Inferno a vicious kick to his stomach, doubling him over. Then with a swift swing, his left fist connected with Inferno's chin, sending him sprawling backwards, a giant arc of flame followed him overhead as his helmet cracked into two. Inferno landed with a hard crash amidst debris and pooling water.

Titan moved in quickly, kicking the weapon out of his hand. Then he grabbed Inferno, and ripped the fuel tank off his back, tossing it aside. Inferno slumped over face first into the street motionless.

Titan looked behind him and saw that the fire department was already at work putting out the fires that Inferno had started. Flames still erupted from several store fronts and apartments. The police were closing in now that it was safe, forming a tight circle around the perimeter so that neither could escape. Titan looked down, seeing several tiny red dots dance over his chest from laser sights of the snipers that were still stationed on the roof.

"You there! Put your hands in the air. Now!" Chief Ross bellowed through his megaphone as he made his way toward Titan. "Get down face first onto the ground."

Titan kept his hands at his sides and remained perfectly still, waiting. Nervously the police officers continued to close in on him. There was no way he could face capture, nor was there any way that he would harm any of them. Seeing the police with guns drawn, Titan could see there would be no reasoning here. The policemen were now only twenty feet away. With officers covering the streets leading to the intersection and snipers on the rooftops, every exit seemed blocked to him.

The street now looked like a war zone. Glass, brick, and other rubble littered the street and fire still sprouted all over. An explosion came from one of the burning store fronts, which seemed to rattle the whole area. Everyone ducked and turned towards the blast. With the officers distracted, Titan leapt high into the air before any of the police were even able to react. He came down several blocks away and was bounding across rooftops before the cuffs had even been put on Inferno.

You did well, Titan. You are learning very quickly.

"Thanks," Titan said, as he bounded over buildings and rooftops glad that no helicopters followed him this time. "Thanks for everything." He felt he was finally getting used to Azure's cryptic guidance. "I just wish I could have put an end to it all sooner."

You mustn't focus on that. You stopped Inferno, and none of the innocent civilians were injured. This was a success. The rest was out of your control.

"Yeah I guess you're right. It did feel pretty good crushing that loser's flamethrower."

As he landed on a rooftop in midtown he pivoted sharply and began to weave his way back to the east side.

"Azure?" asked Titan.

Yes, Titan?

"What do we do now about Mr. Midnight? I mean if Inferno's attack was planned by Midnight to get to me, what do we do now?" Titan inquired. "I don't think Mr. Midnight is the type to just give up after one try. What's our next move against him gonna be?"

As Titan your role is to uphold justice and peace. You must not sink to his level by acting in revenge.

"I'm not talking about sinking to his level," interjected Titan defensively. "I'm talking about finding out who and where he is, and putting an end to his grip on this city once and for all."

Your next move will be to flush him out. Mr. Midnight will be the type of person used to being in control. Now you must turn the tables on him. This will not be easy, and you must find a way to do it that will put no one in harm's way.

Titan thought about this as he sailed across the sky towards the neighborhood. He still felt amazed at the view of the city as it flew by below him. Perhaps he had been doing a better job than he had originally thought. He obviously had Mr. Midnight nervous, or he would not have sent Inferno after him. Now that Inferno had been defeated, Mr. Midnight was bound to be even more uneasy. Perhaps, flushing out Midnight would not be as hard as it sounded. Titan landed in the alley behind Caruthers Grocery.

Until next time, Titan.

"See ya, Azure. Extermino Fortis!" he said, as he transformed.

He felt exhilarated, like he felt the first time he had become Titan. It was his first real triumph against a true villain. Most importantly the city was saved. There may have been massive amounts of property damage, but at least he knew everyone was safe. He only wondered how he would be perceived in the media and among the people of Delta City after this. Surely he would not be seen in the press in the same light as Inferno. Would he?

Michael looked at his watch and saw that he had been gone about five times longer than he should have. He braced himself for Mr. Caruthers' verbal tirade as he went inside.

"Novak!" bellowed Mr. Caruthers as soon as he spotted Michael. "Where have you been? You should have been back ages ago."

"Sorry, Mr. Caruthers," said Michael.

"Well the canned goods weren't stocking themselves while you were out gallivanting, so you better get to it," said Mr. Caruthers, watching the news coverage of Inferno from the little TV at the front of the store.

"I'll get right on it, Mr. Caruthers." He had no real excuse, so he had to listen to Mr. Caruthers rant as he began stocking shelves. Suddenly it was hard to believe that moments ago he had been fighting a crazed super villain.

"You kids today, you have no idea about proper work ethic. Everything's just handed to you on a silver platter, well not in my day. We had to work bloody hard for everything we got," Mr. Caruthers continued, as Michael busied himself around the store. "You have no idea about the value of a dollar earned, that's what it all boils down to."

Michael could tell that what was left of his shift was going to go quite slow. For once, he didn't mind. Suddenly the store seemed a refuge from the outside world. This gave him ample time to be lost in his own thoughts. He thought very little of his battle with Inferno, however. Instead he found himself going over his fight with Carly. When he tried to picture her in his mind all he could see was her standing in the street with that terrified look on her face. By the end of the day so many feelings were swirling around in his head that Michael started to feel dizzy. At last his shift was over and with a heavy heart Michael headed for home.

He wondered if his Grandpa had heard about his battle with Inferno. He could just picture him hunched over in his chair enthralled with the scene being described to him on the radio. He then started to wonder what his grandpa would think of it all. As much as he wanted to talk to Grandpa Dale, he needed to talk to Carly as soon as he could. He had seen her being led away to safety, but still he wouldn't feel satisfied until he was able to talk to her himself. He needed to hear her voice, and see her face.

Suddenly all Michael could think of was getting to Carly and Grandpa Dale. Before he knew it he had started running the several blocks to home. He wanted to get to his grandpa as soon as possible, and then he would find Carly and apologize. Then, as he turned a corner he smashed into a woman holding a bag of fruit from the market. The fruit spilled everywhere and the woman fell backward. Michael felt horrible, but he just couldn't stop, he had to get up and keep going. He tried to apologize as he continued on, but the woman didn't seem to hear as she hollered at Michael.

Just as Michael turned forward and regained his footing for home he glanced across the street and saw Mr. Edwards looking his way. Clearly he had seen Michael's collision with the woman and her scattered bag of fruit and did not approve. He scowled at Michael as he shook his head with disapproval. He was quite sure he would hear about this and it would be used as another example of why Michael was not boyfriend material for Carly. He would just simply have to deal with it when the time came.

As Michael began crossing Fourteenth Street he suddenly stopped in his tracks. He was panting heavily by now and sweat ran from his forehead. There was Carly standing on the opposite sidewalk, looking tired and relieved to see him. For a second all they did was stand and stare at each other. Then Michael took a step closer and Carly ran and jumped into his arms. It wasn't until he could feel her in his arms that he realized how scared he had truly been for her safety.

"Are you okay?" Michael asked, exhilarated at having her in his embrace again.

"I am. Thanks to you. I was so worried until Titan showed up. I didn't want our last conversation together to be an argument," Carly replied.

"I know I was thinking the same thing. As I fought Inferno I was worried if I lost to him that I would never be able to see you again," Michael said.

"Are you kidding? I don't know how I ever doubted you. That creep didn't stand a chance against Titan," said Carly admiringly.

Michael blushed.

"Wow! What happened to old worry wart Carly?" Michael asked.

"Well, previously I may have been a little worried for your safety," Carly began.

"A little? Carly you were a lot worried," Michael said flatly.

"Yeah well, after seeing Titan, um I mean you, up close and in action I can't believe how much power you have. Michael, do you have any idea what you can accomplish with power like that? I mean, you were just incredible," she said.

"That's what I've been trying to tell you all this time. I mean the power part not the incredible part," Michael said, flushing again.

"All I could think about as the police led us all away was that our fight was just so silly and meaningless, and if Titan hadn't come in to save us…" Carly said trailing off as her eyes welled up with tears.

"I'm so sorry about that. I didn't mean to say those things. It's just that I've felt so stressed and out of it lately. I have no idea what's going on anymore. I don't even know what I'm supposed to be doing. This is all just too much. The last thing I want is to lose you or have you angry with me," Michael blurted out.

"Oh, Michael, I'm sorry too, and you know you could never lose me." She paused to lean into him with a kiss. "I guess I never fully realized what you have been going through. I just thought you had everything under control. Frankly I thought you were doing amazingly well under the circumstances. You know with the powers and responsibility and all."

"Don't forget that new guiding voice in my head," added Michael.

"Oh yeah, him too," said Carly.

"Well it's just...I mean...oh who am I kidding? I have no idea what I mean," said Michael, and for the first time Carly seemed to see the anguish on Michael's face.

"Look, I know you're stressed, but you know what? Things could be a lot worse,"

"Yeah right," said Michael under his breath.

"I know you'll find a way to turn everything around and make all this into something great. Don't forget, you're doing good things Michael. All you have to do is hang on and tough it out. Come on, you just saved the city today, and the damsel in distress. You haven't even heard what anyone has said about that. Trust me you were very impressive out there. You're already my hero."

Michael smiled. Carly stepped up and kissed him again. As usual, he knew she was right.

"You see, that's why I need you around, to keep me grounded," Michael said, wrapping his arms tightly around her.

"That's right. So you better smarten up, fly boy," Carly said, all smiles.

"You wanna come over to have dinner with Grandpa and me?" Michael asked as they turned and started to walk again. He simply didn't want to spoil the moment telling her about what her father had seen him do.

"I can think of nothing I would rather do," Carly replied grinning broadly up at Michael.

As they turned towards his grandfather's house, Michael was suddenly looking forward to spending the entire evening with his two favorite people. This quality time with them was long overdue. He couldn't wait to clear his head a little with a simple night of rest and relaxation.

Chapter 15: A Little Support

Michael had been ecstatic after defeating Inferno downtown in full public view, and then meeting Carly on his way home. They then had a wonderful meal with Grandpa Dale, made even better by the fact that Vince was not home to spoil it. They had gone into the living room to watch TV, and practically every channel was showing repeat footage of the Inferno attack. As the newscasts continued, Michael grew quieter and more despondent. Even Grandpa Dale didn't need to see to tell something was wrong with him. As the footage rolled he kept slinking deeper and deeper into the couch. Grandpa shook his head and said, "It's a crazy world we live in." After that, there was nothing that could be said to lift Michael's spirits.

After a night of watching TV with Carly and his grandpa, Michael learned that his public image, as Titan, had yet to change. The newscasts had given him mixed reviews at best. Several people interviewed found the notion of Titan terrifying, and saw him as a public nuisance. They thought his efforts to help only resulted in more destruction to the city and increased menace to its citizens. Furious, the mayor had made capturing Titan his main priority. The mayor became more animated and furious as his speech went on. His face became flushed in a deep red, and his puffy gray hair bounced outrageously back and forth as he carried on. He listed the large sum of money it was believed Titan had at least a part in destroying; also noting that Campbell Park would never be the same. One TV reporter had spoken to a couple of frat boys on the street, and when asked what they thought of the city's new crime fighter, they praised him as being 'way cool'. His only real comfort came from knowing he had saved Carly and Monica from being hurt. Michael found it hard to believe that so many had seemed to miss the fact that he had saved lives during the battle. He felt mad and a little guilty that others in the city felt frightened of him. As though he was there to add to the cities misery instead of help make it a better place to live.

As Michael went to bed he found himself unable to sleep. He simply stared at the ceiling for hours, thinking. Whenever he tried to stop thinking about the news reports and public opinion Vince popped into his head, from there the shootout at the dock and the police chase into Campbell Park ran through his mind's eye, and after that he was once again looking down the barrel of Inferno's flame thrower. On and on it went in an endless loop. Eventually he fell into a restless sleep.

The next day, Michael found himself in a daze. He dragged himself out of bed and got dressed. He brushed aside the photo of his parents, feeling unable to face their smiling faces, and went about his morning routines with his head hung low and his eyes barely open to the world. He slipped out to work without saying goodbye to Grandpa Dale. He just didn't feel he could face him. At least, he thought, Grandpa Dale knew where he would be this time.

Michael faced the day at work feeling much like a zombie. He mindlessly went through his day to day tasks, his body moving on instinct. The whole time only two thoughts swirled through his head. One, how could he draw out Mr. Midnight, and rid the city of him? Two, how could he get the city to stop viewing him as some kind of possible threat? In this way his entire day passed by in a blur. Michael started thinking that Titan was now taking over every facet of his life.

Even Mr. Caruthers hardly seemed to faze Michael. Every time the old shopkeeper would bark an order, Michael would simply nod and move along. He even had to be told when it was lunch time and time to go home.

Michael continued to think on these things as he walked home to his Grandpa's. He found himself wanting to prolong the time that was left until he would head out again as Titan. Only a few days before he had looked forward to becoming Titan with eager anticipation. Now he was starting to dread it. All he wanted now was to spend some time with Carly and Grandpa Dale again, in that perfect world he at least felt safe from scrutiny. Yet, Michael knew he could not do that forever.

As he entered the house, he found his Grandpa in his armchair listening to the news on the radio, and watched him look over as Michael entered the house through the back door off the kitchen. Michael looked around the coat room and saw that Vince was still out. He was thankful for that.

"Michael, is that you?" Grandpa Dale asked. Usually Grandpa Dale knew if it was Michael by the sounds he made. As soon as his grandfather said it, Michael felt a great amount of guilt, realizing just how much he had been preoccupied.

"Yeah it's me, Grandpa," Michael replied.

Just then Mr. Edwards appeared in the kitchen looking into the coat room at Michael. Michael froze, staring at Mr. Edwards not knowing what to say.

"Hello, Michael."

"Hello, Mr. Edwards. Were you looking for Carly? Because I haven't seen her all day; I was at work."

"No, I came by to have a little chat with your grandfather."

"Oh. Should I leave you two then?"

"No, actually I was just leaving. I just wanted to talk to your grandfather about you and Carly. It just seems to me that you two have become more serious than I had realized, and, well, I won't sugar coat it, I was wondering if maybe you two weren't, well, a little young and should maybe take some time apart for now."

"What? Please don't do that I..." Michael instantly began to protest, but Mr. Edwards raised his hand to silence Michael so he could continue.

"Don't worry. After talking to your grandfather I've decided that maybe that would be a little too harsh right now." Michael instantly let out a huge sigh of relief. "You have to understand me though; I am only looking after the best intentions of my daughter."

"I do understand sir, but that's all I care about too," Michael responded.

"Yes, well, it's just that you are both growing up so fast, and I know the kind of elements that can be out there for kids your age these days. I just don't want Carly to fall in with the wrong crowd. I have always liked you, Michael. I want to make sure that Carly keeps a level head on her shoulders. You are both about to enter high school after all. I would hate to see her future get derailed so soon." Michael knew most of this came from the incident the day before, and wondered why Mr. Edwards wouldn't just say so.

"I really don't think that you have to worry too much about Carly."

"Well, anyway, I am going to continue to allow you and Carly to date after talking with your grandfather, but just know that I will continue to keep an eye on things, and if I see any more problematic behavior I will forbid you to see her any more. Am I understood?"

"Yes, sir, perfectly."

With that, Mr. Edwards walked past Michael without a glance or another word and out the door. Michael could hardly believe what had just happened. He stood there running over the scene in his mind wondering if maybe he had imagined it. Slowly he shuffled into the living room and plopped down on the couch beside his grandfather's chair. Grandpa Dale sat solemnly, ear cocked to the radio.

"Well, son how was your day down at the store?" Grandpa Dale asked.

"It was okay I guess. So, what just happened here with Mr. Edwards?"

"Oh, he's just a little concerned about Carly is all."

It was a typical Grandpa Dale response in such matters. Michael simply put his hand out and rested over his grandfather's on the arm of the chair.

"Well, thanks, Grandpa," Michael said, as heartfelt as he could manage.

Grandpa Dale gave a wry smile. "Anytime, son."

They both sat in silence for some time after that, neither seeming to know where to go from there.

"Grandpa, can I ask you something?" Michael ventured, at last.

"Of course, son. You know you can ask me anything."

"Did you ever have to face something where you just didn't know if you were up to the challenge?" Michael paused to think about it, and then continued. "What I mean is, was there ever anything in your life that you wanted to just quit? Even if it was something you believed in doing?"

Grandpa Dale paused for a moment, and Michael sat quietly saying nothing. The old man rubbed his fingers along his weathered chin as though he had been expecting this. Then he looked up and faced Michael. His hand reached out, searching for him. At last he found Michael's arm resting on the couch and patted him gently before beginning.

"Son, from my experience, if you really believe in something, then you should never quit. If there's one thing in life that I've learned it's that anything in life that's worthwhile will never come easily," his Grandpa said, echoing Carly's earlier sentiments. Grandpa Dale sounded as serious as Michael had ever heard him. "The greatest struggle I ever had was getting the custody of you boys. I had plenty of people trying to block my way. They all thought an old blind man would be unfit to raise and care for two young boys. It wasn't easy, but I was able to prove every one of those people wrong. It was one of the hardest things I ever did, and one of the most rewarding."

Grandpa Dale paused and then shifted uneasily in his chair. He adjusted his dark glasses, grabbed a hold of his cane and held onto it, balancing it between his legs.

"There is also your Grandma. The other hardest thing I ever had to do in my life was sit by as the woman I loved wasted away before me. I was left absolutely helpless to do nothing about it as the cancer ate away at her body. In that time I would have done anything to stop her pain and suffering, but I could do nothing at all. Yet, as hard as it was, I wouldn't give up one single second of that time with her. Never give in Michael. If you end up quitting all you will end up with is regrets later in life. Regrets are the only things in life that cannot be fixed." The old man then pulled a comb from his shirt pocket and ran it through his already immaculate hair.

Michael was shocked to hear this confession about his Grandma Emma. It was the first time he had ever heard Grandpa Dale speak of her illness. It had always been a taboo subject in the house. Grandpa Dale always spoke so kindly and lovingly about Grandma Emma, but would never tread openly over the years where she was very sick and near death. It had all happened before Michael was old enough to remember.

"I know you're right, Grandpa," Michael said. "I guess I just needed to hear it."

"Well good, I hope I've helped. Now what else has been going on in your life? How's Carly doing? I never did ask her last night," Grandpa Dale asked.

"She's doing great," replied Michael.

"That's wonderful," Grandpa Dale said. "I really like her. I quite enjoyed having her here last night."

"Grandpa it was the best night I've had in ages," said Michael. At that, it almost looked like tears might roll out from behind his grandpa's dark glasses.

The noise from the radio that always sat beside his grandpa had been turned down low as they spoke. During this pause in their conversation they both heard a story that was talking about the exploits of Titan or the masked man of Delta City as he was known. Grandpa turned it up a little.

"I still can't believe all the news about this masked fella," Grandpa Dale said.

"You know, I hear a lot of people in the media say that he's bad news. As bad as Mr. Midnight," he said, hoping to get a chance to see if his grandfather approved of what he had been doing. He wanted to take what appeared to be his best opportunity to talk about Titan.

"I don't envy anyone associated with him, anyone close to him will be in danger for sure." So far it wasn't quite what Michael had hoped for. He thought of changing the subject quickly then thought against it. "This vigilante has everyone from the police to Mr. Midnight after him. The fella sure has his work cut out for him, but as we were saying about anything worthwhile not coming easy. They sure have been giving him a hard time in the press. Then, when have the reporters of the world ever been known to let something like the facts get in the way of their stories?" asked Grandpa Dale with contempt. "If only someone told the story from his side, maybe then we could see that he may be one of the good guys, which this city could sorely use I might add."

"Sorry what was that?" Michael asked, delightedly shocked.

"I said someone should let them know that this masked fella might be one of the good guys," his grandfather replied.

Any thoughts Michael had of telling his Grandpa the truth about himself and of Titan quickly died away as a fabulous idea suddenly struck him.

"Grandpa I'm really sorry but I have to go. I just forgot that I promised to meet Carly in about five minutes," Michael said, glancing at his watch. He sprang out of his seat and headed for the kitchen.

"That boy, always in such a rush," Dale Novak said to the empty room.

Michael flew through the house heading for the back door. Even with his grandpa's words still ringing in his head, his only thoughts were formulating a plan.

"What's this, loser?" said Vince. He was just stepping in the back door as he knelt in the front entrance scooping something off the ground. "Some dumb cereal prize of yours."

Even from across the kitchen Michael could see the blue glow of the power ring roll around Vince's fingers as he tried to examine it. Michael froze slack jawed in the middle of the kitchen; he could almost feel his heartbeat lower. Michael had been carrying the ring around in his jeans' pocket. He just could not bring himself to put it on unless he was going to use it to transform. He would rub his hand on the outside of his pocket forty times a day just to make sure it was still there. Yet, still, it had somehow fallen out, and now it rested in the hands of Vince. He had no idea what might happen if Vince actually put the ring on. He was sure it wouldn't work for him, but what if it did? Vince was one of the last people he wanted to imagine with such power at his disposal.

"Give that back right now," Michael demanded.

"Or what?" replied Vince, suddenly interested in the ring now that he knew it was Michael's.

"It's nothing to you. Just give it back," Michael repeated. A combination of anger and fear rose up from the base of his stomach and worked into the back of his throat. Vince seemed to relish the torment he was causing his little brother as an evil smile crossed his lips.

"What is it, a present for your little girlfriend?" Vince said tauntingly. Vince then pinched the ring by the band with his index finger and thumb, and looked into the small blue jewel. A look of desire crossed his face, and Michael suddenly knew he was about to do.

"You're being a jerk, Vince. Just let me have it," Michael demanded again. He knew that Vince didn't know how to use the ring, and that naturally he was not worthy to summon its power. Yet the unknown lingered in his mind. Michael still did not have a full understanding of the ring himself.

"I don't see why I should just give it back to you. I think there should be a price for it. After all, I have it and you clearly want it," said Vince, sounding more sophisticated than Michael had ever heard before.

"Well I guess you would know about selling off stolen goods, wouldn't you?" snapped Michael. If he was going to be provoked, he thought, he might as well fight back.

"And just what is that supposed to mean?" asked Vince, trying to play dumb.

Michael noticed Vince rubbing his thumb over the hieroglyphs on the side of the ring. He brought the ring up to a few inches from his eye for closer inspection.

"I think you know what it means. How's your job with Dylan going?"

"Is that why you're so mad, runt? I knew you'd be jealous 'cause your ole Dylan chose me instead of you."

"That's not quite what I mean. I was talking more about the work you do for him."

"Well, what I do is none of your business."

"Look Vince, I need to go so just give the ring back," demanded Michael. He was growing increasingly frustrated. It was quite clear that Vince was not about to let Michael know about anything he did outside of the house.

"If it's so important to you than why did I just find it lying here?"

"Come on, Vince. I just dropped it, that's all. Please give it back," Michael pleaded, suddenly changing tactics. He hated Vince more for making him beg.

"Haven't you ever heard of finder's keepers?" asked Vince, still gazing into the ring. "Besides, it's not all that lame. Maybe I'll just keep it," said Vince, as he gingerly slipped the ring onto the middle finger of his left hand.

"Vince, NO!" Michael shouted.

Nothing happened.

"You boys alright in there?" Grandpa Dale asked from his chair in the living room.

"Yeah we're fine, Grandpa. Nothin' to worry about here. Klutzy old Michael here just dropped something," Vince said, as he took the ring off and lobbed it across the kitchen at Michael. Michael caught it deftly with one hand. A look of disgust spread across Vince's face at having to give up his game so quickly.

"Be careful where you leave things in the future, moron. Next time you just might lose something important," Vince said, as he stormed through the kitchen and headed for his room.

Michael fled out the backdoor with the ring clutched tightly in his hand. He made it all the way through the back yard and out to the back alley before he could open his hand and make sure the ring was actually there. The strength returned to his legs as the ring's blue jewel stared up at him from his palm. He could not believe that he could ever, even by accident, allow the power ring to fall into Vince's hands. Michael then vowed to himself that he would never allow such a foolish thing to happen again. He slid the ring down the middle finger of his left hand. From now on he would wear the ring at all times.

Michael peeled himself off the fence and started to make his way over to Carly's. He did his best to push the incident with Vince from his mind. As he had been talking to Grandpa Dale a plan had popped into his head so clearly he could hardly contain it. He knew it would be bold and he needed Carly's input on it to make sure he executed it correctly. After tonight, he knew that the people of Delta City would no longer doubt Titan. He was so excited that he broke into a full out sprint the rest of the way.

Later that night, Vicki Earnhardt sat in her uptown office at the courier typing away at her computer. She had reluctantly started on a story about this mysterious masked vigilante of Delta City, thereby meeting Charles, her editor, halfway. As a reporter she was duty bound to report the facts and that's all she would do for now. It would probably be boring, even though it was about a real superhero, and if anyone did read the whole thing then they would be able to make up their own minds based on the facts, not a bunch of media spin.

Vicki had written and then deleted the same sentence for the last five minutes, when a brilliant flash of lighting seemed to explode just outside her window, causing her to jump with fright. She recoiled from her computer and went to the window. As she rounded her desk and faced the large window she momentarily froze in place. Sitting on the wide window ledge was the silhouette of a man, who was holding a long staff. Long pieces of fabric flowed out wildly in the wind from the man's waist and head. The silhouette squatted on the ledge unmoving, almost appearing like a gargoyle.

She grabbed the nearest item that would qualify as a weapon, and slowly stepped toward the window. As she stood within inches of it and put her hand on the handle to slide it open she could see from the moonlight that the man on her balcony was the vigilante she had just been writing about. She paused, and then took a step toward the phone on the end table. Then, she suddenly unlocked and slid the window open, leaving absolutely no barrier between herself and the man.

"Who are you? What do you want?" Vicki asked in a shaky voice.

"My name is Titan and I have come to you with a message for the people of Delta City."

"A message? What is it?" Vicki asked. "Because, I'll have you know that I have some very important friends on the police force."

"I have no intentions of hurting you, Ms. Earnhardt, so you can put down the desk lamp."

Vicki glanced at the small table lamp that she had grabbed as her weapon and still held chest high ready to strike. She then seemed willing to take the leap of faith, and lowered the lamp to her side.

"Okay," she said. "I'll take down your message, but you have to answer a few questions for me after." Vicki was surprised to see the reporter in her come out even in the face of fear.

"Very well, I will gladly answer any questions that I can," Titan began, eager to start the speech he had been practicing for three hours. "All I really want to say to everyone is that I am here to help." He paused then and watched for a reaction from Vicki. Whatever she was thinking, she was keeping it well hidden at the moment. "This city is currently being overrun with crime, and all I want is to put a stop to it. I am here to keep the people of this city safe."

"Well, your intentions may be good, but I'm afraid that the police call someone like you a vigilante, and the last I heard that was illegal," Vicki said.

"If you were walking down the street and saw someone being attacked, and you had the power to stop it, would you not help them? Could you sit by while a crime was being committed against the innocent knowing you had the ability to stop it? I hand out no kind of sentence or punishment to these criminals. I simply catch them red handed and stop them. Then it's up to the proper authorities to deal with them and deliver justice. I can't help that most of them don't want to go quietly," said Titan.

"So all you want to say is that you're here to help?" Vicki asked.

"Basically, yes. I just want the citizens and police of this city to know that I am here to help them. The only people who need to fear me are the criminals, which unfortunately are far too plentiful in this city. Surely you must agree that my presence in this city has done some good," Titan said.

"Aside from the millions in property damage that the mayor is intending to fully blame on you, yes, I suppose you're right," Vicki said with a smirk. "Is that the end of your statement?"

"Yes, I suppose it is."

"Good. Now, I have some questions for you."

"Okay, I'll answer what I can," Titan said.

"For starters, who are you? Where do you come from? What exactly are your powers, and how did you get them?" Vicki asked.

"Where I'm from, I'm afraid, is a bit complicated. I'm sorry; I won't be able to go into it with you. My powers are many, and I am willing to demonstrate them to any criminal out there. To tell you their source and how I got them however could possibly put me at a disadvantage to my enemies. So, I'm sorry, again I can't go into that with you," said Titan, trying to sound professional.

"Come on! You've got to give me something. So, are you bullet proof then?" Vicki asked, not ready to give up.

"Well not exactly, although a bullet would not affect me the way that it would a normal human. I would also be able to dodge bullets quite easily in most cases," Titan replied.

"You know, you're being very vague. I don't suppose I could get you to be a little more specific. My readers will be expecting something here. This is the first full interview with Delta City's famed vigilante. People want you to speak. Do you think my publishers are going to believe that you came to see me for an interview like this if I have nothing to go back with?"

"I'm sorry, but for many reasons I cannot say too much about myself. In case you haven't noticed, I do have to wear a mask to hide my identity. All I can really tell you is that I have been granted special powers and I am going to use them to protect this city from crime."

"That is a good point. Why the mask? I think it has only made people more suspicious of you," said Vicki.

"Considering the response I've gotten so far I don't think I could have gotten by without it," replied Titan coolly.

"Good point." Vicki shrugged her shoulders in an understanding gesture. "You know, you do look kind of young."

"I'm old enough." Titan replied, a little defensively.

They spent the next several moments in silence. Titan could sense Vicki sizing him up, trying to probe deep and get answers to some of the big questions about him she felt the public had.

"Well, I'm sorry, but that's not going to create the most exciting article." Titans' eyes went wide in disbelief. "Sorry, I just meant that it's not going to answer the many questions people have about you. Do you have anything else that you can tell me about yourself? Like maybe about the several incidents over the last couple of days. You really haven't given much of a reason to print your statement," said Vicki, clearly ready to play hard ball.

"Those I can explain," said Titan.

Titan then spent the next fifteen minutes telling Vicki all about his exploits. He was very careful to skip everything in the beginning and jump right to the mugger in the alley. He spared no details in describing his deeds, from his saving the young women from the muggers, right up to his battle with Inferno. As he was telling her he began to feel liberated. Titan refused to enter the office when Vicki had offered. Vicki simply sat at the edge of her desk scribbling furiously on a notepad. Titan remained perched on the ledge the entire time.

"That's more like it. I'd like to see Charles keep this issue off the stands. I hope I still have time to make tomorrow's edition. The guys in printing still owe me some favors, so I think we're good," Vicki exclaimed, as soon as Titan had finished.

She thought of her editor's warning; then waved it off. Surely Charles wouldn't deny an exclusive interview. An interview was no editorial piece, and couldn't be edited the same. Certainly this could bypass the mayor's office on its way to newsstands.

"Before I go, I need to ask you what you know about Mr. Midnight," Titan said.

"Wow, okay where do I begin? Why? Are you planning on taking him on?" asked Vicki, finally thinking that she had found the motherlode of all stories.

"He seems to be the source of most of the misery of this city. So I need to know all I can about him. Most of what I know is, are the rumors that circulate among the neighborhoods. It's hard to tell where the rumors end and the truth begins," said Titan.

"Well, you're lucky because I happen to be something of a Mr. Midnight expert. I was working on some Mr. Midnight material a couple years ago. I did a lot of digging and found out a lot. I started to track many of the sightings and the incidents rumored to involve him. I tracked several companies in the city that were supposedly linked to criminal activity and ultimately back to him, like BDC inc. and Camex. The closer I got the more frightening things became. One night I came home to find a couple of creepy brutes hanging out in front of my building. When I got to my building's front door they approached me and asked why I had been asking questions about Mr. Midnight. I didn't really answer. I don't think they were looking for an answer though. All they said was that people shouldn't go snooping around where they didn't belong. That's how people got hurt they said. I told the police, but they did nothing. So I had to stop my story and back off. It's the only story I ever gave up on," said Vicki, looking morose.

"Inferno mentioned that he was sent by Midnight to get rid of me, so I wouldn't get in the way of any more of his plans. I'm almost sure that the guys on that ship were working for him. They had some weird weapons onboard too. I don't have any idea what someone like Midnight would want with them. But whatever it is, it can't be good," explained Titan.

"I know you have some pretty amazing powers, but do you know what you're getting into here?" asked Vicki.

"I do. You don't have to worry about me. For too long everyone has feared Mr. Midnight. Things are about to change. I just need all the information on him I can get," declared Titan.

"So, where do you want me to start?" asked Vicki.

"Start from the beginning. I want to know everything," said Titan.

"Okay, but it's a bit of a long story so I'll try and tell you the abridged version. Mr. Midnight is the boss of Delta City's underworld. Very little is known about the actual man. Stories of his horrible deeds have existed for many years, dating as far back as the sixties. Sightings and stories of him just started sprouting up like wild fire. As you know, the legend of him has never really stopped. Of course no one knows how old he is, because no one has ever known who he really is. The police at first tried to deny that he was real at all. They simply chalked it all up to a bunch of rumour and hearsay. Finally with too many credible eyewitness accounts, they had to admit that he was indeed real and that they were working feverishly to capture him. His real identity has never been known; neither have his origins or background. All that is known is that he wears a mask of solid gold to shield his identity. Any illegal activity that goes on in this city can be traced back to him. Of course someone like this is not to be crossed. So finding anything out is next to impossible.

"The police tried to say about six years back that the real Mr. Midnight had been dead for at least ten years. Of course the police had tried to deny his existence all along. Believe me though; he is very much alive and active today. You don't see people show such fear and loyalty to a dead criminal mastermind. There are still sightings of him, but of course no one will say so on the record.

"His crew is very loyal and very lethal. Most orders are carried out by his number two in command, and his personal bodyguard Kaizen. Kaizen is almost wrapped in as much mystery as Midnight himself. She is feared by practically everyone as one of the most deadly women on the planet. It is rumored that Midnight helped her flee her homeland, don't even ask me where, and she has faithfully served him ever since. She is extremely skilled with weapons and hand to hand combat. Many say that if there is one person who knows the identity of Mr. Midnight that it would be Kaizen. Although, no one has ever dared to try to get that information from her. She bears the unmistakable scar of a metal plate that is visible over the top left-hand side of her face, leaving her with a false eye that glows red. No one knows how she was injured or who gave her those scars. She received the injuries shortly before leaving her homeland. All anyone is certain about is that whoever gave her that scar must have paid dearly for it.

"That's about all I have on the man I'm afraid. I could tell you more about some crimes that his organization has been involved in, but it wouldn't help you find him," Vicki finished.

"If I wanted to find him, and see what he's up to, how would you suggest I go about doing that?" Titan asked.

"Well every time I try to dig up anything on him, anyone who can tell me anything shuts right up. From my information, I would say that his headquarters are near the docks. He has warehouses and other operations all over that area. That's as good a place to start as any. I'm sure someone there will know something. It's just that no one has ever been too eager to find out," said Vicki, wishing she had more. She was excited at the possibility that there was someone capable of taking out Mr. Midnight and his whole criminal empire.

"Now I have a proposition for you. I have given you information, and you have given me information. I suggest we work together," Titan said.

"And how will we work together?" asked Vicki. "I mean I'm just a reporter. What could I do to help you? I'm not about to start running around in a mask and costume here."

"Like I just said, information," said Titan. "You give me whatever information you can when I need it. Just like right now with Mr. Midnight, tonight. In exchange I'll give firsthand information on any other stories I get caught up in."

"Deal," said Vicki, not even needing to think it through.

Titan then stood. He was surefooted and steady even so high up. He turned, faced the city and prepared to take flight.

"Wait!" Vicki shouted, jumping out of her chair. "How am I supposed to get a hold of you?"

"You don't," Titan answered. "I'll get a hold of you."

Then Titan turned to go. Vicki stood back speechless. She covered her face and braced herself for the flash of lightning that had heralded Titan's arrival. Instead there was only a big swoosh, and when Vicki took her hands away from her face, Titan was quickly becoming a small speck in the night sky. For a moment she simply stood there speechless.

She turned, hurried back to her computer and deleted her previous work. She quickly started on a whole new article. With her notebook at her side, she grabbed the phone and dialed.

"Herb, its Vicki. I need a favor. I need you to hold the presses," she said. There was a short pause. "Don't worry; I don't think you'll get in trouble when Charles sees what I'm bringing in."

Not long after his interview with Vicki, Titan and Azure were sitting on a high rooftop overlooking downtown Delta City.

That seemed to go rather well. You may have gained an important ally tonight.

"I sure hope so," said Titan. He was perched on another uptown high-rise window ledge. He looked out over downtown.

You are taking important first steps in your journey as Titan.

"Thanks, Azure. If this works, it will be the first right move I will have made with my public image."

It will work, you will see. The war against evil has never been an easy one for any Titan. Now at least, our enemy has become a little clearer for us. Tomorrow we shall make our first move against him.

Chapter 16: Hunter and Prey

"Michael, are you sure that you're ready for this?" Carly asked. "I mean, I know as Titan you have some awesome powers, but Mr. Midnight is in whole other level from muggers or even Inferno."

"Don't worry. Why are you so frightened for me? Why are you so scared of Mr. Midnight? He's a powerful man, but a man is all he is. When I'm Titan, I'm more than an ordinary man. It's him that should be afraid of me and the power I have," Michael said, trying to reassure her. "I have to do this. Mr. Midnight has to be stopped before we see anyone else from our neighborhood in jail or dead because of him."

Carly simply sat on the ledge of the building staring down at her shoes.

The sun had just set as they sat on their rooftop sanctuary of Carly's building. Just a short time ago the mood between them had been much cheerier. They had finally had a chance to go over that day's news headlines. Michael's plan had seemed to work. Vicki Earnhardt had their interview the night before in the next day's edition. Michael and Carly sat on the bus bench huddled around Carly's laptop reading through the article. TITAN: A HERO FOR DELTA CITY, the headline had splashed across the front page. The article went on to describe her interview with Titan. Finally his side of the story was out there. The article left no doubts about his intentions; it was all there in his own words. When Michael first saw the front page he had felt like a giant weight had been lifted from his shoulders.

After dissecting the entire paper, Michael had told Carly about his plans to flush Mr. Midnight out and bring him to justice. Carly's reaction had been less than he had hoped for, to say the least. She had been trying to talk him out of it from the start.

"I'm sorry. I know you're very powerful as Titan, but it's just so hard to watch you in dangerous scenarios when I know it's still you under that mask. I just worry that maybe you're not quite ready for something this big. I was there when you fought Inferno, remember? I know you kicked butt, but you could have easily been killed. The stakes are a little bigger with Mr. Midnight. You make a mistake facing this bad guy and you could pay for it dearly."

"Listen, this is totally different. Plus you forget I have Azure with me," Michael said, feeling hurt that she would doubt him still.

Feeling bad and wanting to reassure her he said, "Look I accepted the role of Titan and that means ridding the world of evil. Well, around here Mr. Midnight's about as evil as you can get. He's planning something big too, I just know it. So tonight, I'm just gonna go and see what I can find out about his plan. Who knows if I'll even find anything? The whole city knows he's out there and running pretty much every criminal activity in Delta City. Yet no one can find him. He's like a phantom. But, with these powers I'm obligated to try and put a stop to him."

"I know," Carly said. "I guess this whole thing is still just pretty new to me. I just can't bear the thought of bad guys trying to kill you, guys with guns, bombs, and who knows what else. I know you're capable, and that you totally can kick butt as Titan, but still it's hard to see you put your life on the line. Just promise me you'll be careful."

"Don't worry, I always am. I'm a lot safer out there than you think, you know," Michael said. Then he went over and hugged her tightly.

"By the way, my parents saw the Titan article too, before they left for work," Carly said, as she nuzzled into Michael's neck.

"Oh!" Michael replied.

"Yeah, They think Titan's gonna save the city." Carly pulled back so she could watch Michael turn several shades of red. "I think they may be onto something. You should have heard my dad; I think he wants your autograph."

He said nothing; he just stood there with a big broad grin on his face. He thought it would have been interesting to hear her father speak of Titan approvingly, especially after how he has treated Michael the last few days. Michael had already decided not to tell Carly about her fathers' visit to his home the day before. He knew it would just make her upset. The last thing he wanted was to be caught in the middle of a fight between Carly and Mr. Edwards. That was a lose, lose scenario for Michael.

"I bumped into Dave earlier too. I think he and Perminder aren't just part of the Titan fan club, they could be president and vice president," Carly said, holding back her laughter. "Not to mention about half the people I saw today in the neighborhood were talking about how truly amazing Titan was."

"Wow, really?" Michael asked.

"Well I added the truly amazing part myself, but they definitely love Titan."

"So, I guess the article worked."

"I think you did okay," Carly said, trying to hold back a coy smile.

Michael planted a warm kiss on her forehead. Carly's arms were locked tightly around Michael's mid section. Neither of them seemed to want to let go.

"I should get going," Michael said with regret, taking several steps towards the building ledge.

"Yeah, I know. I'm gonna go over to Monica's. It'll help keep my mind off things. I'll see you as soon as you get back?" Carly asked.

"Okay, just, please make sure to let your parents know where you are. I don't want to catch any blame for that."

"Okay, I will." Carly smiled giving Michael a patronizing look.

"I'll come find you first thing in the morning." Michael turned with the city spread out before him.

"Michael..." said Carly anxiously. Michael stopped briefly and faced her. "I just wanted to say, good luck."

Michael simply smiled warmly at her and gave her a little wave. He held out his ring hand instinctively. It had been the first time he had worn the ring all day, and already it was starting to feel natural.

"Exaudio Fortis!" he said, and again the lightning engulfed him. Carly barely flinched this time. Within the blink of an eye he was soaring high into the air leaving Carly below, looking up after him. The ends of his belt and bandana flapped wildly behind him. His heartbeat was quick and his breathing steady; he felt he was already becoming accustomed to the sensations of soaring through the sky over the city. He tried to get Carly out of his mind so he could focus on the task at hand. He angled his body sharply for the coast, heading straight towards the docks.

He knew the dock area only vaguely. It was not a place you went to unless you were looking the kind of activity he would be investigating. Titan landed on the only building familiar to him in the area. It was the same one he had landed on when he stopped the shootout on the ship. He went to the corner and squatted, looking down over the docks area, and listening intently for any activity. A series of wood shacks and small warehouses lined the docks. The entire area was dimly lit. The only sound he heard was that of the water lapping gently against the shore. Farther to Titan's left and a couple blocks back away the real city seemed to start as there were several taller buildings all about seven stories. Behind them he could see the skyscrapers of the city's skyline.

"Well Azure, any suggestions about how to start looking for Midnight and his boys?" Titan asked.

This Mr. Midnight is actually a very high profile man. The problem is that no one goes looking for him because they are afraid of what they might find. Someone like that cannot stay invisible. If you want to find him then we need only look.

"Are you saying the police don't want to find this guy, or haven't even been looking?" Titan asked, shocked.

I am saying they are too scared to find him. This man has created such a mystique for himself that people are not so much afraid of the man as the legend that follows him. However, if we really do wish to find him and destroy his criminal enterprise then all we need to do is keep our eyes open. If we find any illegal activity it should lead us to him.

"Okay then," said Titan. "Let's start looking."

Titan began to comb the docks in earnest, hopping from warehouse to warehouse, searching. He investigated every place that he heard a sound or saw any sign of movement. For the first half hour or so all Titan saw was some dock workers who appeared to be unloading some crates into trucks. It all appeared legal. Otherwise, there were some late night boaters and many, many giant rats. He was about done with chasing rats through abandoned warehouses, and he was thinking of moving his search to the lower east side. Just as Titan began to feel that this venture was turning utterly hopeless he heard a deafening crash a block away.

Titan leapt to the rooftop of the source of the noise and carefully peered down to investigate. As he looked over the ledge he never would have thought catching a crime in action would have made him so happy. Down below was a forklift, a large truck, five men, and most importantly, a crate that had busted open with a load of guns spilling out all over.

"Well, I'm going to go out on a limb and say that these guys work for Mr. Midnight," Titan said, in a low voice.

Yes, at the very least they are up to no good. You must stop them. You should have no problem with this bunch. Do remember to leave one of them awake enough to answer some questions, however.

"Don't worry," Titan said. "I know just how to handle this."

It did appear that Titan was right. The moment he leapt down to the ground the men were so startled they would have done better to simply run away. They scurried about madly, trying to hide any evidence of their crime. The man closest to the back of the truck seemed to think that the police had shown up as he was trying to shovel all of the guns out of sight. The one driving the forklift couldn't seem to figure out whether he should get off and run or make a getaway in the forklift. Titan would be lucky to break a sweat with the five of them together.

"It's him! It's that Titan guy!" exclaimed the punk who had been shoveling guns under the truck.

"That's right, boys. I'm Titan, and I think you all have some explaining to do." He stood surrounded, his staff in hand and ready.

"I bet first we find out just how tough you really are," said the punk riding the forklift. Evidently he had decided to stay and fight.

"Ooh, I'm really scared," said Titan. A coy grin spread over his face, and he crouched poised for battle.

The five men stood by at first as though contemplating what to do. They looked back and forth at each other, waiting for someone to move. Titan stood before them spinning his staff in his hands like a big propeller blade. He smiled full of confidence. Slowly, the men scooped up weapons that were the closest at hand. One of them had a knife; another had a crowbar he had been using on the crates. There was a moment when Titan wasn't sure if they were going to attack him or just prepared to defend themselves. At the end of that moment, four of the five took a run at him.

The only man who sat out was tall, thin and sported a purple mohawk and several piercings on his face. He stood trembling and crept back into the shadows. He watched in wide-eyed horror as Titan toyed with the other four. It was an unfair fight.

Titan was fast and agile; the four of them didn't stand a chance. At first Titan used his staff to simply deflect any attack the men made. Then he was on the offensive, and tossed the men about with ease. Titan's staff shot out a bolt of lightning that connected with the idling forklift and set it ablaze while he was attempting to shoot the blade from one of the men's hands. In short order Titan had all four subdued. He easily flipped all of them into the back of the empty truck, pulled down the door and locked it. Then, seeming to see through the dark, Titan turned and stared straight at the tall thin man with the purple mohawk. Titan, not even out of breath, turned and started walking toward him.

"You and I need to talk," Titan said to him, the glow of the forklift fire engulfing him in an eerie light.

The punk's mouth dropped a few inches lower. His eyes bugged wide. By the time he could have told his legs to move, Titan already had him. He closed his eyes, and his body went rigid as he braced himself for the beating he surely thought would follow, but none came. Titan quickly grabbed him by the waist band, and suddenly, there was no longer solid ground under his feet. The wind rushed past him ruffling his mohawk. When he finally dared to open his eyes his screams could be heard for miles, even from so far above the city.

Titan landed moments later on the roof of a nearby skyscraper. They were now sixty stories above the streets of Delta City. Titan dropped the man on the roof and stood looking down at him, contemplating. The punk scurried up to his knees and turned to face Titan. He had a dark wet spot on the front of his pants.

"P-please don't hurt me, man!" he pleaded.

"What's your name?" Titan asked ignoring his plea.

"Uh…ah…Benny…My name's B-Benny."

"Benny, I have some questions to ask. Do you think you can answer them honestly for me?" Titan asked.

"I don't know, man. I can barely remember my own name," Benny answered, his voice quivering.

"Well, let's just see if you can try for me, okay. Now first, Benny, are you working for Mr. Midnight?"

"Um, well I'm not supposed to say," Benny said. Then he caught Titan's scowl and thought better of it. "Yeah okay, yeah. We were workin' for him. But I don't know nothin' else, man, honest."

"Benny your boss is a bad guy," Titan said. "I am going to put an end to him. Before I can do that I need you to give me some answers."

"You don't understand, man, bad things happen to people who say anything about him to anyone. Please, I can't tell you anything, just let me go. Please! You don't know what will happen to me if I talk," Benny pleaded.

"But Benny, you don't know what will happen to you if you don't," said Titan.

Titan started to walk over to Benny to scare him into cooperating. He simply curled into a ball on the ground, whimpering. Titan reached down, picked him up by the shirt and carried him over to the building's ledge. He paused so Benny could look out and take in what was about to happen. Then he reached out and dangled him over the ledge, with Benny kicking and screaming with all his might. Titan then flipped him completely upside down, holding him firmly by the ankle. Benny now had a perfect view of the busy street below.

"Please, no, man! Put me down! I'm beggin' ya. Please!" Benny yelled, terrified.

Titan, what are you doing? You are not to put this man's life in actual danger.

"Don't worry, I know what I'm doing," Titan said.

It would appear you do not.

"What? Man, are you nuts? Who are you talkin' to?" Benny asked, no doubt thinking that Titan would kill him.

"I wasn't talking to you. Now I want to know what Mr. Midnight is up to," Titan said, loosening his grip ever so slightly as he said it.

Titan, I certainly do not approve of this course of action.

"It's fine. I know what I'm doing here, Azure," Titan responded.

"What? I sure hope you do," Benny said, sounding more confused by the second.

"Tell me, Benny. Tell me what I want to know, and be fast because you're getting mighty heavy here," said Titan.

"Okay, okay. What do you want to know?" Benny gave in much more quickly than Titan had expected.

"He has something big going on. I want to know everything about it. What it is, where it's happening, and who all's involved," Titan demanded.

"Motion inhibitors. It's all about the motion inhibitors," Benny said. The distant sound of the traffic below seemed to be getting ready to swallow him.

"Motion inhibitors? What are those?" Titan asked.

"Look, all I know is that he's found a way to freeze people. It's like a laser, and they get shot with one and they freeze people solid and they have no idea. They just wake up 'bout a half hour later totally clueless. Up till now they've all been small ones that fit in your hand. Those are really only good for one person at a time. But now he's got one massive one. It can freeze over half the city at once for at least half an hour. They say it will give him total control of the whole city," Benny said, tears streaming up his face.

"What?" Titan asked, stunned. "Where is it, and when does he plan on using it?" Titan yelled.

"He plans to do it tomorrow night in the factory he owns at Fifty First Avenue and King Street. That's all I know, I swear," Benny said, frantically gripping at Titan's outstretched arm.

"Thanks, Benny," Titan said, hardly relieved to hear the news. He turned, tossing Benny back to the ground. Benny landed on his face, but still seemed much happier than any of the thieves Titan had seen in a long time. "For a guy who didn't want to talk, you did pretty well."

Benny did not respond. He was far too busy kissing the rooftop after Titan had set him back down.

Your methods were quite unorthodox, and I am afraid I cannot condone them.

"What? No great job on getting the loser to talk?" Titan asked Azure.

You put a man's life in danger. I see there is much I need to discuss with you. I fear your training has gone off course. What you did was not exactly heroic.

"Oh come on, Azzy, I knew what I was doing back there. I was never gonna let him fall," said Titan.

That is not the point, Titan. I fear you have lost focus on your priorities. You have also been using the ring's power for your own personal gain. You seem to forget that we have also yet to speak of the incident at the basketball game. Did you think I was not aware or had forgotten? Also, my name is not Azzy.

"Look, that wasn't a big deal, Azure. I just needed a little energy boost, that's all. Can't I have any perks with having this power ring? Does everything I do have to be completely selfless?"

"Who are you talking to? Man, you're crazy," said Benny, bewildered and more frightened.

Yes, in fact it must be. It is part of the great price I told you would be involved with taking on the responsibility of Titan. I am afraid that you are veering off the path that every Titan must walk. I have seen it only a handful of times over the centuries. I will not have it happen again with you.

"Azure, come on. Look, I know maybe I shouldn't have used the ring's power at the game, but I just couldn't stand the thought of losing to Vince. Then of course we lost anyway, so hey, lesson learned right? As far as Benny here, I know it may have seemed excessive. But it got results, didn't it?" said Titan a little defensively.

Titan, I am putting you on an active performance warning. If I see one more false move from you abusing your powers I will have no choice but to strip you of them. Now, moving on, do you know where this warehouse is?

"Fine, have it your way. We'll do everything your way from now on. Yes, I know exactly where it is and I'll be there waiting." Titan said, defensively.

Very well, let us take Benny to the authorities, and we shall continue this conversation later.

Benny was rolling around on the rooftop laughing hysterically, and failed to notice Titan approach him. Benny's delight at being grounded was short lived, as Titan again grabbed him by the waistband and took to the sky.

A short while later, Chief Ross and Det. Langara exited the police station, and there on the middle of the sidewalk was a young man with a purple mohawk, all tied up with a note attached to him. Ross quickly went over, and all he heard from the man was barely audible mumbles about never wanting to fly again. He read the note quickly, and was quite surprised once he read what this guy had been up to.

"Sam, we need to get some men over to dock nineteen," said Chief Ross.

"What's at dock nineteen, Chief?" replied Frank.

"Well, according to this note there are four more men locked up with a bunch of stolen weapons."

"There's what? Who did this?"

"Well, this note is signed by Titan," Chief Ross answered showing Frank the signature at the bottom of the note.

The look of shock on Detective Langara's face was equal to the shock that Chief Ross was currently feeling. Both men couldn't help but look up into the sky as though they expected Titan to just fly past them at any moment.

Chapter 17: Ambushed

Titan watched cautiously from across the street, as Chief Ross found Benny nicely wrapped on the doorstep of police headquarters. He couldn't help but laugh, as another officer helped a very disoriented Benny to his feet and then handcuffed him. Before Benny could make it all the way inside, he bolted to the edge of the stairs where he released his dinner into the bushes. Titan turned to leave after he saw three squad cars pull out with sirens wailing, presumably headed for dock nineteen, where Benny's friends would be waiting.

"Well, we're right on the trail of Mr. Midnight, and I think we may be well on our way to winning over Delta City's finest. Not a bad night if I do say so myself," Titan boasted.

He was now bounding over rooftops, making his way back home. He felt weightless, as though he could jump over the moon. He had been trying to forget about Azure putting him on a warning. Otherwise he was feeling pleased and decided to take the long way back.

I am not sure that you should be so boastful just yet. It will serve you no good. You must never assume to know anything. Plus, you seem to forget, I am not entirely pleased with your performance this evening.

"Oh come on, Azure, are you still talking about the whole dangling Benny over the building thing? I seriously knew what I was doing. It worked didn't it?" said Titan.

So you have said. Nonetheless it was conduct unbecoming for you, Titan.

Titan leapt over east Second Avenue without even realizing it. He simply carried on as traffic roared up from below.

"Look, I get it. I shouldn't be dangling people from rooftops; even if they are lowlife scumbags. I'll tell you what? In the future I'll make sure to use it as a last resort, okay?" Titan said.

He landed on a high-rise apartment about a half mile away from his neighborhood. He paced briskly across the roof headed for the east side. It was his last stop on patrol, before carrying on to home. He kept one ear trained to the street below, the other to his conversation with Azure.

This is not something to be taken lightly, Titan. While it is important that we track down Mr. Midnight, it is also important that we do not cross a line that will leave outsiders to wonder which one of you is indeed the criminal here.

"You're right. I know you're right," Titan admitted begrudgingly. "It's just that..."

Titan watch...

Suddenly, just as he was approaching the building's edge, Titan was struck hard in the center of his back. It felt like a hard boot had hit him. The force of it sent him sprawling to the ground face first. As he tried to scramble to his feet he caught a glimpse of camouflage pants and army boots walking towards him.

Titan tried frantically to grasp his staff from his back, as he got to his feet. Before he could even get up he felt hands come crashing down on the base of his neck with tremendous force, sending him down on his stomach again. This time he rolled over onto his back, keeping his arm in front of his face to brace himself. As he looked up he saw the face of a woman staring back at him. This however was no ordinary woman. The moon reflected off the metal plate on one side of her face and a glaring red eye stared down at him.

Everything was happening so fast Titan could hardly defend himself. Her foot came down hard onto his stomach. His body arched sharply into V shape. It was all he could do to not yell out in pain. The power behind these blows was simply not normal. All the men he had fought against so far had hit him with less than half the force then she had.

As though she relished the sight of Titan in pain, she attempted to strike at him again. Before she could, Titan rolled away as fast as he could, barely avoiding the blow. He staggered to his feet and back-flipped clumsily into a standing position. Before he could regain stability, a series of blows exploded into his side. When he stuck out his arm to try and block them, the woman grabbed it, twisted it over and flung him over her shoulder and across the roof.

Titan crashed about thirty feet away with a thud. He quickly jumped to his feet, pulled out his staff, faced the woman and braced himself for another attack. Now she stood still and calm. She wasn't even out of breath, even though Titan was panting like a thirsty dog.

Titan something is wrong! This woman is not normal. I was not even able to detect her approaching. You must use extreme caution.

"You're telling me," Titan muttered between gasping breaths.

Kaizen then clenched her fists and started to run at Titan. Holding his staff, Titan charged her as well. He was ready for her this time, but it wasn't her that he needed to be ready for. Out of the corner of his eye, creeping out from the shadows he caught a glint of gold.

Titan get down now!

A flash of light erupted from the shadows and engulfed Titan. Suddenly it felt as though a vat of tar had been dumped over him. No matter how hard he tried, he could not make any words come out of his mouth. His arms and legs would move, but only with the greatest effort, and even then it felt like he was caught in super slow motion. For the time being it seemed that the blast had also managed silence Azure.

Now defenseless, the woman attacked again. She kicked Titan squarely in the chest. Despite the force of the attack his body remained firm and rigid, unable to move. Then she changed her tactics and started punching him in the stomach and chest. Blow after blow exploded across his body. Titan was finally knocked to his knees. He managed to raise his staff up with both arms in a mild attempt at defending himself.

"That is enough, Kaizen," came a voice from the shadows.

Then the figure steeped into the light, where Titan had seen the glint of gold. He wore a black suit and trench coat with a blood red tie, and a black fedora. His face was hidden by a mask of solid gold. In his right hand was a weapon Titan had briefly seen before, and he could only now assume was a motion inhibitor. He had been searching for Mr. Midnight, and now he had found him. The very sight of him sent a chill down his spine.

"I'm very sorry, Titan. My bodyguard Kaizen is highly effective, but sometimes she can become a little overzealous with her prey," Mr. Midnight said.

Kaizen was finally starting to relax and unclench her muscles. Her red mechanical eye glared so brightly it was almost blinding. Her gaze remained fixed on Titan as though she wished that he would break free of the motion inhibitor's hold, so he would be hers once again. Mr. Midnight stood in between Titan and Kaizen. Titan was not sure which one of them gave him more cause for fear.

"I am truly sorry that we must meet this way. I have found you most impressive I must say. Although, you do look much younger than I thought you would. I really had no idea how the inhibitor was going to work on you, or if it would work at all. Well, at least it rendered you immobile, so there's not much more I can ask for. You know, it has a much better impact on normal people. With them I simply could not be having a conversation, at least one they would remember. So it was a gamble. And since you dispatched poor Inferno so rapidly, I thought to myself, leave nothing to chance. Bring nothing but the best. Now you have seen that Kaizen truly is the best at what she does."

Mr. Midnight was pacing back and forth in front of Titan. He barely gave Titan a glance as he continued his speech. He spoke as though it were the most important speech he would ever make and no one present should forget a word of it. Titan could see his image of being stuck, helpless, reflected back in the gold from Mr. Midnight's mask. The mask gave him a soulless, inhuman look. His eyes were barely visible. There was no way of telling what kind of face was hiding under that mask. Kaizen's was equally inhuman as her red mechanical eye glared.

As Mr. Midnight spoke, Titan tried with all his might to force his body into motion, even to simply say something. But, every effort was futile. Turning his back to Titan, Mr. Midnight moved to the building ledge and looked out over the city.

"You see, I simply had to meet you. At first, when I saw your incredible powers, I had briefly hoped we could work together. Together, we could have done anything, conquered anything. But I quickly realized that you would deem us below you. I just cannot have that kind of power out there if it is not under my complete control. This is my city and I control everything in it. I can also not afford to have you running loose with so much at stake. You are far too much of a variable, a wild card if you will. I simply cannot have you ruining the plans I have worked so hard to achieve. I could no longer trust any subordinate to track you so Kaizen and I took care of finding you myself. As one who also likes to maintain a level of privacy shall we say I knew you would not be that hard to locate. So it is with great regret that I say that I will have to now destroy you," Mr. Midnight declared.

At this, Mr. Midnight turned and looked directly at Titan. Still leaning against the ledge, he opened his coat and brought out a square object with coiled wires all around it and an electric mechanism on top. He held the device out as though to show Titan. Mr. Midnight then raised his right arm and fired two more shots from the motion inhibitor at Titan. The shots came out like sonic wall that enveloped him. It felt like tidal waves were crashing down on him, and then it seemed like a giant weight was holding him in place.

"Although, I must admit I am quite disappointed. I thought you would put up much more of a fight than this. So sorry that you are getting such a raw deal here. I usually don't care to use such sneak attacks on my adversaries. Yet as I previously said, with you there are simply too many unknowns in the equation," said Mr. Midnight.

He walked over to Titan and placed the device right between his legs. As he lowered it, Titan saw the mechanism on top was a clock that read four minutes and fifty four seconds, and it was counting down. Even having never actually seen one in his life before, he knew it was a bomb. Mr. Midnight then continued walking past him, back into the shadows.

"Goodbye, Titan. It was nice meeting you. It is truly a shame that your powers must go to waste like this. Come, Kaizen," he said. Then Titan heard the stairwell door open.

Kaizen at last moved. As she walked past, she dealt another quick blow to Titan's ribs. If he could have, he would have winced with the pain it sent through his mid section. Then he could only hear the sounds of their footsteps as they descended the stairs, and finally the crash of the door closing behind them.

As soon as the door slammed shut, Titan began to tug with all his might to move and get to his feet. At first, he pushed and pulled to no avail. He couldn't even grunt or yell. Finally, after several agonizing moments, he was able to lower his arms down to waist height. He pulled his head down so hard he thought for a moment that it might rupture with the pressure. At last he was able to look down at the bomb resting under him. The clock at the top now read two minutes. With all that struggle he had lost nearly three minutes.

He focused all his thoughts on the bomb. He had no idea if this building was empty or not, or how powerful a bomb it was. For once, he wished to have Azure's guiding voice here. Ever since Mr. Midnight shot him with the inhibitor, Azure had fallen silent. It seemed that one of the effects the inhibitor had on his powers, besides immobility, was blocking Azure out of his mind.

The clock now read one minute. Part of him thought, the only thing to do was brace himself the best he could for the blast, and hope that with his powers he would be able withstand it. Yet the way his night had suddenly turned, he no longer liked his odds. He would have to get out of here. He also knew it would take all he had to counter the effects of the inhibitor.

He strained and pulled at every muscle and tendon in his whole body. Just when he thought all his energy was spent, he managed to move his arm in with his staff pointed down. He quickly glanced at the timer. Seventeen seconds. He got the butt of his staff right onto the rooftop, and then he managed to pull his legs into a lifting position. Six seconds. He felt entirely spent with only two seconds remaining. With the last of his energy, he fired a blast from his staff at maximum power. It lifted him off the ground in his frozen state and up into the air just as the timer went to zero.

The blast from his staff sent Titan about fifteen feet further into the air when the bomb went off. As he felt the searing heat of the flames, a cushion of hot air pushed him further from the full blast of the bomb. Titan flew high above the building, still holding his frozen pose in place. He flipped several times through the air, and started coming down just past the edge of the building into the back alley. On his way down, the last of the flames from the blast licked out and grabbed at him as he dropped past. The blast had blown most of the roof away. Titan finally came down onto the top of a closed dumpster, with a thunderous crash. He bounced off the dumpster, and was knocked into the windshield of a parked car, and then rolled off into a thick slimy puddle in the middle of the alley.

"OW!" Titan hollered.

Finally seeming to be loosened from his frozen state, Titan rolled around in real agony, grabbing at his side which had hit the dumpster. He could move again, but was still sluggish. As he continued to move and stretch, his arms and legs slowly regained full mobility. It was the first time he had felt any kind of pain as Titan. It was now that he started thinking that he was wise not to test his durability against the bomb.

Titan are you alright? I am not quite sure what happened there.

Azure's voice came as a welcomed relief. It was faint and distant at first, but got stronger as Azure kept talking. Soon it felt like Azure was once again standing right beside him.

"I think I'll live, but that really sucked," said Titan.

I had a sense of danger, and then was suddenly blocked from you entirely. I could see, hear or feel nothing of you.

"It was Mr. Midnight and his bodyguard Kaizen. They shot me with one of his motion inhibitors," said Titan through deep careful breaths.

I see. Well that would explain some things. What else happened?

"I was jumped by Kaizen, and you're right, she is definitely a little above normal human levels. Before I could even get ready to defend myself, from out of the shadows Mr. Midnight shot me with the inhibitor. I couldn't move, talk, or do anything. Suddenly you weren't around anymore either. He just made this whole crazy speech, which I was barely paying attention to. Then he shot me with two more rounds of the inhibitor, and placed this bomb right under me. I was just able to launch myself out of there with my staff before it went off. As soon as I crash landed here, I could move again and you were back," explained Titan.

Did he seem to know about any of the information that we had learned about him?

"Actually no. He didn't seem to know anything about our man Benny, and what he told us. He just went on about how I was disappointing, and how he was there to destroy me." Titan was now back on his feet and feeling every bump and bruise that Mr. Midnight and Kaizen had given him. He felt like he had been to his first football practice and forgotten his pads. "So he still doesn't know that we know about his plans tomorrow night."

Well, at least that is one good thing that has come of this. Plus now, with any luck, he will think you have died as well.

"Funny, I do feel kinda dead right now. Hopefully I'm feeling a hundred percent by tomorrow night. I have a feeling I'm gonna need all my strength," said Titan, vigorously rubbing his side.

He made an easy jump up to the building across from the bomb blast. It was several stories taller, so he was able to get a good look at the damage. Down on the street in front, three ambulances, two fire trucks, and several police cars were already setting up. From what he could see it seemed as though no one was being put into an ambulance, but he couldn't be sure. He thought he was lucky to not have been spotted. The entire middle of the roof was blown away. A giant black hole was all the bomb left in its wake. Big chunks of charred wood and cement block were everywhere.

I hope that you are ready for tomorrow night. Because, it seems as though this Mr. Midnight may be an even more troublesome adversary than originally thought.

"Oh, he's trouble alright, big trouble. And I need to put a stop to him now. He seems to care less and less for the innocent lives he puts at risk. How long before someone I know gets hurt or killed by this lunatic? Now that he has the inhibitor it seems that it will be much sooner than later. I'm going to put a stop to him, even if it kills me," said Titan.

I could not agree more. It is more important than ever to stop him. But now, what you need is rest. The ring should take care of you as it has done for all its hosts. I trust tomorrow you will feel like new. Then we will again worry about Mr. Midnight.

"Yeah, I agree with you. Let's go home," Titan replied.

With slow easy jumps, Titan made his way back, not to Carly's, but to his own home. He landed softly in the alley behind the house, and no one seemed to notice. It would make his job with Mr. Midnight that much harder if he felt like he had just been run over by a bulldozer. These were the worst injuries he had yet sustained as Titan, and he was about to put the healing properties of the ring to the test. After changing back, he quietly crept into the house and was fast asleep before he knew what hit him.

Chapter 18: The Midnight Hour

"He's got a what?" Carly asked when Michael was finished telling her about his encounter with the motion inhibitor.

"A motion inhibitor," Michael said, kicking a pebble at the bottom step where Carly's foot rested. They were sitting on the front steps of Carly's building enjoying the sunshine.

"Well, you have to stop him," she said.

"Oh, I plan to." He gave the pebble one final kick that sent it shooting across the street.

Michael had been very worried about how Carly would take the news about his encounter with Mr. Midnight, Kaizen, and the bomb. As he had recounted his story to her she simply sat very quiet, her eyes growing narrower in concentration as the tale unfolded. By the time he was done, his brush with death seemed to hardly faze her. He had been especially worried about how she might take the bomb episode with Mr. Midnight and Kaizen. Of course, it had helped a great deal that he now felt better than ever after almost getting blown to pieces last night. As he had stumbled home he had felt like he had been hit by a truck. His muscles had ached all over. Before he went to sleep he had been a little worried, but he had kept the ring on and he had awoken feeling completely refreshed. Michael had in fact not taken the ring off since it had fallen into the hands of Vince. Michael wasn't sure quite how, but he knew that the ring was responsible for his current healthy condition. It seemed to have fully rejuvenated him overnight. Carly had remained silent for sometime after. He was beginning to get a little worried until she finally spoke.

"Do you know where he plans to use this thing?"

"Yeah, you know that old empty warehouse on King Street, the one you're always saying that the city should have torn down?"

"Yes. You mean that old broken down place up town?"

"That's the one all right."

"It's been empty for years," stated Carly.

"Well, it seems not so much recently."

"Are you sure that Benny was telling you the truth? I mean, he did sound pretty scared of betraying Mr. Midnight!" Carly asked.

"Well, I think I was able to convince him that it was me he should be worried about, but I know what you mean and it did cross my mind," Michael said.

"Do you even know what time all this is supposed to go down?" Carly asked.

"All he said was it would be tonight."

"I really think you should learn to ask more questions. You know little things like what time is this happening. At least you found out where this is happening, I guess. So, what's your plan?" Carly asked. Michael simply stared at her speechless. "Michael, please tell me you have some kind of plan to deal with all of this. I mean, I don't think it's wise to just show up on a whim and try and bring down Mr. Midnight and all his crew, especially considering the kind of weapon that he has. You almost got yourself blown up because of it last night."

"I don't know. I haven't really thought about it. I was just gonna show up and stake it out," Michael said.

"Well, I think that you need to get a plan. You know what's happening and where. You have the upper hand here. I say you exploit it for all it's worth," she said flatly. "You should go to this place plenty early and check it out. There will probably be some sort of guard on duty keeping watch most of the day. Go there, Michael, get to know your surroundings, see if there's anything you can use to your advantage." She got up from the steps, walked over to him, and touched the side of his head making him look her in the eyes. "Michael this is huge. You have the power tonight to save the city and bring down Mr. Midnight at the same time. You Michael, a simple kid from the east side, can actually do this. I know you can."

Michael was a little shocked by her words, and then he felt overjoyed in finally seeming to see her come around. Carly was finally expressing her confidence in his abilities, and was now actually encouraging him to go after Mr. Midnight. Then he noticed the slight tremor in her hand as she touched his face, and saw the worried look in her eye.

"You're still worried, aren't you?" Michael asked, taking her quivering hand in his.

"Yes, of course I am. I know you have to do this, but that doesn't mean I'm going to just stop being worried about you. This is going to be incredibly dangerous, but I know you can do it."

"Thanks." Michael wrapped his arms around her waist and drew her in tight. She rested her head on his chest. Neither spoke or moved for several minutes.

"Just try to listen to Azure tonight, maybe if you do he'll end your probation or whatever it is," she said finally.

"Yeah, I guess I'll have to listen to him good, and fly straight for now," Michael replied sheepishly.

"Uh oh, here comes Perminder," Carly said, looking over Michael's shoulder. "Look you can't afford to get sidetracked. Why don't you get going? I'll explain it to Perminder, and find some excuse for why you had to take off."

"I can't just leave. Besides, he already saw me," Michael said. "He doesn't look too happy actually."

"Michael you don't have time for these kinds of distractions. Especially on a day like today," Carly said, grabbing his arm and trying to lead him the other way.

"He's one of my best friends. I can't just run off when I see him coming. I have to at least say hi. Don't worry, it's still early."

"Hey Mike," Perminder hollered as he approached.

"See I told you he saw me. I'll just think of an excuse," Michael whispered.

"Where have you been lately, man?" asked Perminder.

"I'm really sorry. I've just been super busy," Michael replied.

"Yeah something's always coming up with you these days. This is the first I've seen of you since the basketball game. Ever since graduation you've hardly been around to hang with Dave and me. You're just gonna leave your old pals in the dust?"

"What? no way. I'm sorry, Perminder. I know I've been busy, but I promise after today I will totally make it up to you guys. We will have lots of time to all hang out over the summer."

"Why not today? You wanna catch a movie with us?" Michael's silence was answer enough. "You know, you're my best friend, and I want to keep it that way. I don't want us to start to lose touch once we hit high school. I never thought it possible, but it seems like we're all starting to drift apart. I don't want to just pass you in the street three years from now with just a wave or nod. I want us all to still be hanging out together," Perminder stated.

Michael saw that he had been so focused on his role as Titan that he had forgotten about just being Michael Novak. This was exactly why his friends, like Perminder, were so important. They kept him grounded in the real world and now he needed them more than ever.

"We can't," Carly said before Michael could respond, "Sorry, but we can't. Well, I mean he can't today 'cause he's busy. Michael promised to go to lunch with me. So he can't. I'm his girlfriend so how do think I feel. I want to spend time with him too you know," Carly said, sounding convincing enough.

"Oh come on. It's only eleven o'clock. It's too early for lunch. We can just go shoot some hoops at the school. Come on, man," Perminder pleaded.

"No. We have to go now. Michael is taking me to this new place uptown. It gets really busy so we have to go early to get a table," Carly added.

"Sorry, Perminder, but tomorrow I'll be around. I promise."

"Yeah, yeah. I'll believe it when I see it," Perminder replied.

"No, seriously. The three of us should hit the beach or something. I don't even work tomorrow. I hear what you're saying about not being friends anymore, and that is not going to be us. This is just a very busy time right now. The last thing either of us wants for us all to start drifting apart. I won't let that happen, really," Michael said.

"Okay, I'll see you later then."

Michael watched as Perminder turned up the street towards Dave's house. He felt bad, but knew he would have plenty of time to make amends. Then he and Carly turned, darted around the corner, and headed towards uptown.

"Man, poor Perminder," Michael said.

"I know. I feel bad too, but you don't have time..."

"For distractions. I know, I know," Michael finished.

"Michael, be serious. It was nothing, just a little white lie. I just had to get you out of there. Now you have to get uptown and figure this out," Carly said.

"Hey, thank you," Michael said. They both stopped before the next street corner.

"Now get out of here and go save the city," Carly said, breaking into a proud smile.

Michael smiled back and took her hand. He brought her in and kissed her softly on the lips. He savored the soft moist feel of her lips on his, and knew it was something he would never forget. Michael scanned every inch of her delicate palm with his fingertips, until he let go of her hand completely. He walked toward the street corner, staring at her, and etching the sight of her into his mind. Then he crossed the street and went towards the old warehouse, the mass inhibitor, and Mr. Midnight.

With his hands jammed deep into the pockets of his jeans, and his head hung low in deep thought; Michael turned and made his way uptown. He felt completely alone now. The fate of the city was resting on his shoulders and he felt the weight of it bearing down on him.

Michael arrived at the old warehouse several hours before sunset. Feeling quite nervous and uncertain, he found himself detouring slightly, taking his time getting there. His stomach was tied up in knots. He had already faced Mr. Midnight, but it could hardly have been thought of as having gone well. As he saw the faces of hundreds of people he passed on the street, it reminded him he needed to overcome his fears and reservations quickly before Mr. Midnight could do any more damage to the city.

Michael stood on the other side of the street staring at the old warehouse. It was a massive square brick building that took up an entire city block. Rows of windows lined the entire building. Many had long ago been broken or cracked from kids throwing rocks through them. Michael could remember his grandfather telling him that the warehouse had once been used as an auto parts shipping center. When it had gone under, before Michael had been born, it had left a lot of people from his neighborhood unemployed.

Michael staked out the warehouse for about an hour, and saw practically no activity. From the opposite side of the street he paced back and forth around the outside of the building looking for any signs of life or any activity that was supposed to take place. He was starting to wonder if Benny had indeed lied to him about the warehouse. Then he spotted someone he knew all too well walk down the side of the warehouse. This person stopped a couple of times to peek inside the dirty old windows before darting quickly down the alley that ran the length of the warehouse itself. Michael watched and waited about a minute to see if anyone would follow him. Michael waited a minute, when it appeared that he was indeed alone; he crossed the street and followed Vince down the alleyway.

As Michael approached the mouth of the alley all he could think about was how he had been right about his brother all along. No matter what, if Vince was snooping around here that could only mean that he was up to no good. This was all the confirmation that Michael looking for, and hoping he would never get.

As he entered the alley he was just able to find Vince as he turned down the corner out of sight. The alley was an L shape that was clearly designed around the warehouse and its shipping needs that had long since been forgotten. Michael paused as a plan formulated in his mind. Then, as he looked down at the ring, the perfect plan came to him. He held the ring up over his head and said the magic words.

"Exaudio Fortis!"

Titan, are we ready for Mr. Midnight so soon?

"Sorry, Azure, but I just need to get rid of a pest so he doesn't interfere with our plan for tonight," Titan said, as the smoke cleared around him. Azure made no reply.

He was unable to stop himself from smiling as he pulled his staff out and prepared to leap into action. Summoning the power from his staff, lightning sizzled and cracked around the head of the staff. He then leaped easily over the corner of the warehouse hoping to catch Vince completely unaware. This was no longer a simple rivalry between brothers. Vince was now playing on Titan's turf with Titan's rules, and he was about to get a very serious lesson.

Titan landed in the middle of the alley with great force, kicking up clouds of dust and litter. Vince froze in front of a bank of bay doors at the sight of Titan. His eyes widened and his whole body trembled with fear. Titan landed right in front of him with his arms spread high and wide, and his belt and the ends of his bandana flapping wildly about. Bright lightning shot all around Titan as he approached. When Vince finally did move he simply fell right over onto his backside.

"Vincent Novak, I have been looking for you," Titan declared.

"Wha...Wha...what?" stammered Vince. He stared wide-eyed at Titan.

"What are you doing here?" shouted Titan, as small bolts of lightning went off all around.

"I was just having a look around, honest," squealed Vince.

"Were you coming to check things out for Mr. Midnight?" Titan asked.

"I...I was just looking, they just asked me to look," said Vince, gasping and barely able to get out the words. It sounded as though he was near tears.

Titan had heard more than enough. He had wanted nothing more than to finally teach Vince a lesson, but now, seeing him helpless and pathetic, he just wanted to get Vince away from there as fast as possible. Hopefully, if he was convincing enough, it would be the last time he would find his brother in a situation like this one.

"Stay quiet and listen!" shouted Titan. He then shot a quick lightning blast into the wall behind Vince that sent out a dust cloud of broken concrete and brick. "This is your one chance, Vincent Novak. I know what you have been up to, and I am not happy. You are to get far away from here, run home to your grandfather right now. And know this, if I ever catch you running with criminals again I am not going to be so forgiving. Now go!"

Titan then shot two more quick lightning blasts into the wall behind Vince. Vince scrambled, trying to crawl away as bits of brick rained over him. Titan then shot off a massive blast of lightning straight into the air. Vince let out a high pitched scream, and scrambled to his feet. He fell twice as he fled down the alley. As Vince hit the street and vanished from view Titan could still hear his panicked screams drifting farther and farther away.

Titan then leapt to another deserted alley one block away. He hoped that his encounter with Vince had not drawn any more attention to the alley. He now needed to transform back so he could continue his surveillance.

Was that supposed to be funny?

"No it wasn't. I'm sorry, Azure, but that was my brother. I just can't have him around later if I'm to deal with Mr. Midnight. I had to scare him off," Titan responded.

Your brother is a criminal?

"Well, it certainly looks that way."

All criminals must be dealt with no matter our relationship to them. You must put feelings aside.

"I know. I also know Vince. He's nothing more than a two bit thug. He is also my brother, and I can't have him around and deal with Mr. Midnight at the same time. Vince will get what's coming to him in time if he doesn't straighten out, I promise you that."

That is likely a wise decision then. Mr. Midnight and his plans must remain our priority. Good work.

"Thanks. Okay, I'm going to go and transform so I can keep an eye on things. I'll talk to you again when something happens."

Very well.

After he transformed, Michael quickly made it back to the spot where he had originally spotted Vince. He was relieved to find that everything was much as it had been when he had left. He couldn't stop smiling. Scaring Vince had been quite simply the most fun he had had as Titan so far.

Finally the sun began its descent, ducking behind the skyline of Delta City. Michael had been pacing up and down the street opposite the warehouse for some time. He tried to run several plans through his head as he did so. Nothing seemed to come together. He had been pacing for over two hours when he looked up and saw Carly standing in front of him.

"What are you doing here?" asked Michael.

"As soon as you left, I started to think about what you're about to do. How huge all this is, and I just wanted to help," said Carly with conviction.

"What? No way. It's way too dangerous. I'm the one with superpowers, not you," Michael said flatly.

"Look, I can't just sit by while you put your life on the line. I'll just lend a hand from the sidelines, but I am here to help. I am not going home to just sit by and wait for it to all be over. I'm not just some faint hearted cheerleader," Carly said, making it clear to Michael that it was not up for discussion.

"If I let you help, you'll have to stay well out of harm's way. Plus you have to promise me you'll use your cell to call your parents and let them know your okay," said Michael. Carly nodded in agreement.

They ducked into a small diner across the street from the warehouse. They took a booth next to a window so they could keep an eye on the warehouse activity. The waitress came and they ordered a piece of apple pie to share, and furiously went to work on a plan.

"Okay, now if they plan on bringing this thing into that warehouse, it'll probably be from back here," Carly said, pointing to a spot on a blueprint she had just pulled from her purse and uncurled it along the tabletop.

"Where did you get that?" asked Michael, bewildered.

"I stopped at city hall on my way down. You can get all kinds of things like this there. Did you know that?" she continued without hesitation, pointing at the blueprint. "It seems that power and heat were turned on just last week in the name of some company called BDC Inc."

"That's one of the company names Vicki said was linked to Midnight."

"Well, at least we know we're on the right track then. Now also, there seem to be some skylights along the roof that I think will work great for you to observe activity and make your big move."

"You are amazing," Michael said, as he slumped back into the booth and laughed heartily. Carly simply smiled bashfully in reply.

"Thanks. You're pretty super yourself," she replied.

"By the way, something kind of big went down just before you got here. Vince showed up at the warehouse by himself. Then he ducked down the alley over there," said Michael, pointing to the mouth of the alleyway.

"What? I can't believe that you're just telling me now. So, what did you do?" she asked.

"Well, let's just say that thanks to Titan giving him the scare of a lifetime, I think we are going to see a much nicer Vince for the next little while," Michael said, grinning.

"Oh, I would have given anything to be there just to see the look on his face!" Carly said. She was leaning in low over the table gripping either end with both hands.

"One of the highlights of my life so far, I gotta say."

"Are you sure though that he was all alone? That no one else saw anything?" Carly asked.

"I was worried about that too. Don't worry, he was *definitely* alone."

"Michael," said Carly, as she reached out and grabbed his hand. "I am sorry though, that your brother seems to be involved in all this."

"Hey, at least now I know what Vince has been up to. I mean, I may not know for sure if he was at that bank robbery, but at least I know that he has been up to no good. I just hope he smartens up. If he ever gets hurt or arrested Grandpa Dale will be devastated. So, hopefully Titan was able to scare him straight."

"Then I'm glad you were able to get to him first."

The sun had set, and the sidewalks outside had become virtually vacant since they had entered the diner. Finally as the evening sun began to fade into night, Michael stood to leave.

"Well, I guess it's time."

"Just stay focused, Michael, and you'll do fine. Don't worry about me," Carly said, rising with him.

"Just promise me that if things get out of hand you'll go straight to the police."

"I promise. Now, go knock 'em dead, tiger."

Michael pulled her in and kissed her, once again taking in the sweetness of her lips on his.

"Here goes nothing," he said as he began to make his way to the exit.

Michael quickly ducked into the alley behind the diner. He quickly called his grandpa from his cell to say that he would be staying over at Perminder's place. He hated to lie again, but knew the truth would be far scarier to Grandpa Dale. He then took a quick glance to make sure no one was around. Then he held his fist up overhead so the ring faced the sky.

"Exaudio Fortis!"

Before the smoke and lightning had fully cleared he was leaping to the rooftop of the closest building facing the warehouse. He prowled along its edge as he tried to scan the length of the warehouse.

Carly was right. Through the windows he saw a big bald nasty looking guy with a flashlight that seemed to be making the rounds on both floors. Titan watched as the flashlight beam made its way around the building. Other than that, the building still appeared to be deserted. He saw absolutely no sign yet of Kaizen or Mr. Midnight, and that was just fine by Titan. At least he knew that he would have no problem taking out big bald and nasty over there.

We need to get over to that warehouse to locate and destroy this motion inhibitor.

"That may be easier said than done. From the looks of things, I don't even think that it's over there yet."

That is fine. It is just as well if we are to arrive early. We must move to the roof of that warehouse for a closer inspection.

"Fine, but if our cover gets blown because you're the one being too eager, then this time I get to say I told you so," Titan said.

Titan leapt across, keeping low, and began to survey the rooftop area. He moved quickly over to one of the big raised skylights, which was right where Carly said they would be. He peered in.

Through the dirt and grime that clung to the window he could see that the warehouse had a huge open area in the middle, with a large assortment of boxes and crates stacked neatly around the perimeter. The stacked rows faded into vast columns of crates that filled much of the huge warehouse space. Titan thought none of the crates could be the inhibitor. He doubted they would leave something so valuable with only one man to guard it. Circling the outside walls of the main shipping area were the two floors of rooms and offices that the guard was checking in on. The far wall that lead into the alley had several large bay doors for deliveries, and it was there Titan was willing to bet that the inhibitor was going to arrive.

"Well it looks like Mr. Midnight and his inhibitor have yet to arrive to this little party," Titan said to Azure.

Yes, it would appear so. I think it would be best to stay up here to monitor the situation.

It felt to Titan that hours had passed as he watched the back of the warehouse, occasionally peeking through the skylights. Every once in a while he would venture over to the other side of the warehouse. From there he could see Carly huddled in front of the now closed diner. He wished he could have talked her out of this, but to do that he would have had to have left with her, and that he could not do, not on this night. Very little activity had occurred inside the building so far. Another two men showed up to help baldy with the watch duties, but that was about all. From one of the clocks on the inside warehouse walls, Titan saw that the time had crept all the way up to twenty to twelve.

Suddenly, Titan could hear the approach of vehicles moving in from the alley. He quickly ran to the back, keeping out of sight. He looked down, and saw two large black SUV's roll up with a long black limousine following. Titan could only assume that this was Mr. Midnight making his arrival. Then it hit him. How poetic! Mr. Midnight planned to launch his attack on the city at midnight. Of course, he didn't know why Carly, Azure and he hadn't thought of it earlier. About a dozen men got out of the lead vehicles. They all looked around, cautiously scanning the area. Then one of them went over and opened the back door of the limo.

The first person to get out was Kaizen. Her red mechanical eye scanned the area to make sure it was safe. Seeing her instantly brought back memories of their encounter the night before. She took a look around before gesturing back towards the limo, and then Mr. Midnight got out. He stood silently sizing up his surroundings before he went towards the warehouse. It struck Titan again that this man who lived almost solely as an urban legend now stood down below him, very much real.

Once Mr. Midnight stepped out of the car, there was a lot of gesturing and barking of orders. Titan could make out none of it from the rooftop, but the men were all busy running around making sure everything was ready. Mr. Midnight and Kaizen stood off to one side, overseeing everything. The center loading bay door was opened. The men took up strategic positions along the alleyway and warehouse entrance. It looked as though no security measure had been overlooked.

Mr. Midnight would say something to Kaizen and then she would bark the orders to everyone else. From Titan's count there were now two dozen men plus Mr. Midnight and Kaizen present.

Then, with a loud rumble, a large tractor trailer came rolling down the alley. This arrival seemed to have the men more on edge than when Mr. Midnight emerged. The truck backed carefully into the open loading dock. Once the truck was docked several men made sure it was secured by chalking its wheels and checking the truck itself. Then they all quickly made their way inside with Mr. Midnight leading the way.

"Wow, this is huge. Midnight has spared no expense," Titan said.

I agree. We could not have caught up to him at a more opportune time.

Titan looked back in through the skylight. There was a flurry of activity going on inside the warehouse. At the open loading dock, a group of men were unloading the truck's trailer. In another corner of the warehouse a cluster of men were assembling a large glass structure, which resembled a greenhouse, in the middle of the shipping floor. The glass had an odd green tint to it, and the reflective shine coming off of it looked like nothing Titan had ever quite seen before.

"So, when do you think I should jump in and take this whole thing down?" Titan asked Azure.

Not just yet. They are not quite ready.

"We don't want them to be ready though," Titan said, frustrated.

We will wait until the inhibitor is out and on the floor. Are you prepared for this, Titan? There are twenty-six people down there. You will have the element of surprise, but that will wear off quickly. Have you noticed the glass like structure they are erecting?

"Yeah, I figure they're going to all go in there to protect themselves from the inhibitor's effects," Titan said.

I believe so as well. We should wait until just before they are ready to put their plan into full effect. Wait until they are all inside. Then, they will be caught completely off guard.

"Okay, sounds about right to me. Just say the word, and I'm down there," Titan said.

Titan continued to watch Mr. Midnight's men set up through the skylight, waiting to strike. A group of men had now gotten hold of a large

225

crate, which Titan could only assume could be the motion inhibitor. It was brought by forklift into the middle of the warehouse floor. The protective greenhouse was now practically finished as well. Three men with crowbars began carefully taking the crate apart. Within minutes, the inhibitor was fully exposed. It was quite wide and stood about four feet high. Its face looked like an old computer, full of dials and meters and lights. At the top was an opening, like a funnel that Titan assumed would be where the inhibitor's rays would shoot out.

After the motion inhibitor was ready, everyone started to get into the glass shelter. They filed in neatly, two by two, with Mr. Midnight and Kaizen standing outside by the door. One man was over by the inhibitor turning dials and pushing buttons. Once the men were inside, Kaizen filed in with Mr. Midnight waiting by the door for the last man to enter. Titan noticed Mr. Midnight now held a small remote in his hand.

Now, Titan, strike now!

Needing no more motivation, Titan leapt a few feet into the air above the skylight and dove through it with a splintering crash. At first he was aware only of falling, and the tinkling of falling glass all around him. As he was falling, Titan could see everyone below look up in surprise. They started trying frantically to get back out of the glass shelter as he stood in the centre of the warehouse shaking off bits of glass. As Titan landed crouched down between the shelter and the inhibitor, the men had already begun to circle around him before he had even stood and pulled out his staff.

"Sorry guys, mind if I crash your little party?" Titan quipped.

Mr. Midnight's men descended on him in a swarm. He was poised and ready, and he attacked with agility and precision. Flurries of punches, fast kicks and blows from his staff sent Mr. Midnight's men sprawling across the warehouse floor. They attacked from behind and on all sides, yet he brushed them aside like flies. Oddly as Titan fought his men, Mr. Midnight stood back out of sight, and remained calm as though he still believed nothing could stop him. This show of optimism only further fueled Titan's resolve.

Although Titan, surprisingly, saw no guns that could be used against him. Several men did come at him with whatever weapons they could find. These were becoming commonplace for Titan already, and they did not slow him as he continued to fight off the attacking swarm. Titan could see Kaizen nowhere. He remembered his last encounter with her all too well and was alert for an attack from her above all, even against all two dozen men.

Titan left a trail of fallen men behind him and finally found himself face to face with Kaizen once more. The sight of her metal plated face and glowing red eye made him pause; he never got a good look at her the night before. Even when he was frozen, her face was hidden mostly by shadows. Titan's hesitation was more than Kaizen would need. With a swift roundhouse kick to the chest, Titan was sent backwards, his staff flying off in another direction. He landed hard on his back, slightly winded. Just as he went to sit up, she leapt onto his chest and began to pummel him. Her clenched fists were like pistons, delivering blow after blow to his head and upper body. Before he could reach up and grab her arms to stop her, she leaned far back while having a hold of his shoulders and sent him flying up over her head. He landed on his stomach this time. He turned over fast, but she was much faster than any opponent he had faced. Before he could get his bearings and defend himself, she was on him again.

Mr. Midnight seemed to be enjoying the show that Kaizen was putting on. He had stepped closer into the light to get a better look. Many of his men had regrouped and were looking on as though they wanted to jump in and get a piece of Titan for themselves. Mr. Midnight raised his hands and waved them all off. It seemed Kaizen would get Titan all to herself. At last lying breathless and beaten face down on the ground, Kaizen came from behind him, put him in a full nelson and pulled him to his feet to face Mr. Midnight.

"You had more than one warning to stay out of my affairs and yet you persisted. This tells me you are either over confident or ignorant. Either way, you are doomed," Mr. Midnight said. He had pulled out one of the motion inhibitor pistols and held it at Titan; Titan could only wonder if it was the same one he had used the night before. "Now you will sit here and watch helpless as my men and I take this city from right under your nose."

227

"You're mad if you think that you can get away with this," Titan said, trying to stall. He struggled very little in Kaizen's grasp. He let his body go loose.

"Well, you will get to see exactly what I am able to get away with, as you put it," Mr. Midnight said, as he flipped a clasp of some sort on the inhibitor with his thumb and prepared to fire at Titan.

As Mr. Midnight clicked the handheld inhibitor with his thumb, Titan took this as his moment to act. Just as Mr. Midnight fired, Titan pulled down and bent over with all his strength. The result was Kaizen being sent flying forward over Titan's back. She was in the spot Titan should have been when Mr. Midnight fired the inhibitor. The blast hit Kaizen square in the back. Titan could feel her body tighten and grow rigid. When he looked up he saw her fall; her form became frozen even before she landed on the ground, as though she were a statue.

As Kaizen hit the ground Titan went as fast as he could to his staff. It lay ten feet away and Titan dove for it, scooping it up in a mid barrel roll. As soon as he clutched it in his hands, he fired a blast of lightning that hit Mr. Midnight's hand that held the inhibitor. Mr. Midnight dropped to his knees, bellowing in agony. All the other men seemed too shocked to move from the scene they had just witnessed, as though they had been shot with an inhibitor themselves.

"Get him! Kill him! I want his head!" Mr. Midnight hollered at his men while pointing his good hand at Titan.

Just then the power went out. The only light that remained in the warehouse came from the face of the motion inhibitor, and the moonlight that came through the windows. The building blueprint wasn't the only information Carly had gotten from city hall. She now sat huddled by the transformer that she had just disabled, cutting the building's power. Now she would wait. She had her cell phone out, ready to dial the police.

Nervous tremors spread through her arms. Her hands trembled terribly as they tried to clasp the blueprints and her cell phone simultaneously. She had been waiting; sitting huddled in the alley at the back corner of the warehouse. Periodically she would peer in, looking through one of the crud covered windows, to try and look for Titan. There had been very little activity outside for some time. Occasionally a man would walk around the warehouse, checking that all was clear. All

Carly had to do was hide in the shadows until he left again. Then, just when it seemed nothing would happen, the sounds of glass shattering and fighting broke out in the warehouse. Wasting no time, Carly had pulled out the blueprint and had gone to work on the building's power. She had managed the job faster than she had thought she would. Then, trying to see how Titan was doing, Carly tiptoed up to the nearest window and tried to look in.

"Hey! What do you think you're doin'?" said the guard who had been watching the outside of the building. He clasped a firm hand on her shoulder.

Without hesitating, Carly whirled around and slammed her knee into the guard's stomach as hard as she could. He doubled over, gasping for breath. She turned and ran along the back of the warehouse. As she ran, she looked down and realized that she had dropped her cell phone during the struggle. She glanced back over her shoulder and saw it lying on the ground right in front of the wounded guard. However, only a second later she would hear the roar of the guard as he began to follow.

Back inside, Titan flipped backwards through the air and landed in an open area on the warehouse floor. Mr. Midnight's men stumbled about, and eventually started closing in all around him. Titan fought the henchmen easily but now, in the dark, it was even easier. The men were tripping and falling all over themselves.

Titan saw Mr. Midnight head over to the motion inhibitor, his wounded hand clutched tightly to his stomach. His shadow was easy to spot. Once there, he began to madly fumble with the machine's dials and buttons. The inhibitor seemed to spring to life, lights came on and meters suddenly came alive.

With his attention still diverted, Titan blocked two kicks from two henchmen, easily batting them away. Without turning he then shot his left leg out backwards, catching an attacker in the hip, sending him spinning off to the side.

Mr. Midnight quickly pulled the remote out from his jacket pocket with his uninjured hand. A faint blue light emerged from the funnel at the top of the inhibitor.

Using his staff, Titan jabbed a henchman in the stomach and then flipped him up into the air. The man was sent crashing into several others, sending them toppling like bowling pins. Titan turned quickly to locate Mr. Midnight.

Outside, Carly sat huddled in the shadows behind an old dumpster. The guard had proven to be a little quicker on his feet than he appeared. Thankfully, a row of three dumpsters had been close at hand. She quickly ducked behind one before the guard spotted her. There she knelt, not making a sound. Peeking carefully between two of the dumpsters she could now see the large shadow of the guard move up the alley toward her. He was moving slowly, scanning the area for her. Carly pulled herself tighter into a ball behind the dumpster as the guard stood just on the other side. If she did not do something quickly it would only be a matter of time before he caught up to her.

Suddenly, leaning up against the side of the dumpster next to her, Carly spotted a long metal pipe. Quietly, she reached out toward it. The guard was moving slowly, like a cat hunting a little mouse. Every drop of water, every footfall echoed through the alley. Carly slowly extended her arm toward the pipe, trying not to make any noise. At last she grabbed it, and pulled it in silently. The guard was now about ten feet away on the far side of the dumpster and moving up the alley. She quietly got up, moved from behind the dumpster, and approached the guard from behind. Her foot splashed into a puddle just as she came close. The guard turned his head in surprise and Carly swung the pipe with everything she had. Amid the clatter of footsteps from the two, a loud crack echoed through the alley. The guard went down hard, with a thud. With the guard out of the way, Carly ran back to get her phone. She scooped it up on the run, and quickly dialed the police as she continued to run to safety on the other side of the street.

Amid the chaos in warehouse, Mr. Midnight had pressed a button on his remote, and then turned and headed toward the greenhouse hunched over clutching at his injured hand. All his men did not appear to realize what was happening. Mr. Midnight was intent on setting the inhibitor regardless, even using it on his own people if he had to. As the greenhouse door clicked shut, the inhibitor began to make a low deep humming noise that reverberated around the warehouse. All the men stopped suddenly and turned their attention to the inhibitor. With a sharp zapping sound, a blinding white light shot out of the top. The light began to spread and creep across the shipping floor, and up through the air as well. The light fell over several henchmen. They froze instantly, turning rigid and statuesque.

Titan had no idea how much time he had before the inhibitor would spread outside the warehouse and into the city, but he knew he had to act fast. He tried to position himself as far from the inhibitor's rays as he could. The light was less than fifteen feet away and spreading fast. He noticed with satisfaction as Kaizen became engulfed in the blinding light. While Mr. Midnight's henchmen were scrambling, Titan leveled his staff, and shot a brilliant lightning blast straight into the face of the inhibitor, using as much power as he could gather. A huge fireball erupted out of it. Sparks and electric waves shot out from the sides of the giant machine. It was as though a bomb had gone off.

The explosion came with such force that it knocked everyone down to the ground. Titan was rocked, but managed to stay on his feet, the heat from the blast blanketing him. Mr. Midnight had been knocked into the side of the greenhouse and had collapsed to the floor. Glass from the greenhouse was showering down all around him. The henchmen seemed dazed and were slow to get up, and when they did, they were frantically seeking an escape route.

The first explosion ended any hope of the inhibitor striking the city as the rays it had been emitting abruptly vanished. The machine no longer posed any threat to the city, but it continued to wreak havoc upon the warehouse. Several smaller explosions erupted from it, and when they did they sent smoldering pieces of metal scattering all over the building. Flames shot out of the machine and started to climb up the walls of the warehouse with alarming speed. The flames fanned out wildly across the mountains of crates that lined the walls. Some crates clearly contained weapons as they began to explode as well.

The entire building had sprung into chaos. Mr. Midnight's men scrambled about trying to find an exit out of the warehouse. Everyone gave Kaizen a wide berth, as she still lay frozen on the concrete floor. No one seemed to dare go near her, even in this helpless state. The building was being engulfed from within and was rocked with another explosion every few seconds. Scanning the area quickly, Titan couldn't see Mr.

Midnight. He had put an end to the threat of his motion inhibitor, but he was not going to leave without putting him behind bars.

He rushed toward what was left of the greenhouse only to find a small pool of blood amid the shattered glass and rubble. As he inspected the wreckage, Titan spotted the reflection of Mr. Midnight's golden mask dart behind a stack of flaming crates. Titan ran after him just as one final explosion put the mass motion inhibitor to rest. Mr. Midnight was forced to go around the long way of the warehouse to avoid the fiery inhibitor wreckage to make his escape. He quickly looked back over his shoulder where Titan could be seen bearing down on him and turned sharply down another aisle. Another explosion rocked the opposite side of the building. Titan turned quickly and followed.

As explosions erupted throughout the warehouse the rows of stacked crates now started to tumble over, leaving many aisles impassable. He was at once worried for his own safety as well as worried that he might allow Mr. Midnight to escape.

Titan began closing in as Mr. Midnight lumbered up the aisle. Another few steps and he would be able to reach out and grab hold of him. Suddenly, an explosion blasted through some crates directly to Titan's right. The blast sent him flying into a stack of crates on the other side of the aisle. Winded and aching he lay on the ground. Before he could react to what was going on, remnants of the exploding crates came crashing down on him. Titan's body ached as he stretched and pushed at the pile of debris, trying to free himself. He wasn't sure if Mr. Midnight had been trapped under the pile as well or if he had indeed escaped. As he fought and pushed, sharp jagged pieces of metal and wood scraped and tore into him. When at last he broke through the top of the heap, his body was bruised and beaten, and his uniform torn and ripped, but he still managed to get to his feet.

As Titan looked down to the bottom of the crumpled stack he saw that Mr. Midnight had also been partially pinned amidst the rubble. As Titan was gaining his balance on top of the teetering rubble pile, Mr. Midnight was just getting his legs free from the pile of debris. Titan could see the lower half of his pants were shredded and his legs bleeding badly. Still, he managed to get to his shaky feet and limp his way further down. As Mr. Midnight came to the end of the row, he went left toward the front of the building. The street side exit was his last hope for escape. He still clutched his injured hand closely to his chest. Several deep gashes on his arms and chest also bled profusely from where the greenhouse glass had hit him. Titan carefully jumped from the pile and continued his pursuit. He refused to allow this man to escape. Titan was closing in again when Mr. Midnight quickly turned down another corner. Around it he found a dead end, blocked by a large stack of fallen crates. Titan rounded the corner, trapping him. A mess of fallen, flaming crates stood behind Mr. Midnight, and two towering stacks were at either side.

"You're done, Midnight. It's over, give it up!" Titan ordered.

"No, I don't think so. Listen here, boy, this city is mine, it has always been mine, and it will always be mine!" Mr. Midnight said, turning quickly to face Titan. Titan caught a glimmer of humanity through that golden mask as he saw Mr. Midnight's eyes dart about, frantically looking for an escape. He still spoke in a booming, angry, defiant voice echoing through his mask, a voice refusing defeat. "It's not over until I say it's over. Do you hear me? It's not over yet!"

Mr. Midnight then pulled a gun out from his waistband, aiming it with his good hand at Titan. This time it was a real gun, not a motion inhibitor. Both men stood frozen. Titan still clutched his staff, and was now faced with an old west styled standoff against his enemy.

Suddenly, the biggest explosion yet rocked the building. It came from a few rows over. A series of explosions made their way to the end of the row, shaking the crates where Mr. Midnight stood. Titan feared the whole building would soon come down around them. Superpowers or not, he wondered if he could come through something like that unscathed. He knew that Mr. Midnight could not, and wanted only to bring him into police custody.

Titan, he is your enemy, but you must think of his safety also. This building is becoming increasingly unsafe.

"Look, like it or not you're going to have to come out of here with me," Titan pleaded, his hand outstretched to Mr. Midnight as he moved closer.

"Get away from me. I'll....." Before he could finish, an explosion went off that completely engulfed Mr. Midnight. It came from one row over and blew right through the stack of crates to Mr. Midnight's left. There was suddenly nothing but a cloud of debris and shrapnel where he had been. It sent giant shards of wood and metal in all directions.

Titan ducked low to the ground, feeling the shrapnel from the blast sail over his head. As soon as it settled, he jumped up. Mr. Midnight was nowhere to be seen. Where he had been standing was now nothing but a pile of rubble. Titan started tossing debris back, sifting through the wreckage, looking for him. He could feel the heat from the fire that was engulfing the building. Then he reached through to the floor, and all he found was a black fedora with a red stripe around it, and a jagged tear along its front brim. He could see no other sign of Mr. Midnight.

Titan, we must leave here immediately.

At Azure's words, Titan looked around and saw that he was virtually the only one left in the building. He leapt up over the flaming wreckage up into the rafters towards the skylights and to safer ground.

"I can't let him get away," Titan said, still clutching the fedora tightly.

You must not worry about it for now, Titan. If he lives, he will surface again. You did your best to save him. You won this day. That is what matters most.

Titan could hear the approach of police and fire trucks. He thought then that he would still be able to bring down much of Mr. Midnight's empire, if not the man himself. All he needed to do was to find Vicki as soon as possible, and he had a sneaking suspicion that she would not be far away.

Titan made his way over to where the inhibitor once stood, now only a charred flaming wreck. Kaizen still lay frozen in the middle of the floor not far from it.

We must not leave her, Titan.

"It's not like she would save me," Titan replied.

Yes, and that is what makes you better than her.

Titan simply sighed and nodded in silent agreement. He reached down and picked up Kaizen, placing her onto his shoulder. Her body was still rigid in his grip. He looked up through the thick smoke that was gathering around the warehouse roof. He could just make out the skylight and he jumped up through it, the explosions having blown out the rest of the glass. He dropped down to the sidewalk below. Dozens of people had gathered across the street to watch the blaze. Some, Titan was sure, were part of Mr. Midnight's crew that had managed to escape. He spotted Carly among the crowd, relief washing over her as she saw him. His uniform was torn and singed, and he gave a slight nod in her direction to let her know he was indeed oaky. He set Kaizen down and lay the battered fedora on top of her just as the first police cruisers turned the corner. Without hesitation, Titan leapt up high into the city, lost from the spectator's gaze, and into the night.

Sometime later, when the entire area around the warehouse was roped off with police tape and the Delta City fire department was close to putting out the warehouse fire, Chief Ross stood in the center of the police line surveying the damage. Frank was patrolling the perimeter, giving out orders to the police and rescue crews as to what was needed for evidence and what wasn't. The fire had raged for close to two hours. All that remained was the blackened outer walls. Pools of sooty water gathered by Ross' feet. His eyes kept darting back to the battered and torn black fedora in his hands. It had been found at the scene by the arriving officers next to Kaizen. You did not have to be chief of police to guess to whom it belonged.

The police had arrived just in time to catch several of the men involved, only a few blocks away. A woman had been found lying on the sidewalk unable to move when the first policemen had arrived. Many of the policemen at the scene were reluctant to get too close to her. The infamous Kaizen had proven quite difficult to detain once she regained her agility, but his men had managed to restrain her. Hours later the mess was just being set right. Ross was busy trying to piece it all together when he heard a familiar voice behind him among all the other reporters and onlookers gathering around the police tape.

"I'm sorry, Ms. Earnhardt, you know the routine. I'm afraid I have no information to give you at this time, even if I wanted to," Chief Ross said, as he turned to face Vicki.

"Well Chief, that's fine. The thing is, this time I'm the one with information for you," Vicki said, as a satisfied look spread over her face.

Chief Ross paused, in wide-eyed disbelief. Nothing in all his years with the police force could have quite prepared him for what he was about to hear. As he did his best to listen intently to Vicki's entire story, asking her several times to repeat certain parts, a strange sight caught his eye high among the city's buildings in the distance. His eyes barely had time to focus, however, as what he was looking at turned into a streaking blur of yellow and blue across the city skyline.

Chapter 19: Delta City Safe Again

Chief Ross was still busy later the next morning, processing paperwork on the previous night's events. By the time the fire department had been able to put the fire out, the entire warehouse had been reduced to rubble. Ross' men had already started sifting through as much of it as they could, and they were going through it still. So far, what they found was not of much use to them on their case against Mr. Midnight. It was mostly some illegal weapons, but all so charred that the serial numbers were illegible. Most of what he had managed to learn about the fire was what he had learned from Vicki Earnhardt.

With a quick knock, Frank opened the door to Ross' office and peeked inside.

"Chief, you got a second?" Frank asked, looming in the doorway.

"Sure, Frank, come on in," Chief Ross replied.

"You said you wanted reports from the crime scene as soon as they came in. Well, they've just finished going through the place now. They're carting up everything they found of interest," Frank said.

"What did they dig up?" Chief Ross asked.

"Some weapons. Hand guns, assault rifles mostly. They also found some machinery. Everything is pretty badly burned. I don't know if we'll get any fingerprints or serial numbers off any of it," Frank said.

"Well, we'll do with it what we can. I suppose the good news is that Mr. Midnight's crew never got to use it for whatever they intended," Chief Ross said.

"I suppose that's a good way to look at it, Chief," Frank replied.

"What about that woman, Kaizen I believe her name was?" asked Ross.

"Well, they had her examined already before putting her in lockup. I don't know what to tell you, Chief; she's as much a machine as a woman. According to the examiners she has significant cybernetic technology grafted to much of her body. They had never seen anything like it. Her arms and legs are pretty much all robotics. Essentially, our people think that she was badly injured some time ago, and this was their way of repairing her. Whoever did this replaced much of her broken bones with steel piping and hinges. The only thing that may be all human is her brain. They're sending her for more testing later. Right now they're trying to keep her contained until a proper cell can be built to hold her," Frank reported.

"Good lord. How could it happen, Frank? How could all this have been going on right under our own noses?" Chief Ross asked, as he rubbed his head.

"Well sir, I don't think there was anything we could have done. Somehow these people managed to stay off our radar, that's all. Don't blame yourself, sir," Frank replied.

"I suppose you're right. At least their plan failed and the public was kept safe. So how are the rest of our guests down in lockup doing?" asked Chief Ross, referring to Mr. Midnight's men.

"A few have given statements of involvement, basically gave us all they know. We have the addresses of two bases of operations for Mr. Midnight. The rest aren't talking much so far. I think they figure they can walk from the charges. I don't think it's hit them that their boss may not be around to help bail them out," Frank said, pointing to the battered black fedora on Chief Ross' desk.

"Well at least we hope he's gone. I don't see how he could have survived that. But who knows, a character like that, we know so little about him in the first place. I hate to say it, but maybe he did manage to escape," Chief Ross said.

"Don't you believe any of what the reporter told you about Mr. Midnight?"

"I don't know. Do you believe that we've heard the last of him, Frank?" Chief Ross asked.

"I like to think he never really existed in the first place. Of course I've always just been a pessimist. I know most people think he existed, and that last night we may have heard the last of him," Frank replied.

"Well, I don't know what to think about any of that. Honestly, I think this ripped hat says more about the state of Mr. Midnight than some vigilante communicating through a reporter," Chief Ross said. He then swiveled in his chair and gazed out the window at the city. "Still, so far Vicki's story seems to hold up. Plus I can't say I don't like the idea of this Titan being on our side at least. It would seem he managed to wipe out most of Mr. Midnight's organization in a single night. What do you think Frank?"

Frank thought for a moment. Then he smiled broadly and said, "Chief, I couldn't agree more. Of course now the question is, what do we do about Titan?"

"Well, I think the answer to that will present itself in due time. For now, I say we go out and look into these addresses and see if we can prove Mr. Midnight existed then?" Chief Ross asked, standing and heading for the door.

"Sure, Chief," Frank said, as the two of them made their way out of the building.

Several blocks away, Vicki sat behind her desk typing furiously. Ever since Titan had landed at her office with an exclusive interview she'd had no trouble writing at all. In fact, the stories wouldn't stop coming. She had just managed to get a quick blurb out about the warehouse fire the night before, and the battle between Mr. Midnight and Titan. Now she was working on a much more detailed article of the incident with direct quotes from Titan. Her fingers raced across the keyboard. She had rarely been this excited writing, save maybe the first time she had met Titan. That first Titan meeting she had been excited, now she was overjoyed at the fact that Mr. Midnight had been defeated.

So far, the issues featuring Vicki's Titan articles had been among the paper's bestselling. Now she was working on the one that everybody secretly wanted. The city's newest hero against its greatest villain and the hero had prevailed.

It had only been the night before that Titan had been perched at her office window, catching her working late. She had opened the window and let him inside. He had wasted no time telling her all about the events at the warehouse. He had rattled off his account into her tape recorder. Adrenaline still seemed to be flowing through him, having just come from the incident. He appeared a little worse for wear, at least his clothes did. It was then that Titan had asked her for another, even bigger favor than before. As soon as Titan had left she had rushed to the fiery scene herself to report to Chief Ross.

"Vicki, can we talk a second?" Charles asked, coming right into her office.

"You ever hear of knocking, Charles?" Vicki snapped back at him, clearly still mad.

Vicki had stopped typing abruptly and minimized her story on her computer, blocking it from Charles' view. She folded her hands on top of the desk and nodded, waiting for him to continue.

"Oh, sorry. Am I disturbing you? I can just come back," said Charles, heading for the door. All the aggressiveness was gone.

"It's okay, but if this is about laying off the Titan stories because it upsets the mayor then you can just go," Vicki said.

"Actually it's quite the opposite. I came here to apologize," Charles said.

"Apologize? Well then, please go on," Vicki said. This certainly seemed to be turning out to be her day.

"Vicki I should never have let the mayor's office dictate what we print here as news. Your Titan interviews have been outstanding. They're selling like crazy. Titan obviously came to you for a reason. The same reason I hired you in the first place. It seems I just forgot that reason for a while. I was ruling out of fear, and as a news organization that was wrong," Charles said.

"Wow, Charles, I'm flattered. What about the mayor's office?" asked Vicki.

"Forget the mayor. Just keep up the good work," Charles said, as he exited her office.

Vicki broke into a huge smile. She swiveled in her chair and looked over at her first Titan interview, which now rested framed on her office wall. After looking at it she turned and once again began to type furiously at her computer.

Amid the warm sunshine, Michael leaned up against the edge of the roof, looking out over the neighborhood. The hot summer sun was beating down on him. He felt as though a new day had dawned. Below, he watched as two young boys ran around on the sidewalk wearing bandanas on their heads. One held an old broom stick while the other an old hockey stick with the blade cut off.

"I'm Titan!" the first one with the broom handle said.

"No way, you were last time. It's my turn," said the other.

Michael smiled ear to ear as he watched them play below. The neighborhood seemed quiet and serene. It was something he hadn't felt since he was a boy.

Beside him in one of the folding chairs sat Carly, reading Vicki's latest story off her laptop of the events from the night before. The two of them were up late into the night, and finally fell asleep with Carly curled on the old bus bench, her head resting in Michael's lap close to sunrise. As soon as they woke Carly snagged her laptop from her room and headed for the roof so she could read over the whole account with Michael, and without disruption.

He was terribly afraid that after last night Titan might be in as much hot water as Mr. Midnight, and he would find himself back in the same situation as he had in the beginning. After all an entire building had been leveled and he knew that blame would be placed on someone. However, Carly had kept saying not to worry, and she had been right. "TITAN TRIUMPHANT, MR. MIDNIGHT BELIEVED DEAD!" the headline had read. He had trusted that Vicki would report the events as he had told them to her. It turned out that he had been right.

"Oh, Michael, this is wonderful," Carly said, finally putting the paper aside. "It says here that the dense criminal network that was controlled by Mr. Midnight was virtually wiped out in a single stroke with last night's warehouse fire. A large number of Mr. Midnight's underlings have been apprehended, and it appears a serious civilian threat wiped out, and all thanks to Delta City's new hero, Titan. She even makes it sound like the Chief was grateful to Titan that Midnight's plan was stopped. It seems the only one who still really thinks that you're a threat is the mayor. The mayor says that Titan is as big a threat and liability as Mr. Midnight, but what does he know?"

"Yeah well maybe he's right. I let Midnight get away. He was right there, and I let him slip through my fingers," Michael said, hanging his head.

"Michael, how could you say that? You make it sound as though you lost last night. You aren't even sure that he did escape. For all

243

you know he died under that pile of rubble. If it wasn't for you, who knows what might have become of this city last night? It probably wouldn't have ended last night either. We could have been in his grip for a long time. I mean, as long as that thing was in Midnight's grasp we were all in danger. And you, Titan, saved us all," Carly said, raising his head up with her fingers under his chin.

"Yeah plus..." Michael said pointing to below. "I am pretty big with the kids you know."

Carly laughed out loud in response.

"On the bright side Vince couldn't have been nicer this morning. It was almost sickening," said Michael.

"Well let's hope he's learned his lesson for good. Do you think that Dylan was involved somehow too? He was cozying up to Vince at the basketball game," asked Carly.

"I sure hope not. It's bad enough that I have a brother mixed up in criminal activity I would hate to have someone I look up to mixed up in it too."

Then, they saw Perminder and Dave with Monica trailing behind, heading towards the building, no doubt wondering if they had heard all the news about last night.

"I wonder what the guys have to say about all this," Michael said, watching his friends approach.

"I'm sure they loved it. They already went down there to check out the scene themselves," Carly said.

"I suppose it is pretty cool that I stopped Midnight all on my own," Michael said, then after a slight pause, "Well, me and Azure,"

"Pardon me?" Carly said, looking hurt.

"Just kidding. You were an amazing help last night too, partner. I couldn't have done it without you. Thank you."

"We do make a good team," said Carly.

"We sure do. Azure even lifted that whole warning thing against me."

"Michael, that's good news! I told you that you could overcome all this negativity. Of course you know, this does mean that if he is in fact alive that at some point Mr. Midnight will be back," Carly said. "Someone like that just doesn't give up, and go away."

"Yeah he'll be back, I'm sure of it," Michael said, taking Carly into his arms. They embraced, and Michael kissed her squarely on the lips. He pulled back, still holding her tightly and then said, "and when he does, Titan will be there waiting for him."

Watch for the ongoing saga of TITAN.

titanseries.blogspot.com

Made in the USA
Charleston, SC
21 September 2012